THE VEIN TO THE HEART

Beaver County Rocks!

THE VEIN
TO
THE HEART

C. P. HOLSINGER

Foremost Press
Cedarburg, Wisconsin

Also by C. P. Holsinger

All the Bishop's Men

Published by Foremost Press
www.foremostpress.com

ISBN-10: 1-939870-02-X
ISBN-13: 978-1-939870-02-5

To my wife, Judy,
for forty-five years as the love of my life

CHAPTER 1

The Awakening

The ringing of his cell phone jolted Nick Greer out of a deep sleep. He had driven in from Disneyland late last night. He'd been dead-tired, and his head had no sooner hit the pillow than he had fallen asleep.

He reached out and groped the nightstand until he felt the edge of the cell phone. Grabbing it, he almost ripped it from its charger. His fingers felt the vibration of the hostile ringing. Through sleep-deprived eyes, he glared at the large blue letters on the screen. It read: Sonny. The time read: 3:57 a.m.

Though still groggy, he knew it was Sunday. Why the hell would Sonny be calling him in the middle of the night? His thumb found the answer button on his Android. "This better be important. I'm still on vacation, and it's the middle of the goddamn night!"

"Oh, it's important all right," came the response from the other end. I need you to meet me at Forty-Third Avenue and Peoria. They just fished a body out of the canal and you need to see it."

"Come on, Sonny. You can handle it. I'm on vaca—"

"It's Pete!"

"What's Pete?"

"The body. It's Pete Mendoza!"

Shock seized him when he heard the name. He dropped the cell phone as he sprang straight up in bed—he was wide-awake. He reached down and grabbed the cord that was still attached to the Android, and pulled it back up from between the nightstand and the bed where it had fallen. He brought the phone back to his ear and tried to speak, but the words didn't come.

Lieutenant Nick Greer and Sergeant Sonny Madison were both homicide detectives for the Phoenix Police Department. Up until four months ago, Pete Mendoza had been their captain.

"Nick, Nick, are you there?" Sonny's voice came through the speaker.

"Uhhh . . . yeah. What?" Again, Nick was speechless as the shock of the news echoed throughout his entire being. "You're telling me Pete is dead? Pete Mendoza? Our Pete?"

"Yep, and there's more, Nick," Sonny said. "I really need you here. You have to see this."

"What do you mean, more?"

"Nick, not now. When you get here."

Nick felt the intenseness in his friend and ex-partner's voice and said, "I'm on my way."

Nick pushed the end call button on his phone. By now he was sitting on the edge of the bed. He stretched out his tired arms and stood up as he tried to mentally digest the news. Not only had Pete Mendoza been their captain, but he was also a long-time friend. He had been Nick's first training officer. He and his wife, Elena, were godparents to Nick's youngest daughter.

Nick Greer was born and raised in Phoenix. He graduated from Moon Valley High School and obtained a basketball scholarship to Arizona State University where he then earned a master's degree in criminology. He had been scouted by several professional teams, but during his last year in college, he blew out his knee, keeping him out of the draft. He didn't mind so much, because, though he loved the sport, he didn't want to play basketball forever. The more he learned about criminology, the more he wanted to be a cop. Upon graduation, he had been offered a position as a field agent with the FBI. He knew a career with such an organization would be exciting and could take him to many interesting places, and he fully considered their offer. But he loved the city he grew up in, and it was his love for Phoenix that was the deciding factor in his choice to join the Phoenix Police Department.

Agapito Mendoza had retired as a captain from the Phoenix Police Department a little over four months ago. He was an avid gun collector and a gunsmith. It was his fascination for firearms that caused him to open a gun store in Phoenix. He was so happy. Nick remembered what his friend had said the day he opened the gun store: "I am finally living my dream!"

Pete's Pistols 'N Parts was a new store. But due to his association with the Phoenix police, and friends he had with the Maricopa County Sheriff's Department and other city police departments, it was off to a great start. Police were known to support their own, and this was no exception.

Sue Kim was standing at the foot of the bed, holding a towel. As Nick stood up, she tossed it to him and said, "Go ahead and take a shower. I'll make you some coffee." He looked at her with puzzled eyes. "You had your phone on speaker," she said. "I heard it all. They need you. Go!"

Sue Kim was born in Okinawa. Her parents immigrated to San Diego, California, when she was two years old. The only child of a software engineer, Sue Kim studied music and forensic science at Stanford University and held a degree in both. She loved her job as a crime lab technician, but her real passion was her music. She was a concert cellist and a proud and respected member of the Phoenix Symphony Orchestra.

Her first job had been as an assistant in the Maricopa County morgue. It was there she first met Nick Greer. Although their relationship had gotten off to a rocky start, they had been together now for a little over a year. She knew the long hours and the middle of the night calls that plagued the life of a police detective had cost Nick his first marriage. She understood the nature of his job and was supportive.

He quickly showered and threw on a shirt and jeans. As he left the bedroom and walked into the kitchen of the townhouse, he saw her standing there with a thermo-cup of coffee in one hand and his car keys in the other. He kissed her and said, "Thanks, sweetie. I don't know when I'll be back. Tell the kids—"

"Go," she said. "Don't worry about it. The kids will be fine. Call me when you know anything."

* * *

The canal was less than ten minutes from Nick's townhouse. It is part of a canal system that carries water, mostly for irrigation, and runs at an angle through the cities of Phoenix, Glendale, and beyond.

From a half-mile away, Nick's eyes caught the red and blue lights flashing brightly against the dark, starless sky. There were several police cars from both Phoenix and Glendale, along with an ambulance and a rescue truck. Southbound traffic was blocked off at Forty-Third Avenue, and the northbound lane was blocked off from the south. His concern was on which side of Forty-Third the body was found. He knew Forty-Third Avenue was the boundary between Phoenix and

Glendale. If the body was on the Glendale side, it would be within their jurisdiction, and they probably wouldn't want Nick involved. If it was truly Pete Mendoza, and if it was not an accident, this detective wanted the case. This was his ex-captain, his mentor, and his friend.

Nick got out of his car and walked briskly across the street. He flashed his gold badge as he made his way through the small crowd. There were only a few onlookers at this time of the morning, but as the sun rose, Nick knew there would be plenty more. There weren't any news reporters here yet, but they were sure to show up soon. Though both sides of the street were covered with police and other emergency personnel, Nick was glad to see that most of them were on the east side, making it come under Phoenix jurisdiction.

"Hey, Nick, over here," a familiar voice rang out. He saw Sonny waving to him.

Sonny Madison and Nick Greer had once been partners. But due to cost cuts, they had worked alone for some time now, though they sometimes partnered-up, depending on the need. Even when on separate cases, they would consult each other at times. Both of their talents complemented the other. They both were good detectives, but as a team, they were unstoppable. There would be no doubt they would work this one together.

"I'm sorry to cut your vacation short," Sonny said, "but I figured you would want in on this from the beginning."

"Are you sure it's him?" Nick asked.

Even in the dark, he could see the sadness in Sonny's eyes as the red and blue lights flashed across his face. Sonny nodded and looked in the direction of the body covered with a white sheet. It was lying next to the sloping gray walls of the canal.

Nick could hear the water slowly rolling its way through the concrete channel as he walked over to the body. He squatted and lifted the sheet just enough to expose the victim's head. He recognized the face of his ex-boss and friend. Pulling the sheet down farther, he saw what appeared to be a small stab wound in the center of his chest.

Nick shook his head and sighed as he pulled the sheet back over the victim's face. He looked up at Sonny and said, "You said there was more?"

Sonny nodded. "Take a look at his left hand."

Nick reached out and pulled the sheet up from the left side of the victim. He was shocked at what he saw when he lifted the victim's hand. Pete Mendoza's left ring finger was missing. It was cut off at the base where it had once met the hand. He looked closely at the severed area. It was clean. It didn't look like it was ripped or chewed off. Nick put the hand back, covered the body again, and asked Sonny, "Who is lead CSI?"

Sonny pointed to two men standing along the edge of the canal. The white letters on their shirts said: Crime Scene Unit. "The one on the left—Jeremy Kramer."

Nick stood up and walked over to the two men. He showed them his badge, introduced himself, and said, "Make sure Jack gets this one. I know it's Sunday but call him in. Tell him it's Pete Mendoza. He won't give you any trouble. I guarantee it." Both CSIs nodded.

Jack Konesky was the senior medical examiner and was considered one of the best at his trade. He was also a close friend of Pete Mendoza. Nick knew him well and respected his abilities. There was no one else this detective wanted on the case.

The sun was beginning to peek out over the eastern mountains, and a news crew had arrived on the scene. The distant sound of helicopter rotors told the lieutenant that the scene would soon be crawling with reporters.

"Well, it looks like my vacation is over," Nick said to Sonny, who nodded. Nick continued, "You know we gotta tell Elena."

"I'll meet you there," Sonny said.

* * *

Both of the police officers arrived at the Mendoza home at the same time. Sonny looked at Nick and slowly shook his head. "I think this is the hardest part of the job," he said.

Sonny Madison had been on the Phoenix Police Department five years longer than Nick. He was considered one of the best investigators the Phoenix Police Department ever had. He knew his way around a computer keyboard. He would dig and dig until he found what he was looking for. If it weren't for his in-your-face attitude, he might be Nick's boss, but he didn't care. He loved what he did, and he knew he was good at it. It was authority that he had trouble with.

Elena and Pete Mendoza had been married almost thirty years. They had three grown children, but only one lived at home. Pete and Elena both came from strict Catholic families and raised their children the same.

Nick looked at his watch as he pushed on the doorbell. It read: 6:33. They waited about a minute and rang the doorbell again. Sonny saw the mini-blind part and said, "She's here."

The door opened, and Elena stood there in her nightgown and robe. The look on her face told the two detectives she knew why they were there.

Nick began, "Elena, I know it's early, but can we come in?"

She nodded and pointed toward the living room. The house was a typical ranch-style Phoenix home, about forty years old, and very welcoming and comfortable. They stepped down into the sunken living room. The two detectives took their seats on a brown leather sofa that sat against a bay window looking out onto the street. Elena sat in a matching love seat across from her visitors.

"I knew something was wrong. He didn't come home last night. Is he . . . ?"

Nick sighed as he nodded. "I'm afraid so, Elena."

Tears began rolling down her cheeks, and Sonny's eyes spotted a box of tissues sitting on the oval, glass coffee table in front of them. He got up, picked up the box, and put it on her lap. As she took a tissue from the box, she said, "For thirty years I worried. Every time I heard of a police-involved shooting, my heart pounded. Even after he took the captain's job, he'd still be out in the field as much as possible. You guys know that." Both detectives nodded as she continued, "I was so happy when he retired; I thought it was over. I didn't have to worry anymore. What happened?" She dabbed at her eyes with the tissue and wiped the tears from her face. "Was it a car accident?"

"Uhh . . . no, Elena. It wasn't that," Sonny said gently as he reached for her hand. "He was found in the canal at Forty-Third and Peoria."

Sonny handed her another tissue. "I'm so sorry, Elena."

Elena shook her head. "Somebody must have run him off the road, or he must have lost control of the car."

Sonny looked across to Nick, who said gently, "Elena, Pete's car wasn't there. It's not here, is it?" She shook her head.

"We're going to check the store after we leave here, and see if it's there," said Sonny.

Her voice cracked as she asked, "What do you mean?"

Nick sighed again, stood up, walked over to Elena, and knelt in front of her. He could feel her hands tremble as he took them into his, and said, "Elena, it doesn't look like it was an accident."

Her mouth flew open. "What? A robbery? A mugging? No, not my Pete. He was too smart for that. You've got be wrong."

Nick shook his head. "I wish we were, Elena. God knows I wish we were."

She looked at Nick, then to Sonny, and back at Nick. "I want to see him," she said with conviction.

Sonny spoke, "Elena, you know the procedure. You'll be able to see him when the ME says it's okay. Until then, you shouldn't be alone. I called April, and she's on her way over."

Sonny knew his wife, April, had taken courses in grief counseling, and she would be able to provide some comfort to the widow. She and Elena had always gotten along well. Elena nodded in agreement.

"Where is Jordana?" Nick asked. He knew their daughter still lived at home.

"She spent the night with a friend. I'll have to call her. Oh, God! What will I say? How do I tell her—" Her words were interrupted by the sound of the doorbell.

Sonny went to the door. It was April. She came in, went straight to Elena, sat down and hugged her. Elena began sobbing. April nodded to the two policemen and said, "Go, guys. We'll be fine here. Go do what you do."

Nick Greer and Sonny Madison left. They knew they had work to do. But neither had any idea what lay ahead, nor did they know this would be the biggest case of their careers.

CHAPTER 2

The Crime Scene

Pete's Pistols 'N Parts was a little over a mile from the Mendoza residence and only two blocks from the canal where the body had been found. Sonny was the first to arrive, with Nick close behind. Both detectives immediately recognized Pete's SUV sitting alone in the parking lot. Sonny got out of his car and went over to it. He slowly walked around it while his eyes carefully inspected every inch.

Nick got out of his car and walked toward the gun store. He stopped when he saw several red spots on the sidewalk. He took care to walk around them so as not to compromise the scene. The detective looked through the window. He saw the ceiling lights were still on in the store, so he looked at the edge of the door. He could see the dead bolt was not locked, so he reached to his side, pulled his Glock, and said, "Sonny." He nodded his head toward the door.

Sonny knew the drill. He pulled his Glock from his side and joined his partner at the door. Nick pushed on the door with his shoulder; it gave no resistance. Nick entered and his partner followed. With their guns drawn, the two policemen went through the entire premises; first the lobby, then behind the counters, and then the back, even the restroom. After the final "clear," both detectives holstered their side arms.

Sonny pointed to several blood drops on the floor. Nick said, "There are more on the counter, too."

"The alarm wasn't set," Sonny remarked. "It must have been a customer or maybe Pete knew the perp."

Nick pulled his Android from his belt and called for a crime scene crew. He put the cell phone back into its holder and said to Sonny, "CSI's on their way. Stay here until they arrive."

"Where are you going?" Sonny asked.

"To the morgue. The body should be there by now. If it's not, I want to be there when it arrives. I want to be sure Jack gets it."

"I'll see you there when I'm done here," Sonny said. Nick nodded.

* * *

Jack Konesky was standing over the body when Nick Greer entered the room. The body, covered with a light blue sheet, was lying on a metal table. So many times the detective had viewed this scene, but this time it was different. This time it was his friend and mentor lying on the cold autopsy table.

Nick watched the medical examiner as he stood there, staring down at the corpse. Jack Konesky was a jovial man who was always smiling and was known for cracking jokes about the cadavers on his table. He once told Nick that was what kept him from going insane. But today, Nick Greer saw a different person standing there. His face was sullen. His eyes were sad. He hadn't noticed Nick come into the room; he just stood, staring at the body.

Nick broke the eerie silence. "Jack, are you okay?"

Jack looked at his visitor, and then he looked back down at the body. "He was my best friend for over thirty years. Did you know I am Jordana's godfather? I should be with Elena instead of here, cutting her husband open."

Nick put his hand on his friend's shoulder and said, "Jack, Elena is in good hands. April Madison is with her. She's a grief counselor, and they're also good friends. She'll take care of her, I promise."

Nick sensed conflict within the man standing next to him. For the first time since Nick had known him, he seemed unsure of himself. He said to his friend, "Jack, you're right where you need to be."

Konesky shook his head. He looked at the instrument tray next to him, looked back at the body, and shook his head again. "I can't, Nick. I can't pick up a scalpel. I can't cut my friend open. I just can't."

Nick put his hands on both of Jack's shoulders, and gently turned him so he could face him. He looked through the medical examiner's silver-rimmed glasses into his cloudy eyes. "Jack, if you can't do this, I will respect that. I know he was your best friend, but you are the best ME we have. Pete Mendoza, your friend, deserves the best and only the best. Sonny and I will work this case until we find the perp, I promise. But we need you. I need you. What's more, Pete needs you. But don't do it for me. Do it for Pete."

Jack took a breath, nodded, and looked toward the instrument tray, and then back at Nick. "Okay, Nick. I'll do it. But it will be my last. When this is over, I'll be giving the county what they want."

Nick knew what his friend meant. The county had been pressuring Jack to retire. Thus far he had refused. About a year ago he told Nick, "I'll retire when I'm damn good and ready. Not one day before. They all can kiss my ass."

Nick nodded. "Do your thing, Jack. Call me when you've got something." He turned, left the morgue, and headed for the station.

* * *

It was nine-thirty when Nick Greer opened the squad room door. He was reminded it was Sunday morning when he saw how empty the room was. He reached to the wall, switched on the lights, walked toward his desk and stopped. He looked at the closed door at the back of the room. The black letters on the frosted glass door read: Spencer J. Lovett, Captain. Nick remembered when it had once read: Agapito Mendoza, Captain. He shook his head and sat down at his desk. He put his elbows on the desk, put his face in his hands, and closed his eyes. His mind wandered back to his first meeting with the then Sergeant Mendoza. Several scenes passed through his mind as he thought about his ex-boss and friend. He remembered cases they had worked on together and the many talks they had in Pete's office, some about cases, some about family, and some just about stuff. He already missed his friend. He finally looked up. The clock on the wall read: 10:15. He had been sitting there for forty-five minutes. He looked down to his desk and saw the tri-fold frame that held pictures of his children. He was reminded that he needed to get them home to Prescott.

Cassie, Nick's ex-wife, once the divorce papers were filed, had taken their kids and moved in with her mother and father in Prescott, a move that Nick was not at all comfortable with. His lawyer had told him that he could fight it because Arizona law stated that a spouse could not move the children more than one hundred miles away without the other parent's permission. Prescott is about one hundred twenty-five miles from Phoenix. He decided not to fight it. Cassie could be a real bitch when she wanted to, and he knew she would figure a way to make it worse. So he did the best he could to go to Prescott every other weekend. He would either pick the girls up and drive them to Phoenix, or often he would stay at a hotel. Right now they were at his townhouse with Sue Kim.

Nick and Sue Kim had taken them to Disneyland. They had a good time, and the girls bonded well with her. She liked the kids and loved to spend time with them, and they seemed to like her.

The problem was he was supposed to take them back today. How could he do that and work the case at the same time? He thought about it and decided to call Sue Kim.

"Hello," she answered. "Where are you?"

"At my desk. Just trying to work things out in my head. I needed some alone time, I guess."

"You loved him, didn't you?" she said.

"Guys don't love guys," he responded. "But he was—"

"Bull!" she interrupted. "He was your friend and you loved him. That doesn't break the man-code."

"Okay, maybe, but there's a small problem."

"Okay, what?"

"You know I need to get the girls back to Prescott today and—"

"It's all taken care of," she cut in.

"Huh?"

"I talked with your ex. I'm bringing the girls by the precinct to say good-bye to you. Then we're meeting Cassie at Cordes Junction."

"How the hell did you arrange that? Cassie hates you . . . and me."

"Well, when I called her she was not happy. The first thing she said was why the . . . well, I can't say it now; the girls might be listening . . . was I calling her? You know she has a mouth on her? Yeah, you know." She giggled. "Anyway, as soon as I told her what happened to Pete, she became silent. It was several seconds before she spoke, and then she was as nice as can be. It was her idea for us to meet in Cordes Junction."

"Amazing. But she did like Pete and Elena, you know. She and Elena were friends. They played bunko together."

"She said to tell you to find the bastard who did it!"

Nick said, "Thank you, sweetie. You're great."

"Yeah, I know," she said. "I'll bring the girls by there before we leave, okay?"

"Sure. I'll be right here." Nick hit the end button on his phone, and dropped it onto his desk. He put his elbows back onto his desk and put his head in his hands again and said out loud, "This sucks!"

Just then his cell phone rang. He picked it up, and looked at it. The blue letters read: ME. "Hi, Jack," Nick answered.

"I got some prelim info for you. I'm on my way over."

"You know where I am?"

"At your desk, I assume. Waiting for me."

"How did you know?"

"I know you. Where else would you be!"

It was about ten minutes later when Jack Konesky came through the squad room door. He sat in a chair next to Nick's gray desk. "Are you okay?" Nick asked.

"Yeah, for now." He sighed. "I had to stop, Nick. I couldn't take it anymore. I'll try to finish up tomorrow. He's in the drawer, but I do have some info for you."

"Fire away."

"I figure the time of death was between seven and eight last night. The good news is he didn't suffer, at least not much. It looks like the weapon was an ice pick, or something of the sort that was thrust dead center into his aorta. It went in deep, all the way, I believe. I figure he was dead in seconds."

Nick shook his head. "What about the finger?"

"Yes, the finger," Jack continued. "It was cut off clean. Sliced clean through the bone."

"How? With what?" Nick asked.

"I'm not sure. It's going to take some research. The lab should be able to figure it out. That little one of yours is pretty smart. I'll have her work on it. I'll see you tomorrow." Konesky turned and began to leave just as Sue Kim came through the door with Nick's three daughters following close behind.

"Ahh, and here she is now," Jack said. "Hello, young lady. How are you?"

"Well, hello, Dr. Konesky. I'm glad to see you. I'm fine, and how are you?" Sue Kim responded with a smile.

"Fine, I guess, considering. Take care of him," he said, as he looked toward Nick.

"Yeah, I will. Since somebody has to, it might as well be me." She giggled as the medical examiner left the room.

All three of the kids ran to their dad. Kaitlin, the youngest, had a Mickey Mouse hat on her head. "How are my girls?" Nick said as he hugged each one. Kelly, the oldest one, held onto her dad and said, "I'm sorry about Uncle Pete."

Nick hugged her tight. "Thank you, baby."

Just then Sonny came through the door. "Uncle Sonny!" Kaitlin exclaimed as she ran to him. Her sisters followed. They hugged him as he bent down to them. "Right here," Sonny said as he pointed to his cheek. Each of the girls kissed him.

"Hello, beautiful," Sonny said to Sue Kim.

"Mr. Sonny." She smiled and nodded to him.

Nick spoke, "This is almost like a family reunion."

Sonny looked at him and said sadly, "Yeah, with one missing."

The mood turned somber again. Sue Kim spoke, "Okay, girls. It's time to take you home. Say good-bye to your dad."

All three girls hugged their father, said good-bye to Sonny, and left with Sue Kim. Sonny sat in the chair next to his partner's desk.

"What ya got so far?" Nick asked.

"They're still processing the scene. They have the whole complex roped off. One of the storekeepers got a little pissy about it. But when I was done with him, he was sweet as a spoonful of sugar."

"What did you say to him?" Nick asked.

Sonny looked at his partner. The look in his eyes said: you don't want to know. "It looks like it went down inside the store. The lights were still on, and the alarm wasn't set. You know. You saw it."

"Tell me something I don't know," Nick said.

"Well, the blood on the top of the case? I think it came from the severed finger. There were scratch marks on the edge of the case. Could be from whatever the perp used to hack it off. There was no sign of the finger inside the store, so I got a crew checking the parking lot and the dumpsters out back."

"Did you check his car?" Nick asked.

"I had it impounded. They'll get a team on it in the morning."

"Anything else?" Nick questioned.

"That's all I have for now. The pictures and the report should be available in the morning."

"Who could possibly have done this?" Nick asked. "Pete was a good and well-trained cop. How could someone get the drop on him? Could you tell if anything was missing?"

"The cash register was full. It wasn't a robbery, or at least not someone who cared about the cash," Sonny answered. "I was thinking maybe guns, but the big ones were still on the wall. It didn't look as though any were missing from the showcase. We'll have to get an inventory. Maybe that will tell us something."

"Maybe," Nick said. "But why stab him?"

"Quieter than a gun," Sonny answered.

"How did the perp get close enough?" Nick asked. "You know Pete was an instructor in hand to hand. At the academy, he gave me a knife and ordered me to stick him. I'm quite a bit taller than he is and my arms are longer. But before I knew, it I was flat on my back on the ground, and Pete was on top of me. He jammed the knife into the ground about an inch from my ear. I'll never forget that day. The only way a person with a weapon of that type could get that close to him is if he knew him, or if he was somehow caught by total surprise. I don't think it was robbery at all. And why the finger? Why the hell cut off a finger? Not for the ring, that's for sure. The guns were worth much more than his wedding band."

"We'll know more tomorrow." Sonny stood up. "Are you okay?"

"Yeah. I'm okay. I just gotta think this out."

"Yeah, me, too. I'll see you in the morning, buddy," Sonny said. "We should know more then."

"Tomorrow," Nick replied. "Tell April thanks, and let me know how Elena is doing."

"Will do." Sonny left the room.

Nick sat there for a couple of minutes, then he got up, turned off the lights, and shut the squad room door behind him as he left. He headed for his townhouse, but decided to make a detour on the way.

Nick Greer had been raised Catholic. He had gone to a Catholic grade school and made all of the sacraments. But he hadn't been to church in years. Today he decided to stop at St. Raphael's.

It was shortly after noon when he pulled into the parking lot. There were a few cars scattered across the lot, but there were plenty of empty spaces. He pulled into one, killed his engine, and went into the church. He knew this was the church Pete and his family had attended for many years.

As he pushed open one of the large double doors, he immediately caught the aroma of incense and candles. There were about a dozen people milling around doing various things. He dropped into the back pew and knelt. Nick put his face in his hands and said a short prayer for his friend. Then he got up and left for home.

CHAPTER 3

The Lady In The Lake

The squad room was unusually quiet when Detective Lieutenant Nick Greer walked in. The normal Monday morning hubbub was replaced by an almost eerie silence. Other than the occasional sounds of shuffling paper or the sliding of a desk drawer opening or closing, you could have heard that proverbial pin drop. Everyone in the room had known and admired their ex-captain. He had always treated them with respect.

Rosa, the receptionist, looked up at Nick. Her reddened eyes were clouded by tears as she nodded to Nick, got up from her seat, and hugged him tightly. He wrapped his arms around her and held her for a moment. When she let go, she looked up to Nick and through teary eyes said, "You find the guy who did it. Promise me."

"I won't stop until I do. I promise."

Rosa went back to her seat behind her desk. She reached into a box of tissues, wiped her eyes and blew her nose.

It was eight-twenty and Nick was late. Though he had tried to sleep last night, his thoughts about his friend invaded his efforts. His dreams were haunted by the scene from Sunday morning. Each time he came to the part where he saw the severed finger, he awoke and sat up. Sue Kim's attempts to comfort him were fruitless.

Nick went directly to Sonny, who was sitting at his desk looking at his computer screen. "Anything?"

"I'm just reading the departmental announcement. The whole place is pretty well down. By the way, the boss wants to see us right away."

Nick tossed his keys onto his desk and went into the captain's office. Sonny followed.

Captain Lovett was waiting for them and motioned for his detectives to sit down. Nick took a chair on the right and Sonny on the left. With the exception of a few personal items, the office hadn't changed since Pete's retirement. The office was small but well organized. A five-foot wooden desk sat in the center of the room just far enough away from the rear wall to comfortably accommodate the large, brown leather swivel-chair in which the captain now sat. The pictures and credentials hanging on the wall behind him had changed, but the insignia of the Phoenix Bird and the motto—To Protect and to Serve—still stood out. The large bookshelf on the wall to Nick's left still contained department instruction and training manuals. Nick had sat there many times in the past, mostly discussing cases with his old boss and his new one. He looked at the nameplate on the desk. It seemed particularly out of place today. Spencer J. Lovett, Captain.

The captain was the first to speak. "I don't know what to say to either of you at this time. I know you are both grieving for Pete, as am I, and as is the entire department."

Nick and Sonny nodded silently.

"I want both of you on this. You're the best detectives we have and arguably the best there is, and as a team you're even better. But I need to know if you can handle it. I only ask because each of you had a personal relationship with Pete and his family, and I want to be sure you're both up to this."

Nick began to speak, but Sonny leaned forward and interrupted before a sound came out. "We're already on it, Captain. What's there to be sure of? Don't you even—"

"Just don't let feelings get in the way," the captain interjected.

Sonny pursed his lips and stared at his boss, who said, "Okay, Sergeant Madison. I got it." He looked to his left at Nick.

"What he said," Nick stated as he motioned his head to the detective sitting next to him.

"Okay. Good." The captain picked up a sheet of paper from his desk. "I have something for you. Perhaps a place to start. It seems there was a similar incident a few months ago."

Both detectives leaned toward the desk as Lovett continued, "A floater was found about eight months ago in the Tempe Town Lake."

"Yeah, I remember seeing it on the news," Sonny responded. "Robbery-murder I thought they said."

"Yeah, you're right, Detective," the captain responded. "That's what they said, but they left one part out." He looked back and forth between them and added, "The victim's left ring finger was missing."

"Wow," Nick said. A shocked Sonny shook his head.

The captain reached to the left side of his desk and handed each of his detectives a manila folder. "It's all in there. Go to Tempe. Talk with the investigators. See what they have to say."

Both detectives got up and left their captain's office. Sonny stopped, turned around, and looked like he was going to say something to Lovett. But he shook his head, turned back around, and followed Nick into the squad room.

Nick said to Sonny, "What were you going to say to Spence?"

"Well, believe it or not, I was about to apologize for my attitude with him, but I decided against it."

Rosa was standing at Nick's desk. "Lieutenant," she said, "the ME's office just called. Elena Mendoza is on her way there to ID the body. They said to let you know."

Nick grabbed his keys and headed for the door. Sonny yelled behind him, "Wait for me!"

Nick and Sonny were waiting as Elena arrived. April Madison was with her along with Jordana, the Mendoza's only daughter. As they walked over to the viewing window, Nick said, "Elena, you don't have to do this."

"Yes, Nick, I do." She nodded. "I really must do this."

Sonny's eyes found the button to the right of the six-foot-wide window. He had pushed it so many times in the past, signaling the attendant to open the screen covering the window. But this time he hesitated as he looked at Elena. She nodded. He pushed the button. A few moments later the blinds were pulled open. Directly inside the window was a gurney with a body on it. The body was covered with a light blue sheet. Jack Konesky stood beside the gurney. Nick nodded, and Jack removed the sheet from the dead man's face.

Jordana began sobbing, as she saw her father's face. April wrapped her arms around her and said, "Let it out, baby. Let it out."

A straight-faced Elena nodded to Nick. Sonny knocked on the window. Jack put the cover back over the head of the cadaver, and the blinds closed.

Jordana was still crying, but she was now hugging her mother. Elena's face was unusually emotionless. April said to Elena, "Come on, I'll take you both home." They left without another word being said.

Nick looked at Sonny. "Let's go to Tempe. They're waiting for us."

"Huh?" Sonny questioned.

Nick held up his phone for his partner to see the text message from Captain Lovett: *Tempe is waiting for you. Detective Cruz 480-555-2322.*

"Got your keys?" Nick asked.

"Yeah," Sonny answered.

"You're driving."

"I figured that."

As Sonny pulled out of the parking lot, Nick called Detective Cruz. They agreed to meet at the Denny's restaurant at Thirteenth and Broadway in Tempe.

* * *

As they walked through the door of the restaurant, they saw a young lady sitting alone in the front booth. Above the booth was a sign that read: Reserved for the Tempe Police Department. Some of the restaurants around Maricopa County reserved a courtesy booth for their men and women in blue. It was mostly beat cops who would come in and fill out reports, but others came, too. They were given complimentary coffee or tea.

Sonny and Nick walked over to the booth, and Nick said, "Detective Cruz, I presume?"

She reached out her hand to both of the visiting policemen and said, "Carmen, Carmen Cruz. Please have a seat."

Carmen Cruz was an attractive Hispanic lady. She looked to be in her early to mid-thirties. Some of her long, black hair rested on her shoulders, the rest hung down her back. She had been promoted to detective and assigned to the Tempe PD homicide division less than a year ago.

Sonny slid across the orange seat and Nick followed. "I'm Lieutenant Nick Greer. This is my partner, Sergeant Sonny Madison."

A server came to the table and Nick said, "Just coffee for me, please, black."

"Coffee for me, too, cream," Sonny said.

The waitress left and Nick said to Carmen, "Thank you for meeting us on such short notice."

"Partners? We haven't had partners for a long time, budget cuts you know. Maybe I should move to Phoenix," she said with a grin.

"Us, too. This is a special case so we're working it together. Actually the whole department wants to help," Nick responded.

“Yes, I heard. Let me say, I’m sorry to hear about your loss. I met your Captain Mendoza once at a lecture about a year ago. He seemed like a nice man. He was very knowledgeable and an excellent speaker. So, how can I be of help to you?”

“We understand you worked on a case about eight months ago,” Nick said. “A floater in the lake.”

“Yes, I remember it well,” she answered. “It was my first case as a detective. Morgan Montgomery was her name. We never did find the perp. The case is still open, but it’s gone cold.”

“Did you have any leads at all?”

“Nothing! Not a clue. It went down as a robbery-homicide.”

Sonny spoke, “We understand there was something unusual about the condition of the body—a missing digit?”

“Yes,” Carmen answered. “Her left ring finger was gone.”

“Didn’t you think that was a little unusual?” Sonny questioned.

“Yes, I did, but my sergeant said the perp probably couldn’t get her ring off so he took the finger and all. Our investigation found her to be pretty well-to-do, and she wore a good-sized stone. Her husband was an investment banker in Scottsdale, you know.”

“Again, you didn’t think that was strange—the finger missing?’ Nick questioned.

“Yes, I did, but like I said, it was my first case. My sergeant said the finger was probably in the water; it was fish food. He was pretty adamant about it so I let it go. But there was one thing that bothered me.”

“Sonny leaned forward. “That was?”

“When we fished her out of the water, she was wearing an expensive diamond necklace. I thought, if it was a robbery, why didn’t the perp take it? My sergeant said the perp either didn’t see it, or he was interrupted and didn’t have time to take it. I told him it would have been quicker and easier to pull the chain off than to cut off a finger, but he dismissed the idea. He said he had over twenty years as a detective, and he didn’t like being second-guessed, especially by a newbie. I think he had a problem with female detectives, if you ask me.”

“So you don’t think it was a robbery,” Nick stated, more than asked.

“No, sir, I don’t.”

“Do you think your lieutenant would cooperate with us?” Nick asked.

"I doubt it, unless you can talk to the dead." She took a sip of coffee, looked up at her guests, and said, "A heart attack took him two months ago."

The waitress returned with two beige coffee cups and set them in front of both men. She filled the cups from a brown plastic pitcher and set a small bowl with cream packets in it on the table. She topped off the cup sitting in front of Carmen and left.

"Do you remember how she was dressed?" Nick questioned. "Would the necklace have been easily visible?"

"Yep. You don't wear a piece of bling like that and hide it under a turtleneck sweater. It would have been plainly visible. She was wearing a pullover knit top. The neckline was low enough to easily expose the diamond, and more, if you know what I mean. It would have been hard to miss, especially for a thief."

"What about the husband? Did you clear him?" Sonny asked.

"Yeah, he was clean. He was in Seattle at a seminar. He was one of the main speakers. We were able to account for his whole time there. The ME said she was killed Friday, early evening. She floated up Sunday afternoon around five o'clock. The husband flew in Sunday morning. We checked into him thoroughly and found absolutely nothing to implicate him. He didn't even have a life insurance policy on her. There's no way he did it."

"Anything else? A purse maybe?" Sonny asked.

Cruz shook her head. "Nope. We figured the perp took it. It's all in the report." She reached down to the seat beside her and pulled up a manila folder. She tossed it, along with two of her cards, onto the white table, and said, "It's all yours, Detectives. I copied every page. Find the bastard who killed Pete." She dropped two one-dollar bills on the table, got up, and abruptly left.

The two detectives looked at each other. "Uh, was it something we said?" Sonny asked.

Nick shrugged his shoulders and motioned for the check. The waitress came over to the table and said, "For you guys, the coffee is always on us."

"Thank you," Nick said as he dropped two ones on the table.

As the two detectives walked to the parking lot, they saw Cruz's car rolling away. Sonny said, "Did you get a load of that?"

"Of what?"

"Detective Cruz."

"Yeah," Nick said. "She's a lot better looking than you."

"Oh, partner, I'm hurt." Sonny grinned.

They got into Sonny's car and headed back to Phoenix. Nick read over the report as Sonny navigated his Chevy through the traffic and on to the precinct.

"Does anything stick out at you?" Sonny asked as they merged from Interstate 10 onto the Black Canyon Freeway.

"Yeah," Nick answered. "It looks like both were stabbed in the heart, and both had their left ring finger sliced off. It says here the fatal wound was nine inches deep and zero-point-zero-two-inches wide, and went directly into the aorta. It looks to be the same with Pete. We'll know more tomorrow when the final ME report comes in."

"Uhhh," Sonny said, "you don't think . . . ?"

"Think what?"

"Please tell me it's not another serial killer."

"Christ, I hope not!" Nick said. "First the Baseline killer, then Hausener and Dieteman, then the Tucson massacre. And let's not forget the Jodi Arias trial. They all went national. All we need is another scandal, and even the airliners will go around Arizona. They won't even want to enter our airspace."

Both Nick Greer and Sonny Madison spent the rest of the afternoon searching for any other cases involving missing fingers, but they found nothing.

* * *

On his way home, Nick decided to check on Elena. He rang the doorbell, and Jordana came to the door. "Hi, Nick. What's up?"

"Is your mom home?"

"Yeah, come on in. Have a seat in the living room. I'll get her."

Nick sat on the sofa and waited for Elena. When she came in, he stood and hugged her. "Are you okay, Elena? I just came by to check on you."

"Yeah, I'm okay, I guess, considering the circumstances. Jordana is a big help and April was wonderful."

"What about the boys?"

"Pete Jr. is flying in from San Antonio. He should be here in the morning. Jordana will pick him up at the airport. We haven't gotten ahold of Pete's mother yet. She's in Mexico City. She's been there ever since Pete's father died, you know."

"What about Miguel? Have they found him yet?" Nick knew Miguel Mendoza, their second oldest, was on deployment somewhere in Afghanistan.

"They called this morning. They are pulling him out of his unit, and they said I should expect a call this afternoon or this evening. I've been waiting by the phone all day. His dad was so proud of him. How do I tell him?"

"Elena, he'll probably already know when he calls. I'm sure they will have a chaplain meet with him before he calls you. He's a good boy. He'll be worried about you and Jordana. Remember that when he calls, okay?"

She nodded. "That's what April said."

"Is there anything you need? Anything I can do or get for you?"

"Not unless you can make the phone ring."

"Okay, I'm going to go now. Call me if you need anything. I'll see my way out."

She nodded. He hugged her, left the room, and headed for the door.

Jordana followed him outside and said, "Nick, I'm worried about something."

"What?" he asked.

"Mama cried when she first heard the news, but since then she has shown no emotion, none at all. But I see anger in her eyes. I mentioned it to Mrs. Madison. She said it is a way of coping, but not my mama. She should be crying. She loved him more than I could ever imagine."

"April is probably right," Nick responded. "She knows about that stuff. Don't push her. She's had a major shock to her emotions, and she has a lot to deal with. I think when the family all gets together you'll see a change."

"Funny. That's what Mrs. Madison said." Nick kissed her on the forehead and left.

* * *

It was six-thirty when he arrived home. Sue Kim was waiting for him. He bent his lanky frame down and kissed her. Her long, black hair was still damp from the shower she had just taken. She held him tight and said, "Are you all right, baby?"

"Yeah. I'm a little hungry," he answered.

"I got chicken in the oven."

"Ooooh! Smells good. I noticed it when I came in," he said. "When did you have time to bake a chicken?"

"Boston Market. I got your favorite, buttered corn and carrots. Should be ready in"—he heard the beeping of the microwave as she punched in the time and pushed start—"about sixty seconds." He smiled.

Sue Kim opened the refrigerator and pulled out a Bud Light. She handed it to him and said, "This should hold you until then."

"Thank you, my dear." He took the bottle from her hand, twisted the cap, raised the bottle to his lips, and took a long drink. He walked to the end of the kitchen counter and looked at the oval wicker basket that contained mail and bills. "Any mail?"

"Just junk. I dumped it." Sue Kim removed the chicken from the oven and placed it in the middle of the table.

Just then the microwave dinged. Sue Kim said, "Have a seat. Dinner is served."

The small kitchen table was set. Nick sat as Sue Kim put a spoon in both bowls of vegetables and set them on the table. She went to the refrigerator, pulled another beer out, reached into the freezer for a frosted glass, and sat across from Nick.

"You sure went out of your way today," Nick said as he attacked the chicken.

"Yep." She giggled. "The line at the drive-through was super long. I actually had to go inside. I hope you appreciate it."

After they were finished eating, Nick got up and put his dishes into the dishwasher. Sue Kim did the same and wiped off the kitchen table. "Sit down. I have something for you," she said.

His brows came together as he squinted. "What?"

She pointed to one of the chairs at the table. "Sit."

Nick sat in his chair as Sue Kim left the room. A few seconds later she came back with a manila folder. She tossed it onto the table in front of Nick. "Have at it, Detective."

Nick opened the file and looked up at her. The file contained the lab report on Pete Mendoza. She sat and watched him as he read the report.

Nick read over it carefully. It mirrored the report from Tempe. The cause of death was a puncture to the upper aortic arch. The wound was nine-inches deep, zero-point-zero-two-inches thick. The size of a common everyday ice pick, he thought. The finger was chopped off clean. Just like in the Tempe case.

"You should know he didn't suffer much," she stated.

"He was stabbed in the heart. How could he not have suffered?"

"Nick, if you stab someone in the heart, though they don't die right away, they lose consciousness almost immediately. Death would occur in about five minutes, but he would have lost consciousness after ten or fifteen seconds. You see, the brain can only survive for about five minutes without oxygen. With no blood pumping to it, the brain is deprived of that needed oxygen, and that's when death occurs. Whoever stabbed him was either lucky, or knew what he was doing. The puncture went straight in, not at an angle."

She was sitting across from him. Nick got up and went over to her. "So, if he was sitting in the chair and the perp was standing"—he brought his hand down and shoved it forward to the center of her chest—"it would've had a downward thrust. Even if Pete was standing"—she stood up for him—"and the perp hit him this way"—he lifted his right arm and brought it down to the same spot—"it would still have entered at a downward angle." He thought for a moment. "So Pete must have been lying on his back. But how could that be?"

She smiled. "Keep reading. You'll find something interesting in there. It just might answer your question. It'll be in the system in the morning, but I thought I'd give you a head start. I'll be on Facebook if you need me." She got up and went into the living room where she opened her laptop and powered it up.

Nick turned the page to the toxicology report. He stopped, looked back at it a second time, and called out, "Sue! Come here."

Sue Kim closed her laptop and went into the kitchen. She stood behind Nick and put her hands on his shoulders, rubbing them lightly. "What's up, baby?"

"Is this what I think it is?" He pointed to the statement: traces of Rohypnol. "Are you sure?"

"Yep! I did the test myself. I checked it twice, and then I checked it again."

"What would Pete be doing with a date rape drug in his system?"

"I don't know, baby. That's your area of expertise. All I can tell you is it definitely was in his system. Someone slipped Pete Mendoza a rufie."

"That would explain how the perp got the drop on him in the first place." He thought for a moment. "And why he was lying on the floor."

She kissed him on the cheek and spoke lightly in his ear, "Thank you, Sue. Oh, you're welcome."

He turned around and kissed her. "Thank you, baby. You're great."

"Yeah, I know." She giggled as she turned and headed back into the living room.

Nick thought for a moment and said, "Hold on a minute. Come back. I need to tell you something."

"You sound serious," she said as she sat across from him.

"There was a case in Tempe a few months ago. A female vic was stabbed in the heart, and her left ring finger was missing. Tempe thought it was a robbery-murder. Sonny and I interviewed the investigator today, and she gave us a copy of the file. It was the same size weapon, and, like I said, the ring finger was gone. But there was nothing in the tox report about any Rohypnol."

"How long was she dead?"

"They found her floating in the lake. They figure a couple of days."

"Rohypnol dissipates from the system pretty fast. It is usually gone and untraceable after about forty-eight hours. By the time the ME got it, there would have been no trace. Unless they thought to check the hair, but that would be unusual."

"The hair?"

"Rohypnol can remain in the hair follicles for months," she stated.

"You're not only beautiful, but you're smart," Nick stated.

"I thought you already knew all that." She got up and went back into the living room. Nick looked at her, shook his head, and smiled.

CHAPTER 4

The Wash

It was Tuesday morning. Nick walked into the squad room and checked the message slot with his name on it. It was empty. He looked up and noticed that Rosa wasn't at her desk. Her desk was empty and all her personal items were gone. He wondered what was going on as he went to his desk and sat down. Just then, Sonny came in. He stopped and looked at the bare desk.

Sonny looked at Nick and said, "Hey, Gumby, where's Rosa?"

Nick shrugged. Nick hated to be called Gumby. Someone, he didn't remember who, had hung that moniker on him in Junior High School because he was already six feet tall and very thin. Sonny Madison was the only one who called him that now, and the only one who could get away with it.

Four other detectives were at their desks working at their computers or on the phone. There were eight gray desks positioned throughout the room, each contained a computer and a phone, except one had only a phone.

"Sonny, I got something for you." He handed Sonny the Mendoza file.

Sonny sat at his desk and began reading the file, but he was interrupted as Captain Lovett came into the room. "Everybody listen up. I have an announcement."

All attention was on the captain, who continued, "As you have already noticed, Rosa is not here. I'm sorry to inform you, but due to departmental budget cuts, her position has been eliminated." He waited until the groans subsided. "Your messages will be channeled through the main phone system and sent to your department-issued phones. I'm sorry, but it is what it is." As he turned to go back into his office, he motioned for Nick and Sonny to follow him.

"Anything happening?" the captain asked as the two detectives sat down and Lovett took his seat behind his desk.

"Yeah," Nick answered. "Both the Tempe case and Pete's seem to be the same MO." The captain leaned forward as Nick continued, "The ME report is in, and it looks like the same perp. It was the same type of weapon, and both were stabbed in the heart. And they both had the same finger severed."

Spencer reached for a file on his desk. "Yeah, I got it here. Give me a moment while I take a look at it." He looked at Nick with puzzled eyes as he opened the manila folder and read it over.

Sonny wondered why Nick suddenly got up, closed the captain's door, and sat back down. A few seconds later, he got his answer as their captain spoke in a louder than normal manner, "A rufie? Pete Mendoza? How the hell could that happen?"

Sonny looked puzzled. Nick looked at him and said, "There's Rohypnol in the tox report, Sonny. I didn't get a chance to tell you."

"You gotta be shitting me. No way!" Sonny shook his head vehemently. "Huh-uh, Pete wouldn't let that happen! No way."

"Apparently he did," Lovett responded. "Well, Nick, you seem to have known all about this before any of us. I guess knowing someone in the crime lab has its advantages."

"I know a lot of people in the crime lab," the detective responded.

Lovett smiled as he looked at the signature on the report. "Yeah, I'm sure you do.

"Okay, gentlemen, check with your contact in Tempe. Find out why they didn't check for Rohypnol."

"I already know the answer, Captain."

"And?"

"Rohypnol only stays in the system for a couple of days. It would have been gone by the time the ME got to it. Besides, they were convinced it was a robbery-murder. But Rohypnol can remain in the hair follicles for several months. Maybe we'll get lucky and have some hair samples. Maybe we can have the body exhumed."

"Hmmm," the captain said as he rubbed his chin, "your contact in the lab is a pretty smart cookie." Nick shrugged. Spencer added, "And cute, too."

Sonny chuckled and shook his head. "You got that right."

"Let me know what you find," the captain said in a tone of dismissal.

The two detectives stood and began to leave when they heard their boss say, "Wait a second."

They turned around. Lovett continued, "Pete's widow, does she know about the finger?"

"Her name is Elena," Sonny interjected.

Nick responded to their boss's question. "Not yet, but we'll have to release the body soon. I'm sure she'll notice."

"No one knows about that except us and Tempe. We need to keep that information under wraps for as long as we can. All we need is for the press to get wind of it."

Both detectives knew what their boss meant. Once word got out that there was a pattern in the murders, all the television and radio stations, along with the newspapers, would be running it as their lead story. History has shown that when such an item goes public, the police end up dealing with the nuts who claim to be the killer. But as long as the public didn't know about the fingers, it would be easier for the police to weed out the false confessions.

"I'll talk with her," Nick said. "I think it will be okay. I don't see a problem. She's a cop's wife. She knows the drill."

The detectives left the room and returned to their desks. Sonny finished reading the report while Nick pondered on how he would tell Elena about the missing finger. He knew he needed to do it soon before she found out herself. He decided to go see her, but then he remembered Pete Jr. was flying in this morning. Let them be together for a while, he thought. This afternoon should work.

Nick pulled his Android from his belt and called the number on Carmen Cruz's card. The phone rang, but it went straight to voice mail: "I can't answer the phone right now. Please leave a message, and I will return your call as soon as I can." Nick left a message for her to call him, and he pushed the end call button on his phone.

Sonny came over to Nick and sat in the gray chair beside his partner's desk. He held the Mendoza file in his hand. It was open, and he looked at it and shook his head. "You know, this tox report explains a lot."

"What are you thinking, Sonny?"

"Pete was too savvy to let a stranger slip him a Mickey Finn. I'm thinking it must have been someone he knew, someone he trusted, someone he would've never thought would do something like that."

"I agree," Nick responded. "Call the crime lab. Tell them to put a team together and meet you at Pete's store. Go through the trash. Get DNA and prints on every cup, straw, spoon, and napkin in there. Run them all through CODIS. Shake the tree. Let's see what falls out."

"Got it." Sonny headed for his desk to make the call.

"One more thing," Nick said.

Sonny turned and looked at his partner. "Get Sue Kim over there. I want her on this."

Sonny nodded. "Where will you be?"

"I'll join you later. I'm going to go see Elena."

Just then Captain Lovett came into the room. "Greer! Madison!" He motioned for the two detectives to follow him into his office. The captain closed the door behind him, sat at his desk and said, "We got another one! It's in a desert wash north of Happy Valley Road." He reached to his computer keyboard, pushed print, and the printer behind him came alive. Spencer took a sheet of paper from the printer and handed it to Nick. "Here's the info. There's a team there now. It sounds like the body has been there for quite a while, but they say there's a finger missing. The left ring finger. One of you needs to go."

"That'll be me, I guess." Nick answered.

Both detectives left. Sonny made arrangements for a crime team to meet him at Pete's Pistols 'N Parts, and he asked for Sue Kim to be among them. Nick got into his car and headed to the crime scene.

About twenty minutes later he turned right off of Happy Valley Road and drove about half a mile north until he saw several police cars, emergency vehicles, and a forensics SUV, all parked along a dry wash about a hundred yards off of the road. He pulled off of the road, drove his Taurus as close to the scene as he could, killed the engine, and walked the rest of the way. Nick knew this wash channeled huge amounts of water when it rained. He also knew it had been dry for quite a while.

A uniformed officer met him as he approached. He looked at the gold shield hanging from Nick's belt. "Lieutenant Greer, I presume. "I'm Sergeant Thomas, Chris Thomas."

"What do we have, Sergeant?" Nick asked.

"Some kids were riding their bikes in the wash and found a foot sticking up. When the crime scene crew got here and pulled the body up, we saw a finger was missing. Someone on the crime scene team said to call you guys."

Nick knew the missing finger was to be kept secret so he asked, "Who told you to call us?"

The sergeant pointed one of the team members. "Her."

Sue Kim turned her head, looked at him, and said, "Hello Lieutenant Greer." She giggled, turned back around and continued her work.

Nick smiled. "I guess you're not with Sonny."

She looked up at him and said, puzzled, "Huh? Why would I be with Sonny?"

Nick shook his head. "Never mind. I'll explain later. What can you tell me? What have we got?"

The body was lying on a sheet. She said, "It looks like he was stabbed in the heart. He's been here a while. The body could have washed down here from about anywhere. The last rain caused a lot of flooding, you'll remember, but this is why you're here." Sue Kim held up the dead man's left hand. The left ring finger was completely gone, just like Pete's.

Nick nodded. "Be sure to check the hair for, well, you know."

"Of course!"

"And see that Jack gets this one," Nick said.

"I'll see to it myself, Lieutenant." Sue Kim reached into her forensics case, pulled out a plastic bag, covered the dead man's left hand with it, and secured it with tape.

Nick turned, went back to his car and drove back to the precinct. He needed to talk with his captain.

* * *

Sonny drove to Pete's gun store and waited for the crime team to arrive. When twenty minutes had passed, he decided to call and see where they were. Just as he pulled his cell phone from its holder, an SUV arrived. The letters on the outside of the vehicle read: Phoenix Crime Scene Unit.

Sonny got out of his Malibu, walked to the gun store's door, and removed the yellow police tape. He reached into his pocket and pulled out the key he had removed from the store two days before.

Two men got out of the SUV and walked toward Sonny, who said, "Where is Sue Kim? I specifically asked for her."

"She's busy on another call. We're perfectly capable of handling it."

Sonny could tell the man was upset and said, "I didn't mean . . . Oh, never mind. I'm Sergeant Madison." He held his hand out to the man. He shook the detective's hand, but Sonny could feel the tension.

"I'm CSI Barrera." He looked toward his partner. "This is CSI Macy." Macy shook Sonny's hand.

"Okay, gentlemen, let's get to it," Sonny said as he unlocked the door. "We're looking for anything that may have DNA or might possibly contain Rohypnol."

* * *

He was almost at the station when his cell phone rang through his car speakers. "Nick Greer," he answered.

"It's Carmen, Detective Cruz, Tempe PD. You called?"

"Yes, ma'am, I had a couple of questions for you."

"I'm sorry I didn't return your call earlier. I've been busy all day. What can I do for you?"

"Your lake lady, could she have had any Rohypnol in her system?"

"A date rape drug? I'm sure you read the tox report. There were no drugs in her system, but Rohypnol wouldn't show after a couple of days, anyway. Why do you ask?"

"Just a hunch. How about her personal effects? Maybe a hairbrush or lipstick?"

"No effects, remember? No purse. Nothing."

Nick thought for a moment, then said, "Do you think the family would give us a problem if we wanted to exhume the body?"

"That would be a little hard to do."

"Why?"

"She's ashes. She was cremated and scattered over Lake Tahoe, if I remember correctly. What's going on? Does this have something to do with Pe . . . your captain?"

"Keep this under your hat, but Pete had traces of Rohypnol in his system."

"What? No way!" she exclaimed. "Are you sure?"

"Positive."

"That would explain how someone got the drop on him."

"Yeah, and there's more."

"What?"

"We need to keep the finger bit under wraps, because I think we have a serial killer. We don't want the public to know about the finger."

"Do you think two vics are enough to declare it a serial killer?"

"Three. I just came from another one. The left ring finger is gone."

"Wow! Where?"

"North Phoenix. It'll be on the news. I saw the Channel Five van coming as I left. I'm sure more followed."

"Uh, stabbed in the chest, like the others?" Carmen asked.

"Oh, yeah," he answered.

"Keep me in the loop."

"Will do." He disconnected the phone call as he pulled into the police parking lot.

Nick Greer walked into his captain's office and sat down. He looked at his boss and said, "Well, Cap, we got ourselves a serial killer."

"You're sure?" Lovett asked.

Nick took a breath, exhaled, and nodded. "I wish I wasn't."

"Okay, I'll inform the chief." Captain Lovett smiled and added, "By the way, Lieutenant, welcome back to hell!"

CHAPTER 5

The Leak

Nick pressed his finger on the doorbell and waited for a moment. He was about to ring it a second time when his ears caught the sound of the dead bolt being released. The door opened, and Jordana Mendoza greeted him. "Hi, Nick. Come on in."

Nick walked into the foyer. Jordana closed the door behind him and reached her arms out to him. He bent his lanky frame down, gave her a hug, and asked, "How are you, sweetie?"

"We're coping."

"What about your mom. How is she handling it?"

"Mama's in the kitchen with Petey. I picked him up at the airport this morning. Let's go in there."

Nick followed her into the kitchen. Elena and Pete Jr. were sitting at the kitchen table drinking coffee. Pete got up and shook Nick's hand. "I'm sorry for your loss doesn't quite cut it," Nick stated.

"I know," young Pete responded. "I understand. You loved him, too."

You're the second person who has said that, he thought. He looked toward Elena Mendoza. "How are you holding up, Elena?"

"I'm okay. We're still waiting to hear from Miguel."

"Is there anything you need?" Nick asked. "Is there anything I can do? Anything I can get you?"

"No, Nick, but we need to talk." She looked at her children and said, "Leave us alone for a few minutes, please."

Pete looked more puzzled by their mother's request than did his sister. "Okay, Mama," Jordana said. She looked at her brother. "Come on, Petey. Let's go into the family room and let them talk."

"Have a seat," Elena said to her guest. "Would you like a cup of coffee or tea?"

"No, thank you, Elena. I'm fine. I have something to tell you. But first, is there something you wanted to talk to me about?"

She looked at Nick. Her eyes exhibited a mixture of disappointment and accusation as she asked, "Why didn't you tell me about my husband's finger?"

Her question caught the detective by surprise. "Uhh . . . that's why I'm here. How did you know?"

"Do you think, after all the years he'd been a cop, and all the people I know, that I wouldn't find out?"

"No, Elena, that's not it at all. I wanted to tell you myself. That's why I came here today." He took her hands in his and looked into her brown eyes. "Tell me, how did you know?"

"How I know is not important. What I want to know is why you didn't tell me sooner?"

Nick knew not to push her. He would find out the leak later. "I couldn't, Elena. I wanted to, but please understand, I couldn't. We have to keep that part under wraps." He squeezed her hands lightly. "I must ask you. Who else knows?"

"Just Jordy. We haven't told Petey yet. Why? What's going on?"

Nick paused for a moment. He wanted to choose his words carefully. "Elena, I'm afraid Pete isn't the only one this has happened to."

She looked puzzled. "What do you mean, not the only one?"

"There have been two more cases in the county where a body has been found and the left ring finger was missing. I'm afraid there appears to be a pattern."

"A serial killer?" Her voice was raised. "Are you telling me my Pete was a victim of a serial killer? How could that be possible?"

"I don't know, Elena. I honestly don't know, but I promise you I won't stop until I find out."

Just then Pete Jr. and Jordana came into the room. They had heard their mother's voice from the next room. "What are you talking about? What about a serial killer?" Pete asked.

Nick looked up at the two siblings and said, "Why don't you both sit, and I'll explain as much as I can."

"Yeah, you better," Pete said. "Jordy just told me one of Dad's fingers is missing. That's mafia stuff. I guarantee you my father wasn't involved with anything illegal or sinister—"

"Pete, your father was a fine man. He was a good cop, husband, father, and friend. He was an honorable man. I guarantee you he wasn't involved with any bad people. Please sit. Let me explain to you what I can." Pete and Jordana sat down at the table.

"First of all, when I came here on Sunday morning to tell you, Elena, I didn't say anything because I figured you would have enough grief to deal with. And besides, we didn't know whether or not it would be an issue."

"An issue?" Pete yelled. "My father's finger was chopped off, and you didn't know if it would be an issue?"

Nick looked at the young man. "Pete, I meant a police issue. Sometimes information has to be withheld until we can sort it out."

He looked at Elena. "I'm sorry I didn't tell you sooner, but I couldn't at the time." He looked back and forth to all those sitting at the table. "Actually, this is something I must ask you to keep within the walls of this household. I realize you will need to tell Miguel, but no one else can know. No one, at least not until we find the person who did it. If the media gets wind of it, it would not help us at all. Do you understand?"

Nick looked at each person, and they all nodded in agreement.

"Okay," Nick continued. "Here's what I have so far. There have been two other cases where we have found bodies with the same finger missing. One was in Tempe a few months ago, and the other one came up in a wash in the desert in North Phoenix just this morning. It will probably be all over the news tonight, if it isn't already." He paused and looked around the table. "I believe we have a serial killer."

All three looked at him with curious looks on their faces. "Once it gets out that there's another serial killer in Phoenix, all the nuts will come out. People will come in to the station and confess, just to get attention. Or some will blame a neighbor, or a co-worker they don't like. It happens every time something like this surfaces. But as long as no one knows about the fingers, it will help us weed out the crazies and help us find the real perpetrator. You all understand that, right?"

Elena said, "Yes, Nick. We are the family of a police captain. We understand completely." She looked at both of her children and stated with authority, "No one in this family will leak the information. I promise." Then, she looked directly into the detective's eyes and with total resolve in her voice stated, "Pete said many times that you and Sonny were two of the best detectives he had ever worked with, and that the two of you together were unstoppable. You and Sonny do whatever you have to, but find the son of a bitch who killed my husband." The look in her eyes and throughout her face was as serious as he had ever seen, and he had never, in the many years he had known Elena Mendoza, heard her use foul language of any type.

Nick looked at his hostess and said, "Elena, I promise you, I will not stop until we do. You have my word."

Elena nodded. "Does April Madison know about the finger?"

"Uh, I don't know," Nick responded. "Sonny doesn't talk about his cases with her. He's always made it a point to keep his work and his personal life separate, but this is so close to all of us. I really don't know for sure, but my guess is, no."

"She should know." Elena nodded her head with conviction. "She should know!"

"Okay, I'll tell Sonny what you said," Nick stated.

She nodded.

Nick got up and left the kitchen. Jordana followed him. As they neared the door, she said, "Nick, I'm really worried about Mama. She's not acting right."

"Well, yeah," Nick answered. "She just lost the love of her life."

"Yeah, Nick, I know. But it's more than that. She has been acting strangely for the past three or four weeks. She seems angry. I asked her a couple of times what was wrong. She just shrugged and said, 'Nothing, *mija*, nothing. Everything is fine.' I wonder if she is sick."

Nick said, "I don't know, honey. If you find out anything, will you let me know?"

"Of course," she said, as he left the house. She closed the door behind him.

CHAPTER 6

The House of Gold

Sonny's crew was meticulous in their work. A second CSI van pulled up about twenty minutes after Sonny arrived. The two crews processed the entire store: every scrap of paper, every pencil, every pen, every cup and glass. Sonny removed the laptop computer that sat on Pete's desk, bagged it, tagged it, and took it with him. He would take it to the geeks and have them go through it for any possible clues.

After about an hour and a half, everything was collected and deposited in Barrera and Macy's van. Sonny locked the door and reapplied the police tape. He thought about going to Barrera and apologizing again for the Sue Kim comment, but his cell phone rang. He pulled it from his belt. The screen said: Nick. Sonny answered, "Where be you, partner?"

"I'm on my way back. How are things going there?"

"We're just wrapping up. I'm getting ready to head back to the precinct. You know there were two crews here, but Sue Kim never showed?"

"Yeah, they sent her up north. She was there when I got there. That's why they called us. I'll explain when I see you."

"Got another one, I presume?"

"Yeah." Nick took a breath and exhaled. "We've got another one."

* * *

Sonny Madison was sitting at his desk, typing on his keyboard, when Nick Greer came into the squad room and sat behind his desk. Sonny got up and walked over to him. He grabbed a chair, pulled it up beside Nick's desk and sat down. "Okay, fill me in."

"The vic was a male Caucasian. A couple of kids found him in a wash. He was covered with mud. It looks like he'd been there since the last big rain, about a month ago, I think."

"The left ring finger was hacked off," Sonny stated.

"Oh, yeah!" Nick rubbed his forehead. "Chopped off clean."

Sonny said, "Let's see what we have for common denominators."

Nick reached into his desk drawer and removed a yellow legal-sized notepad and tossed it onto the desk. He then reached into his shirt pocket and pulled out a pen. He took a deep breath, exhaled, and said, "Okay, let's see what we got."

Sonny began, "We have two males and one female, so it's not limited to one sex. All three of them were stabbed in the heart one time, and they all were missing their left ring finger. What else?"

"All three vics were dumped in water," Nick replied.

"The last vic was in the desert," Sonny said. "There's not a whole helluva lot of water there."

"He was found in a wash, remember?"

"Oh, yeah, that's right," Sonny replied. "So they all were dumped in water, but neither Pete nor the Tempe vic had any water in their lungs. I'll bet today's vic didn't either. Hmmm." He scratched his head. "What do you make of that?"

"I don't know. It could be part of his MO or maybe just coincidence. What's your take on the ring fingers?"

Sonny shrugged. "I don't know, man. It really doesn't make sense." He thought for a moment, then continued, "So the three things we have are the fatal wounds to the heart, the severed ring fingers, and the bodies dumped in water."

"Probably the weapon, too," Nick added. "I'm willing to bet the autopsy will show the exact same-sized wound."

"There may be one more thing," Sonny sort of whispered.

"What?"

"I'm not sure, yet. Let me check one more thing before I tell you something you don't want to hear."

Nick looked at his partner. "What is it, Sonny?"

"Nick, trust me. It's just a hunch. I shouldn't have even mentioned it. I gotta check on something first. I promise, I'll let you know what I find as soon as I find it."

Sonny got up and left the squad room. He heard Nick call after him, "Madison!" But he just kept going.

* * *

Sonny got into his car and drove straight to the county morgue. He pushed the door open and went in. Jack Konesky was sitting at his desk going over some paperwork. He looked up and saw the detective. "Well, Detective Madison. To what do I owe the pleasure of your company?"

"Hey, Jack. You're getting a new stiff. He should be here any time now. Some kids found him in a wash up north. The left ring finger is gone. Sue Kim was to see that it went straight to you. When you get—"

"Already got it," the medical examiner said. He pointed to a body lying on a metal table in the center of the room. It was covered with a blue sheet.

Just then, Sue Kim came through the back door. "Well, hello there, Mr. Sonny. What brings you to this little corner of the world?"

"I heard there was some free beer around here," he answered.

Her long, black hair blew across her face as she giggled and pointed to the corner of the room. "The third drawer on the left. Don't worry about the cadaver. He won't bother you."

Sonny's eyes were as big as golf balls. He opened his mouth to speak, but nothing came out.

Jack said with a surprised tone in his voice, "Well, I'll be dipped. Sonny Madison, speechless!" He looked toward Sue Kim and back to Sonny. "I gotta write this down in my journal. The smart ass of smart asses upstaged by a girl! Hey, maybe it'll make the department news bulletin."

Sonny laughed. "It looks like you taught her well. She'll fit in here just fine."

"Oh, no, I'm only here to help," Sue Kim said. "I work upstairs, remember? What did you want to know about this one, anyway?" She pointed to the body on the table.

"Do you have an ID yet?" Sonny asked. "There's something I want to check out."

"He just got here, so hold on a sec." Sue Kim walked to the end of the room, reached into a box and pulled out a pair of surgical gloves. She slipped them on as she walked back to the body. She uncovered the corpse. Jack, who had already donned a pair of gloves, joined her. He turned the body on its right side, and Sue Kim reached into the left rear pocket and removed the victim's wallet. Jack let the body go back to its original position.

"Let's see what we have here," she said as she took a pair of forceps and carefully pulled out the victim's driver's license. She held it up by the corner and said, "Richard Joseph Perrotta, 6733 West Casa Del Oro Drive, Phoenix." She looked closer at the driver's license and said, "Hmm, guess what? He was an organ donor."

"It looks like that ship has sailed," Jack responded.

Sonny retrieved a sheet of paper from the desk and wrote the name and address on it. "Thank you. I'll check missing persons."

"What about the next of kin?" Jack asked.

"I'll handle that," Sonny said. He turned, left the morgue, and headed back to the squad room.

* * *

Sonny fired up his computer and checked missing person's reports. He discovered that a Richard Perrotta was reported missing thirty-seven days ago. The report said he was last seen going to his office. He was a real estate broker and the owner of Perrotta Realty in Phoenix. His wife reported him missing. It appeared he had been gone for over a week before she reported him to missing persons, right after his car had been found in a strip center, not far from where the body was found.

He printed the information and walked over to Nick. "Here's some info on the guy in the wash. I think we should talk to the widow."

Nick read the information, nodded, and said, "You're driving."

"So, what else is new!" Sonny responded as he walked over to his desk and grabbed his keys.

They turned onto Casa Del Oro Drive from Sixty-Seventh Avenue to the address on the report, stopped the car, and got out. They walked to the front door of the upscale multi-level home. Sonny said, "Wow, what nice digs! This street sure is properly named." They both knew the Spanish translation for Casa Del Oro was house of gold.

Sonny pushed the doorbell. In a few seconds, a female voice came through a speaker above their heads: "Can I help you?"

"We are police officers from the Phoenix Police Department. We would like to speak to Kathleen Perrotta, please."

"There's a camera to your left. Show me your identifications, please, both of you."

The two detectives held their badges up to the camera. In a few seconds, the door opened and a middle-aged lady appeared. The look on her face said: why are you disturbing me? "What do you want, Officers?"

"Uh, ma'am, we need to speak to you. It's about your husband. May we come in, please," Nick asked.

She looked at the two men, thought for a moment, then said, "I was on my way out, but I guess its okay."

The interior of the home was exquisite. Richard Perrotta was obviously successful. They followed her past a spiral staircase and into the living room. Sonny noticed the paintings on the wall. He knew enough about art to recognize them as expensive pieces. At least two of them appeared to be DeGrazia originals.

They sat in a living room that was lavishly furnished. Sonny thought the sofa they sat in cost more than all the furnishings in the whole Madison house. "You have a very nice home," he said.

"Thank you," she responded. "I assume you are here with news on the whereabouts of my husband."

Nick said, "Ma'am, I'm afraid we have some bad news."

She sat perfectly straight and looked at Nick. "He's dead, isn't he?"

"I'm afraid so. Please accept our condolences."

"What happened?" she asked.

She exhibited absolutely no emotion whatsoever, neither in her voice, nor on her face. This bothered both detectives. "He was found in a wash not far from here," Sonny replied.

"The news said there was a body found just north of Happy Valley. They said it was found in a wash. I suppose that was him?"

"Yes, ma'am. It was."

She continued to show no emotion. "What happened? How did he die?"

Nick answered, "We don't know yet. We're waiting for the results from the medical examiner. We have a couple of questions for you, if you don't mind."

Her mind seemed to be preoccupied as she answered, "Go ahead."

"I understand you reported him missing after his car was found in the Walmart parking lot. Is that correct?"

"Yes."

"The report says he had been missing for a week prior. Can you explain why it took so long to report him missing?"

"I figured he was on one of his trysts. Besides, I'm in the process of divorcing him, anyway."

"May I ask why?" Nick asked.

"I found out that the business trips he was taking were for monkey business. Then, I accidentally came across one of his company credit card bills and found out the son of a bitch was hiring high-class hookers. He was taking them to Laughlin and Las Vegas. One trip was to Lake Tahoe."

Nick thought for a moment, then asked, "Ma'am, excuse me for asking, but wouldn't a divorce be rough on you financially? I mean, this is a nice place, and you seem to be used to a rather comfortable lifestyle."

"Yes, sir, I am used to a comfortable lifestyle. Look around you. Everything you see is mine. This house, the furnishings, everything is in my name."

She saw the puzzled look on the detectives' faces. "My maiden name was Mancuso, Kathleen Mancuso."

The detectives recognized the name. The Mancuso family owned a ton of real estate and several businesses throughout the state and across the nation. They were one of the largest commercial builders in the country. She came from old money. The family had been in Phoenix since the eighteen-hundreds.

"Before you ask, yes, there was a pre-nup. He gets nothing if he cheats. I filed for divorce three days before the car was found. My God! In a Walmart parking lot even. How embarrassing!"

The detectives looked at each other, then back to their hostess, who said, "If you have no more questions, I have a Pilates appointment."

They both stood up. Nick handed her his card. "I wrote the phone number of the medical examiner's office on the back. You'll need to call them. You'll need to identify the body."

She took the card from the detective's hand, looked at it, and said, "Sure, when I get the time."

Sonny asked, "By the way, did you and your husband have any children?"

"Oh God, no!" she exclaimed.

"Thank you, ma'am," Nick said. "We'll see ourselves out."

The only sounds were the roar of the engine and the tires rolling on the asphalt surface as Sonny maneuvered the car down the street to Happy Valley Road. He turned left and headed back to the precinct. Finally, he broke the silence. "Wow! I've seen winners in my time, but she gets the trophy for bitch of the year, maybe the century. Where's the remorse? Her husband is dead, for Christ sake. Even if he was screwing around on her, she should show something. I've seen more emotion caused by the death of a hamster."

"Most people love people. Some only love money," Nick responded.

"Or themselves," Sonny added.

They returned to the squad room. Nick went to his desk and Sonny said, "I'll be back in a bit. I gotta get rid of lunch."

CHAPTER 7

The Agenda

When Sonny Madison came back, his eyes scanned the room for his partner. Nick was not at his desk, so Sonny decided to call him. Just as he reached for his cell phone, he heard his name called: "Sonny, we're in here."

It was Nick's voice, and it came from Captain Lovett's office. Sonny went in and sat in the chair next to his partner. "What's up?"

The captain spoke first. "Nick and I have been talking. I think we could use some outside help."

Sonny looked at his partner and back to his captain. "Help? What kind of help? From whom? I don't believe in psychics."

"I'm not talking about a psychic. I want you two to meet with a profiler," the captain stated.

Sonny's eyes began glaring as he slowly said, "What profiler?"

"I have a friend who's a profiler. He works downtown in the Phoenix FBI office."

"Bullshit!" Sonny said. "We don't need the feds diddling around in our case. Huh-uh. No. We don't need them. We're perfectly capable of handling it ourselves."

"First of all, Sergeant Madison, it's not your call." Lovett leaned forward and pointed to the word Captain on the nameplate on his desk. He looked his detective in the eyes and stated, "We need to find out as much as we can about the type of person we're looking for." He sat back and addressed both detectives. "You two have an appointment to meet with Special Agent Sean Barclay tomorrow at one o'clock. He already has a copy of the file."

Sonny looked at his partner. He could see that Nick was okay with this. He was silent as he leaned back in his chair and crossed his arms.

"Like I said, he's a friend of mine. There's no reason for him to want to get involved. He's willing to help us out, that's all," Lovett said. "This is our case. All he is going to do is read the file and give you an idea what he thinks makes the perp tick." He looked at Sonny.

"You will give him the respect he deserves, Detective. Am I making myself clear?"

Sonny still had his arms crossed. He took a breath and nodded so lightly his head barely moved. Both detectives got up and left their boss's office. On their way out they heard: "One o'clock. Don't be late."

They each went to their own desk. Nick knew Sonny was pissed and needed to calm down before they talked about it. He knew his partner and friend very well, and understood his disdain for the FBI.

A little over three years ago, the feds got involved in one of Sonny's cases. Sonny had worked hard on the case for about four months, and he was just about to arrest a high-profile mortgage banker who had killed his business partner. When he arrived at the perp's business, with a warrant and with two uniformed police officers as back up, the feds were escorting the suspect out. He was later granted immunity for testifying against a massive human smuggling ring that stretched from the Arizona–Mexico border to Chicago. After the trial was over, he disappeared and was never heard from. Sonny assumed he was put into witness protection.

It was about an hour later when Sonny finally went over to his partner and said, "Thanks for the support."

"The captain's mind was made up," Nick responded. "I tried, but I couldn't talk him out of it. Besides, you know he's right. Maybe we can get something from the feds that can help us get Pete's killer."

"Yeah, I know. I just hate the feds."

* * *

What the two detectives didn't know was their new boss didn't care for Sonny and expected he would cause a problem tomorrow. Spencer Lovett saw his detective as an arrogant cop, who had no respect for authority. Sonny Madison was a seasoned investigator, and one of the best the Phoenix Police Department had. But Captain Lovett, due to his Marine Corps history, was a strict disciplinarian, and Sonny was not one to easily surrender to authority. The captain was aware of Sonny's feelings toward the FBI, and he had told Nick, "If Madison keeps with the attitude, as soon as this case is over, I'll suspend him, or I'll have him transferred."

"That's not a good idea," the lieutenant had responded.

"Why?" Lovett had questioned. "I can replace him. There are a lot of good cops out there. He's a maverick! He does his own thing. He has no respect for authority. He doesn't conform."

Nick had bent his lanky frame forward and looked his boss in the eyes. "Yes, he's a maverick. Yes, he does things his own way. That's what makes Sonny, Sonny. That's what makes him a good cop. There's no one as good as Sonny Madison. He makes us all look better, you included, and you know it."

The look on the captain's face had been one of shock. He never expected this detective to talk to him that way. Nick had continued, "And replacing two of your best detectives at the same time? I wouldn't want to try to explain that to the chief of detectives."

"You wouldn't!"

Nick had placed both of his elbows on his boss's desk, folded his hands, and rested his chin on them as he looked his captain in the eyes again. "With all due respect, Captain, you most certainly do not want me to have to make that decision."

It was then that Sonny had come into the squad room.

CHAPTER 8

The Vein To The Heart

"We're going see the feds tomorrow," Nick told Sue Kim. "The captain wants Sonny and me to meet with a FBI profiler."

There was a concerned look on her face. "How do you feel about that?" she asked, as the server delivered their chimichangas to the table.

"I'm okay with it, I guess. I mean, we really have no choice. Lovett's the boss. It's Sonny I'm worried about. I hope he doesn't get out of control. He doesn't like the feds, you know."

"Yeah, I know. That's going to be interesting."

"There's more," Nick added.

She dipped a chip into her salsa and looked across the table at him. "Go ahead."

"The new captain doesn't like Sonny. I think he has an agenda, and Sonny isn't on it," said Nick. "I'm wondering if he might be expecting Sonny to give the feds a bunch of trouble so he can use it against him."

Sue Kim answered, "I think Captain Lovett spent too much time in the Marine Corps. He's all discipline. Someone like him would consider anyone like Sonny a misfit. He doesn't understand Sonny and how valuable he is to the department, and that's too bad."

"Wow, you have a better view than I thought."

"April and I talk. She's always afraid Sonny is going to get in the wrong person's face and end up getting fired."

"When do you two talk?" Nick asked.

"What do you think I do when you and Sonny are working at night or Saturdays on a case? Watch soap operas? We talk on the phone, and sometimes we meet at Dairy Queen for a milk shake. She likes strawberry!" She looked at Nick. "What will you do if he cuts him loose?"

"He won't. He needs us both too much."

Sue Kim froze for a slight moment as her brain processed his words. "You wouldn't . . . ?" She looked into Nick's eyes and nodded. "Yeah, you probably would."

Nick changed the subject. "Anything on the Rohypnol?"

"Yeah, there were traces in the hair follicles. The report will be ready tomorrow."

"What's your take on this finger stuff?" he asked.

"You're asking me? Wow! The big bad detective asks the little crime lab girl for advice."

Sue Kim held her hand and rubbed her ring finger. "Do you know the story of the wedding ring and how it started in the first place?"

Nick looked at her, puzzled. "Enlighten me."

"A long time ago, the ancient Romans somehow thought the vein in the fourth finger on the left hand ran directly to the heart so they thought the wedding ring should be on that finger. They called it the vein to the heart.

Nick dropped his fork. "How do you know all this stuff?"

She giggled. "You always said I was more than just a pretty face."

CHAPTER 9

The Cross

They had a couple of hours before the scheduled meeting at the federal building. Nick decided to go to the computer lab and see if the techs had made any headway with the computer from Pete's store. Jerry Petrella was going over the laptop when he arrived. Jerry had been with the Phoenix cyber-crime unit for seven years. He knew most of the detectives, and he had known Pete Mendoza.

"Hey, Jerry, did you guys find anything for me in the computer?" Nick asked.

"Nada," Jerry replied. "Nothing unusual at all. The vic . . ."—he paused for a moment—"Captain Mendoza, kept good books, straight as an arrow. The finances were stable and the inventory matches. I checked his email. I didn't find anything unusual except a couple of questionable emails to a ladyd at hotmail dot com. But there was nothing to implicate her."

"Questionable?" Nick asked.

The tech turned the screen so his visitor could read it clearly. Nick looked at the emails, and Jerry said, "It looks to me like Pete was getting a little something on the side. What do you think?"

"Pete? I doubt it. He wasn't the type. He's been married forever. He loved Elena. He was a devout Catholic. I remember one time when there was a retirement celebration and the guys all went to a strip club. Pete wouldn't go. He really looked down on anyone who cheated on his wife. He said marriage was sacred, blessed by God."

"Yeah, well, tell that to my ex. The bitch left me for my next-door neighbor. We were all friends until my neighbor's wife walked in on them and caught them sucking face."

Jerry's words caused Nick's mind to reflect back on his own past. He had felt sick and gone home early one afternoon and caught his wife, Cassie, in bed with her boss. He moved out the next day. The divorce was final a few months later. Cassie was a real problem through it all. She acted as if Nick was the offender. She even moved in with her parents in Prescott and took their three daughters with her. Though

Nick tried to keep their situation amicable, Cassie would have nothing of it.

Nick's mind came back to the situation at hand. "Send a copy of the emails to me. How about prints?"

"The lab said there were no prints on it except the captain's. Even the mark on the screen was his. They checked the DNA."

"What mark on the screen?" the detective asked.

"The screen was dusty, and there was a plus sign on the screen. He probably traced it to see how dusty it was. At least that's my guess."

"Can I see it?" Nick said.

Jerry pointed to the mark still on the screen and said, "Sure. See? Right here."

Nick looked at the screen; in the middle were traced two lines, one horizontal and one vertical, dissecting each other. He immediately noticed the horizontal line was not in the middle, but about halfway toward the top. "Get a good picture of that screen. That's not a plus sign," the detective stated.

"What is it?" he asked.

"Do you see how high the horizontal line is? What does that look like to you?"

Jerry leaned forward in his chair, looked at the screen, and said, "A cross. It looks more like a cross than a plus sign."

"Bingo!"

"Do you think he meant it to be a cross? Maybe it just turned out that way. Or maybe he knew he was dying and that was his final prayer. He probably couldn't talk, you know."

"That makes sense, but I'll check it out anyway. Get a copy of the pix to me as soon as you can. Copy Detective Madison and Captain Lovett, too."

"I'll send it all to them."

"Just send the picture of the screen to them. Send the copies of the emails to me—me only."

"Will do, Lieutenant."

Nick left and went back to the squad room.

CHAPTER 10

The Feds

Lieutenant Nick Greer and Sergeant Sonny Madison arrived at the FBI building at twelve-fifty and, after the procedural security screening, were led into a small room with a conference table and six chairs. "Do you think this will do any good?" Sonny asked.

"It can't do any harm. The worse that can happen is nothing, which is what we've got so far. Who knows, these guys are pretty good; maybe he can shed some light on the subject. Maybe he can give us a place to start."

A man wearing a blue suit came into the room. He was carrying a manila folder in his hand. "Good morning, gentlemen. I'm Special Agent Sean Barclay."

"I'm Lieutenant Nick Greer." Nick looked toward Sonny. "This is my partner, Sergeant Sonny Madison."

The agent shook hands with the detectives and sat across from them.

"So, how do you know our captain?" Sonny asked.

"He's my brother-in-law. His wife and my wife are sisters."

Sonny looked at his partner, who just shook his head. A friend in the FBI? he thought.

Lieutenant Greer looked back to Special Agent Barclay. "I assume you have reviewed the information we sent you?"

"Yes, Lieutenant, I have." He opened the folder and looked at it again. "This is an interesting case." He thumbed through the papers as he continued, "I'm sure none of these were robberies. It is possible the wedding rings were the target, but most likely, not for their monetary value, but for some other reason. The female vic pulled from the Tempe lake had an expensive diamond ring, but both of the men had plain gold bands."

Sonny interjected, "Gold is about twelve hundred dollars an ounce, last I checked. That's nothing to sneeze at."

"Yes, Sergeant, but neither of their wallets or watches were taken. Your real estate broker . . ." He paused while he looked at the file.

"Richard Perrotta," Sonny said.

"Yes, thank you. Richard Perrotta." The special agent continued, "He had a Rolex Oyster on his wrist and a good amount of cash in his wallet. The female had a pretty noticeable diamond around her neck and a diamond tennis bracelet on her wrist. If this was a robbery, they would have been easily taken. No thief would have missed that."

"That's obvious to a rookie beat cop. Tell us something we don't know," said Sonny.

The agent glared at Sonny, then said, "The un-sub"—both detectives knew un-sub was a FBI term for unidentified subject—"wanted the rings, or the fingers, or maybe both. And he probably still has them, at least the rings. Souvenirs, I'll bet. Adding the fact that all three of the victims were stabbed in the heart, tells me the un-sub had a traumatic experience of some sort that has something to do with a relationship or perhaps a marriage. Perhaps he was jilted by a girlfriend, a fiancée, or more likely a wife. The un-sub is most likely a male, between twenty-five and thirty-five."

"Is there anything else?" Nick asked.

"Yes, Lieutenant, there is. As your captain requested, we ran the information through our database. We found something interesting."

Both detectives were attentive as the agent continued, "It appears there have been two other cases with the same MO. They're cold, now. One is eight years old, the other six. The last one was in Baltimore, Maryland, and the first one was in western Pennsylvania. Both of the victims were stabbed in the heart, and both were missing their left ring finger."

"Where were the bodies found?" Nick questioned.

"The Baltimore vic was found bobbing in the harbor, and the Pennsylvania, uhh, let's see." He leafed through the pages. "Oh, yes, a small lake in Beaver County, Pennsylvania, Brady's Run Park. It's all here in our report." He closed the folder and tossed it onto the table in front of the detectives. "At your captain's request, I have included all the info we have on the two victims. It's all yours."

Nick reached for the file, but Barclay put his hand on it, looked at the two detectives, and said, "Detectives, I understand your need to work this case. I realize your ex-captain was one of the victims, but I must advise you that our people will now be looking into it."

Sonny almost knocked the table over as he jumped up from his seat. "This is our case. We'll handle it. You keep your fed noses out of it." He looked at his partner. "I told you they'd pull something, Nick. I told you! We should have never come here!"

The agent was calm as he looked at Sonny and said, "Sergeant, I have no control over bureau policy, but in respect for your captain, I'll make you a deal." He looked at Nick and continued, "You have my permission to continue your investigation, and we'll do our best to stay out of your way. But we will need you to keep us informed of any and all information you find. And please try to stay out of our way. If you do that, we'll all get along fine."

Nick saw fire in his partner's eyes. He hoped he wouldn't have to restrain him. Sonny looked into the agent's face and yelled, "We have your permission? Stay out of your way? You stay out of ours!" Sonny pushed the door so hard the glass rattled as he stormed out of the room.

Nick grabbed the folder from under Special Agent Barclay's hand, looked at him, and pointed toward Sonny. "What he said!" Nick turned and left the room.

* * *

They were halfway back to the precinct and neither detective had spoken. Sonny had been intensely studying the information in the folder. Periodically he would pick up his cell phone and enter something into its notepad. He finally broke the silence. "I told you the bastards would stick their big, fat fed noses into our case. They want us to share our info with them, but did he say they would do the same? No! Fuck 'em!"

"Do you think you might have been a little rough on him?" Nick asked. "He did give us some information that might help."

Sonny looked over to the driver and said, "Do I . . . ? Rough on him . . . ? Let me think . . . Uhhh . . ." His eyes widened, and he shook his head. "No!"

"I didn't think you would," Nick responded. Sonny laughed.

After they arrived at the squad room, each detective went to his own desk. Nick read and reread the FBI report. Sonny pulled out his cell phone and scribbled down the notes he had entered into it, then he did some research on the computer.

About thirty minutes later, Nick said, "By the way, the tox report on our latest vic is going to show Rohypnol. Just a trace, but it's there."

"Yeah, it just came down," Sonny said. "I'm looking at it now. That's something Special Agent Barclay and his fed cronies don't know about, at least not yet."

"Yeah," Nick responded. "But they'll eventually ask for the report and see it." He grabbed a yellow notepad from his desk, took it and the manila folder with him, and sat in the chair beside Sonny's desk. "Okay, let's see what we have so far. Let's look for some sort of common denominator. There's gotta be something they all have in common." Nick laid the pad on Sonny's desk, pulled a pen from his pocket, and began writing as he spoke, "They all were married, of course. What else?"

"Yes," Sonny answered while still looking at the computer screen. "They all three were dumped in water of some sort."

"Tell me something I don't know. Keep going."

Sonny shrugged. "You know they all had the ring finger missing."

"Like I said, tell me something I don't know. By the way, did you know the Romans started the tradition of placing the ring on that finger?" Nick asked.

Sonny looked up from the computer screen toward his partner. "Huh?"

"It seems they thought the vein in the fourth finger of the left hand ran directly to the heart."

"Yeah, *vena amoris*. The vein of love, they called it," Sonny responded.

"You knew that?" Nick asked with surprise in his voice.

"Uhh, yeah. Doesn't everybody?" Sonny smiled.

Nick shook his head. "So all we know is they were all married, dumped in water, and short a finger. That doesn't give us much of a place to start."

"Well, there may be one thing more," Sonny said as he stared at the computer screen.

"What's that?" Nick bent over to look at the screen. It was the obituary notice of the victim in Pennsylvania, James Robert Widmann.

"You ain't gonna like this, Nick. Not even a little."

Just then, Sonny's cell phone rang. He picked it up and saw it was April. "Yeah, babe . . . Uh-huh . . . You sure? How much? . . . Wow!" He took in a deep breath and let it out. "I don't see where we have a choice. Tell him okay. Just put it on plastic, I guess." Sonny pushed the disconnect button on his phone. "Shit!"

"Uh, is everything okay?"

"The Romans got it wrong!"

"Huh? What are you talking about?" Nick questioned.

"The wedding ring? The vein to the heart? It doesn't run from the finger directly to the heart; it stops by the wallet on the way! My air conditioner is shot. It's gonna cost six grand for a new one. My credit cards are already stretched so far, I'm wondering which one of them will be the first to snap back and knock me flat on my ass!"

Just then they heard: "Greer, Madison, get in here."

Sonny looked toward their boss's office. "Ahh, his master's voice."

"Let's go and see what he wants," said Nick. "He doesn't sound happy."

Captain Lovett's door was open, and he motioned for his two detectives to come in. "Sit, Detectives. We have some things to discuss."

They both sat down. "Before we do, do you have anything new?" The tone in his voice told them their captain was not in the best of moods.

"The agent said there were two more cases like these back east," Nick answered.

"Yeah, I know all about it. Agent Barclay sent me a copy of their report."

"You mean your *friend* at the FBI?" Sonny taunted.

The captain looked at Sonny. The fire in his eyes could have ignited an inferno.

Nick intervened, "The only common denominators are: stabbed in the heart, missing ring finger, found in water, and none of them looked like robberies."

"Is there any type of Arizona connection to the vics back east?" the captain questioned.

"None so far, but I've not finished looking," Sonny stated.

"See if you can connect the dots." Lovett looked back and forth between his detectives. "Is there anything else?"

"That's it for now," Nick answered.

"Thank you. Go back to work." They got up to leave. Lovett said, "Madison, stay!"

Nick left and Sonny sat back down. "Yeah, Cap?"

"Madison, I explicitly ordered you to behave yourself with the feds, did I not?"

"Uh, I didn't consider it an order."

"Shut up and don't interrupt me, Madison!" There was still fire in his eyes. "You disobeyed my orders and went off on Special Agent Barclay."

"Oh, you mean Special Agent Brother-in-Law?"

Spencer Lovett's face turned as red as a ripe tomato as the anger within him grew. "That has nothing to do with it. And I said do not interrupt me, Sergeant!" He reached his hand out and pointed to the part of his nameplate that said: Captain. "I don't know how Pete Mendoza ran this squad, but I run a tight ship, and I'm tired of your insubordinate attitude. You will follow my orders to a tee, or you will be in a patrol car in South Phoenix! Am I making myself clear?"

"Pete Mendoza knew more about running a detective unit than you'll ever dream of knowing." The voice came from behind Sonny. It was Nick. The look on his face was more intense than Sonny had ever seen it. "I don't know what your problem is, Captain, but this is not the Marine Corps. Unless you lighten up, you're liable to have one giant mutiny on your hands!" He looked at Sonny. "Come on, partner, we have a killer to find!"

Both detectives got up and left their captain's office. As they walked to their desks, Sonny said, "Thanks for covering my back, partner."

"It's not your back I should be covering, it's your mouth. Sometimes I think you should have been born with a roll of duct tape. I know he's a hard ass, and it's obvious you're not his favorite person. But he is our captain, like it or not. Don't you think you might want to lighten up on him a little?"

"Uhhh . . . Lighten up? He's a prick."

Nick shook his head. "At least think about it. You don't want him to suspend you. You have an a/c bill to pay."

"He's still a prick."

"Yeah, I know."

CHAPTER 11

The Operation

Nick Greer had picked up some fast food and brought it home to his townhouse. He knew Sue Kim was at practice. The Phoenix Symphony was having a guest conductor, and they were preparing. Nick ran the events of the day through his head. He was worried about his friend. It was obvious that Spencer Lovett was going to do whatever he could to get rid of Sonny. Nick could read the writing on the wall, even if Sonny couldn't. Their captain wanted people he could break down and control, but Sonny was not one who could be broken. What the new captain didn't realize was that Nick couldn't be broken either.

The door opened, and Sue Kim came in lugging her cello case. Nick got up, kissed her, and took the case from her. "Here, let me get that for you. How was band practice?"

"Band practice?" she yelled. "I don't play in no fucking band! I play in the Phoenix Symphony. It's a symphony orchestra, not a bunch of high school kids marching across a football field!" She threw her purse on the table. "How would you like it if I asked you how many parking tickets you gave out today, Mister Big-Shot Detective?"

"Uhh, it wouldn't bother me . . ." Oops! Wrong answer, he thought, as he heard the sound of the bedroom door slam.

He stood there for a moment, then he went to the refrigerator and pulled out a beer. He twisted off the cap, took a long drink, and sat at the table. After taking another swallow, and a couple of bites of fried chicken, he thought, let's see, today I pissed off an FBI agent, then I pissed off my captain, and now my girlfriend. What the hell else can happen?

His question was no sooner asked than answered as his cell phone rang. He picked it up from the table. The readout said: Cassie. What did his ex-wife want?

"Kelly's in the hospital. It's her appendix. They have to remove it."

Nick was silent as he let the words sink in. "I'll be there as soon as I can."

"They're prepping her now. I gotta go."

"Which hosp—" The phone went silent.

Just then Sue Kim came out of the bedroom. She had just showered and her hair was wrapped in a towel. So was the rest of her. "I gotta go to Prescott," he said.

"When? Why?" she asked.

"It's Kelly; she's having an appendectomy. Cassie just called. I'm gonna head up there now."

"I'll go with you," she said.

"You don't have to. I can—"

"I'll only be a minute. Pack a bag. We'll probably have to stay," she said as she disappeared into the bedroom.

Nick followed her. He grabbed an overnight bag and stuffed it with a change of clothing and toiletries. Sue Kim got dressed and did the same. They locked the townhouse, got into his car, and headed for Prescott. Nick turned on his chase lights, hit the gas, and made it to Prescott in record time. The ride was silent except when he phoned Cassie several times on the way. He finally got an answer just as he hit the Prescott city limits. Kelly was out of surgery and was doing fine. She was at the Yavapai County Hospital.

It was shortly after eight o'clock when they arrived at the hospital. They entered through a set of double doors, and Sue Kim followed Nick to the receptionist desk. A security guard looked up and asked, "Can I help you, sir?"

"Greer, Kelly Greer? I'm her father."

The guard punched some keys on his computer and said, "She's in room two twenty-six." He pointed to the right. "Just take the elevator to the second floor and follow the signs."

Nick turned toward the elevator. Sue Kim looked at the guard and said, "Thank you." He nodded. They rode the elevator to the fourth floor and followed the signs to room two twenty-six. There was a small waiting lobby to the right, and Sue Kim sat down. "Go, be with your daughter. I'll wait here. She needs her dad."

Kelly was sitting up in the bed when Nick walked into the room. It was a two-bed room, but the other one was empty. Cassie and her mother were sitting in chairs next to the bed.

"Dad!" Kelly exclaimed. "Boy, you sure made it up here fast." He gave her a hug and kissed her on the cheek. She looked around. "Where's Sue Kim? Did she come?"

"She's out in the lobby. She'll be in later. The rules say only two visitors per room, and I make three." He looked at Cassie's mother, hoping she would get the hint and leave.

Dolores Metzler seemed to plant herself more solidly into the chair. Her glaring eyes showed her disdain for his presence there. Her voice could've turned water into ice cubes as she said, "Hello, Nick."

Far be it for you to get up off your fat ass and let me visit my daughter, he thought. But he said, "Hello, Dolores." His eyes caught the empty chair where Cassie had been seated. He wondered where she had gone. "How are you?"

"I'm fine except my blood pressure is up again, and my diabetes is acting up."

"I'm sure you'll be fine," Nick answered as he turned to his daughter and asked, "Where are your sisters?"

"They just left. Grandpa took them home. They'll be back tomorrow morning, but the doctor said I can go home tomorrow."

"I'm proud of you, pumpkin."

"Thanks, Dad. Can you send Sue Kim in? I want to see her."

"Uh . . . sure." He left the room and went out into the lobby. He couldn't believe what he saw. Sue Kim and Cassie were sitting together, having a conversation, and Cassie was laughing. This is a sight he thought he would never see. He didn't know what to do. This was uncharted waters for him. "Uhhh, sorry to interrupt," he said, "but Kelly wants to see you, Sue Kim."

She looked at Cassie. "Is it all right?"

"Of course, go ahead," Cassie answered.

Sue Kim got up and went into the room. Nick said to Cassie, "Uhhh, are you two okay? You actually seemed to be getting along."

"Of course, we're getting along. She's a nice girl," Cassie said. "The girls like her. I like her. It's you I can't stand."

Nick's brain was still processing the information his ears had just delivered to it, when Cassie stood up and said, "But Mom may not feel that way." She immediately headed for Kelly's room.

Cassie could feel the tenseness in the air as she entered the room. She didn't know what her mother had said, but she could tell by the look on Sue Kim and Kelly's faces that it wasn't good. "I'm glad you're here, Mom," Kelly said as she looked at her grandmother. "Can Dad come in?"

Cassie looked at her mother and said, “Would you excuse us for a minute, Mom? And send Nick in, please.”

Dolores’s eyes were like daggers as they pierced her daughter’s being. She got up and left the room. She saw Nick sitting in a chair as she entered the lobby. “They want you,” she said as she sat at the opposite end of the small lobby.

Nick went into the room. Kelly crossed her arms and said with a tone of authority, “Okay. Let’s talk. Mom, Dad.” She looked back and forth at her parents as she continued, “Kaitlin, Kasey, and I have accepted your divorce. We understand, at least I do, more than you think. Now, we all like Sue Kim.” She looked at her father as she continued, “and I think you two are happy together.” Nick nodded.

“Okay, now that we have that straight.” Kelly looked at her mother. “Mom, we gotta do something about Grandma. She wasn’t very nice to Sue Kim. I thought she was going to make her cry. What does gook mean anyway?”

Nick’s eyes widened as he looked at his ex-wife and anger began to build inside him. “Not anything nice, Kelly. Nothing nice at all.” He looked back at Sue Kim, and he could see tears beginning to form in her eyes.

Even Cassie thought her mother had gone too far and said, “I’ll talk to Grandma. Until then, let’s try to keep them away from each other.”

Cassie looked at Nick and said, “Not bad for a thirteen-year-old.”

“Oh, there’s more, Mom,” Kelly said. Her parents looked at her with questioning eyes. “You two need to be nicer to each other. We love you both, and we hate it when you fight.”

“Uh, we’ll work on it,” Nick said as he looked at Cassie. Cassie nodded.

“Okay,” Kelly said. “You can all go now. I’m tired. I’ll see you in the morning.”

All three of them kissed her and left the room. As they did, Nick looked at his ex-wife and chuckled as he said, “Our little girl is growing up. I think we were just dismissed.”

Cassie smiled and nodded. Sue Kim giggled.

* * *

Nick and Sue Kim got a room at Bucky's. They would see the girls in the morning after Kelly went home, and then they would head back to Phoenix. Nick called Sonny and explained the situation to him. Sonny said he would let the captain know. Sue Kim sent a text to her boss and let him know she would be late.

Sue Kim was lying on the bed, watching television, when Nick came out of the shower. "Uhh, sorry about earlier today. The band bit, I mean."

She looked up at him. "I'm proud of what I do. It takes a lot of work, practice, and talent. I am, and work hard to be, a professional musician, and I don't like being made fun of."

"You know, I was only kidding."

"Yeah, I might have overreacted a little."

"Ya think?"

"I was in a bad mood when I got home. They kicked Carol out." Carol Schmidt was Sue Kim's best friend, and a flutist in the symphony.

"Uh, what happened?" Nick sat on the edge of the bed beside her.

"The new conductor has a niece who is a flutist. She isn't nearly as good as Carol, but he gave her the seat. It's all politics."

"It's everywhere, baby, it's everywhere." He looked into her eyes. "So, we're good?"

"Oh, yeah." She reached up to him, and wrapped her arms around his neck. Her kiss was soft and sweet as she pulled him to her.

CHAPTER 12

The Suspension

The next morning, Kelly was home from the hospital and bragging about her surgery. The girls were happy they got to see their dad, but they seemed happier to see Sue Kim. Nick and Sue Kim left Prescott at ten-thirty.

Sue Kim decided to take the entire day off. She told Nick she wanted to talk with Carol. She was pretty worked up about her dismissal. "I'll take her to Mimi's. That's her favorite restaurant."

Nick had called Sonny, but he had received no answer, so he left a voice mail message. He also sent him a text, but it wasn't returned either. He wondered why. That wasn't like Sonny Madison.

He walked into the squad room and immediately looked at Sonny's desk. It was empty. He went to Captain Lovett's office and knocked on the door.

"Come on in, Lieutenant. I didn't expect you until tomorrow. How is your daughter?"

"She's fine. She's home and telling everyone about her operation. Do you know where Sonny is?"

"He's gone."

* * *

It was eight a.m. Thursday when Sonny walked into the squad room. As he sat at his desk, his eyes caught a note taped to his computer screen. It read: *See me immediately. Captain Lovett.* He got up, walked over to the captain's office and knocked on the door.

"Come in, Sergeant."

Sonny opened the door and entered. He began to sit down but his boss stopped him. "Don't bother sitting down, Madison. You won't be in here that long. As of this moment, you are on suspension. I want your badge and your service piece now."

Sonny was stunned. He reached into his pocket and pulled out his badge He then removed his Glock from his belt. He dropped the badge and the gun onto his boss's desk. "Why? Why are you doing this? All because I gave the feds some shit?"

"You're not a team player, Madison. You're a maverick, and I don't have any room for mavericks on my team. You got two weeks without pay to think about your future. That ought to give you time to think about things. You better have a major attitude adjustment before you come back here, if you do."

Sonny shook his head and said, "You have absolutely no grounds for this, and you know it. Do you think PLEA is going to put up with this?"

Spencer Lovett knew what his detective meant. Sonny Madison was a member of the police union, the Phoenix Law Enforcement Association. He figured the union would back Sonny, but he didn't care. The worst that would happen was Sonny would be out of homicide, and that was fine with the captain. "I'll deal with that when the time comes. Now get out of my office and clean out your desk." He reached down to the floor and picked up a cardboard box. He tossed it to Sonny. "You'll need this. Get out!"

Sonny caught the box, looked at the captain, and said, "You're an asshole, Lovett."

The captain stood up and yelled, "Get out! Get out of my fucking office. Now!"

* * *

"Gone? Gone where?"

"Out of here. He's suspended," the captain responded.

"What for?"

"Insubordination and disobeying a direct order."

"What the hell are you thinking? We need him to find Pete's killer."

"You'll get another partner."

"No, I won't! I have one."

"Not anymore, you don't. Not if you think his name is Sonny Madison. He's gone and he's not coming back. Not as long as I'm sitting at this desk!"

Detective Lieutenant Nick Greer reached for his badge. Every fiber in his body and soul told him to toss it onto Lovett's desk and tell him to shove it up his ass. But he thought about Pete Mendoza, Elena,

Jordana and her brothers. He had to see this case through. When it was all over and he had Pete's killer in jail, he could turn in his badge. But until then he would push on and stay off of Captain Lovett's radar as much as possible. He turned and stormed out of the captain's office. He needed to find Sonny.

* * *

When Nick Greer left the squad room, it was after three o'clock. Maybe Sonny was at Charlie's tavern, he thought. Charlie Cates was a retired Phoenix cop. His tavern was a favorite hangout for a lot of the Phoenix police officers, and it was where Sonny often went when he needed to get away. Nick decided to check there first.

Charlie was behind the bar when Nick came through the door. Nick's eyes were adjusting from the brightness of the outside world to the darker ambience of the bar room, as he scanned the room in search of Sonny. Charlie handed Nick a bottle of Budweiser, pointed to where Sonny was seated, and said, "This one's on me."

Nick pulled up a chair and sat at the table across from Sonny, who was nursing a bourbon and water. "Am I gonna need to drive you home?"

"I doubt it," Sonny replied. "I've been staring at this one for over half an hour. I guess you heard."

"Yeah. He's an asshole among assholes. How long did he suspend you for?"

"Two weeks without pay. That ain't gonna go over well with April."

"You know if you need money, all you have to do it ask."

"Hey, you got child support and your own expenses. We'll manage."

"I've got a few bucks put away," Nick said as he lifted the bottle and took a generous drink. "It's yours if you need it."

"I appreciate it, buddy, but we'll be okay. April has a pretty good job, and it's only for a couple of weeks. I'll stick Lovett with some OT to make up for it."

"Sonny, you know you're not going back to homicide; at least not as long as Lovett is there." He took another swig of beer and continued, "The union will jump all over this and you'll be reinstated. But if you go back there, there's no way you can work with him after all that has happened. He'll want his ass kissed, and I know you well enough to know that ain't gonna happen. You'll move to vice or robbery, or maybe cyber. I think that's what's bothering you more than losing a couple of weeks' pay."

Sonny knew his best friend was right. He loved his job, and he gave it his all. That's what made him so good at it. If he were to be assigned to another department, could he give it the same effort? He looked up at his friend. "Who died and made you Doctor Phil?"

"Bud," Nick answered.

"What? Bud who?"

Nick turned the label of his beer bottle toward Sonny and said, "Weiser, Bud Weiser."

Sonny laughed, picked up his drink, chugged it, and said, "I'm going home."

As they began to get up, Nick's Android buzzed. He pulled it from his belt and looked at the screen. He had a text message from Deputy Chief Bruce Mannion, Chief of Detectives. He looked at Sonny. "What would the C of Ds want with me?"

Just then, Sonny's Android rang. He picked it up and looked at the readout and back at Nick, puzzled. "Or me?"

The message was the same. It read: *Meet me in my office at ten a.m. Monday.*

CHAPTER 13

The Affair

The drive to Prescott always seemed therapeutic to Nick. He liked to leave early, roll the windows down, and watch the sun come up as he drove north along Interstate 17. He headed west at Cordes Junction onto Route 69 through Mayer and Dewey and on to Prescott Valley. As the sun spread its rays across the tops of the Bradshaw Mountains, he was reminded of their original name, The Silver Mountain Range. Though the moniker was due to their mineral content, today their peaks glistened as if they were coated with silver.

This morning his mind was on what he was going to do when he came back from seeing the girls. He had a lot to deal with. First was finding Pete's killer. A close second was Sonny Madison. He needed Sonny's help. Nick knew Sonny wanted to nab Pete's killer, too, and he assumed he would continue to work behind the scenes during his suspension. But he had no idea how Captain Lovett would react. He also didn't know what Sonny would do after his suspension. He knew his partner well enough to know he wasn't coming back to homicide as long as Lovett was the boss. Sonny couldn't just up and quit the force; he had a family to support. Where would he go? Would Nick get a new partner? Would Nick remain on the force?

As he pulled into Bucky's, he wondered where he should take the girls. He figured Kelly would still be tender from her operation. Maybe a movie would work. They had talked about going fishing, but he knew that was not an option. Maybe the next time. He walked through the casino to the hotel check-in counter. A lady greeted him from behind the counter. "Good morning, Mr. Greer."

"You remembered my name? I'm impressed."

"Oh, yes, sir. You're famous." Nick was puzzled. "I'm Melanie Steele. Your daughter Kaitlin and my daughter Mariah are friends. They're in the same class at school. All she talks about is her dad, the detective. She sure is proud of you. She's a nice girl."

"Thank you. I kind of like her."

She handed him his room keycard and a coupon book. "Here, this is on the house. Have a nice weekend."

He thanked her and headed for his room. He tossed the coupon book onto the round table that sat in the corner of the hotel room, unzipped his bag and dumped its contents onto the bed. He looked at his watch. Sue Kim would be on her way to Palm Springs by now. A couple of months ago, Sue Kim, Carole Schmidt, and two other women from the symphony had won a spa weekend in Palm Springs. This was the weekend they had reserved. "A girls' weekend out," Sue Kim had called it.

Just then his cell phone rang. He pulled it from his belt. It read: Cassie. "Hello."

"Nick, where are you?"

"I'm in my hotel room. I just got here. What do you want?"

"Nick, I apologize, but I forgot to tell you—"

"Tell me what?" he asked.

"The girls have a birthday party to go to this afternoon at two. They'll only be gone for a couple of hours, but they really want to go."

"Why didn't you tell me about it?"

"Truthfully, I forgot about it with the ordeal with Kelly and all. I really am sorry. I'm pulling into Walmart now to buy a gift. I'll be home soon. Why don't you come over and spend the day with the kids here at the house?"

"Uhhh . . ." He thought for a moment. Why is she being so nice? "What about your mom? You know how she is with me."

"Mom and Dad are going to a wedding in Flagstaff. The daughter of one of their friends is getting married. They won't be back until tomorrow."

He hesitated. "Well, I guess so, if your mom doesn't have mines buried somewhere."

"Don't worry; I know where they're at. See you in an hour. The girls will be thrilled."

I don't trust her, he thought.

He remembered the coupon book he had tossed onto the table and thought, I have an hour to kill. Let's see what happens.

* * *

The blackjack tables were crowded, but he found a spot at a ten-dollar table and sat down. He tossed two twenty-dollar bills onto the table, and the dealer gave him eight red chips. He laid a two-for-one coupon on the table and covered it with two chips. The dealer distributed the cards around the table. Nick looked at his, a nine and an eight. He looked at the dealer's up card, a five. The entire table stayed, and the dealer turned her hole card over, a king. She pulled a card from the shoe. It was another king. Bust. Cool, he thought. I won forty bucks.

He let the twenty dollars in chips ride, and the next hand was dealt. He looked at his cards and turned them over: a ten and an ace, twenty-one. The dealer placed one green and one red chip in front of him. Thirty bucks, he thought, cool. The dealer drew a nineteen.

The next hand offered Nick a ten and a nine. He waved the stay sign with his hand, and the dealer also drew a nineteen. She turned her hand upwards and tapped her finger on the table two times. "Push," she said, as she pulled in the other bets from the table and redealt the cards. The next hand graced the dealer with a twenty-one, and the whole table lost. He had only bet two chips.

Nick thought she was due to bust so he played eight five-dollar chips. Her up card was a five. He looked at this hand and saw two aces. He turned them over and dropped eight more chips on the table. He knew he was splitting and would get one card on each ace. He hoped one would be a winner. The dealer laid a nine on the first ace and an eight on the second. The rest of the players stayed their hands, and the dealer turned over her hole card, another five. He heard everyone at the table groan as they all expected the next card to be a face card. She looked around the table, reached into the shoe, and pulled out a seven. "Seventeen," she said as she paid the table.

Nick looked at his watch. It was time to leave so he tossed a five-dollar chip on the table and left. He figured he was ahead so would quit. That would pay for the room and the gas.

* * *

He pulled up to the Metzler home and saw their Lexus parked in the driveway in front of the closed garage door. He thought about driving around until they left. He preferred not to run into his ex-mother-in-law. Screw it, he thought. He parked his Taurus in the front of the house, got out, and pushed the lock button on his key. He heard the sound of the doors locking and the short beep of the horn as he stepped onto the sidewalk of his ex-in-laws' home.

Just then, the garage door opened, and both Rod and Dolores Metzler came out toward the car. Rod looked up and saw Nick. "Nick, my boy. How are you? Did you have a nice drive?" Rod had always liked Nick. He considered him the son he never had. He was not happy about the divorce; however, he did stand behind his daughter's wishes.

"I'm fine, Rod." Nick looked toward his ex-mother-in-law. "How are you, Dolores?"

"I'm fine, Nicholas," she answered, as she got into the passenger side of the car and shut the door.

Rod said, "I didn't expect you so soon. The girls are inside. Did you know they have a party to go to this afternoon?"

"Yeah, Cassie called me a while ago. That's why I'm here. She said it was okay to come."

"It's okay with me. Just you and Cassie try not to kill each other, okay?" Nick nodded.

Rod Metzler opened the driver's side door. "Have a good time. The girls will be glad to see you." He shut the door and Nick heard the engine come to life. Nick traveled the sidewalk to the front door and rang the bell.

The door swung open. Kasey hugged her dad and pulled him into the house. Cassie was standing in the foyer. She called out, "Kelly, Kaitlin, your father is here."

Kaitlin came running to Nick. Kelly followed at a slow walk. He hugged them and said to Kelly, "How are you feeling, pumpkin?"

"I'm a little sore," she answered as she touched her right side. "I won't be shooting hoops for a while, but I'm okay."

"Come on, Daddy," Kasey said as she tugged at him. "Let's go out back."

Nick looked at Cassie. "They have a pitcher of iced tea and a bowl of chips on the porch waiting for you. I'll leave you all alone."

Nick nodded to his ex-wife. He wondered why the change in attitude. Ever since Kelly's surgery, Cassie had been nice to him. He wondered if she wanted something.

Nick and the three girls talked, laughed, and were having a good time until Cassie came out on the porch and said, "I hate to break this party up, but you girls have to get ready for Alyssa's party. Your dad will be here when you get back." All three girls hugged their father and left to get ready.

Nick stood and said, "What time should I come back?"

Cassie looked at him and smiled. "You don't have to leave, Nick. I'll take them to the party and come back. We can talk. You can stay here while we're gone. I know you won't steal anything; you're a cop." She laughed.

Nick sat down and took a sip of iced tea. Cassie left the porch and went into the house to finish getting the kids ready for the party. About ten minutes later, she returned with all three girls in tow. "Say bye to your dad. He'll wait here for you." The girls hugged Nick and then left with their mother.

Nick leaned back and took a deep breath. The clean mountain air filled his lungs. He held it in as long as he could, then he exhaled. It felt good. He stood up and walked to the edge of the redwood porch. He put both hands on the railing, and took another deep breath as he gazed at the scenic surroundings. The Metzler home was on an acre of prime land. The view was fantastic, and the smell of freshly cut grass teased his olfactory senses. The green grass ran from the bottom of the porch about fifty yards to a grove of Ponderosa pines that enclosed all three sides of the large yard. A stream ran across the rear of the yard rolling its way along in front of the trees. He could hear birds chirping their songs and the peaceful sound of water slapping against the rocks as it made its way to he didn't know where. Above the trees, the Bradshaw Mountains stood statuesque in the distance. He understood why Rod and Dolores moved here. There was a peace and tranquility that only nature could provide. It was something you would never find in the big city. He stood there gazing.

All of a sudden he heard a sound. He turned around and saw Cassie standing behind him. She walked across the porch and stood beside him. She looked out at the landscape and said, "It's beautiful, isn't it?"

Nick took a breath, exhaled, and nodded. He said, "You wanted to talk about something?"

"Let's go inside." She turned and he followed her into the living room. He sat on the sofa and Cassie sat beside him. She reached for his hand, but he pulled it back. "It's okay, Nick. I'm not going to bite it. I just want to say I'm sorry for what happened." She reached out and took his hand between hers. "I'm sorry I have been such a stinker about things, especially the kids. I realize how much they love you and how much you love them. I intend to try to do better."

Nick didn't know what to do or say. He wondered if he was dreaming. Ever since he caught her in bed with her boss, she had done everything she could to hurt him. Now, all of a sudden she was repentant. Did Kelly's operation scare her that much? Did Kelly's candid statements in the hospital really get to her? He looked into her blue eyes. Remembering it was her beautiful eyes that had first attracted him to her, he gently pulled his hand from hers and said, "Uhh . . . I need to use the bathroom."

She pointed to a hallway to the left of the room and said, "My room is the first one on the left. Go ahead and use that one." Nick got up and left the living room.

Nick finished washing his hands and dried them on a hand towel. He turned, opened the door to leave but stopped in his tracks as he saw what was standing before him. Cassie was standing at the bottom edge of the bed with her hands to her side wearing a sheer black teddy. Her blonde hair teased her bare shoulders as she looked at him with seductive eyes. "Cassie, what are you doing?" Nick asked.

The nipples on her ample breasts poked through the sheer fabric that barely covered them as she walked toward him. He looked behind her as if seeking an escape route, but she continued toward him. Her top fell on one side, exposing her left breast as she reached her arms up to his neck and kissed him. Her kiss was as soft and as sweet as he had ever remembered it. He knew he needed to push her away and leave. But her tongue parted his lips, and she pulled him down onto the bed.

It was four-fifteen when the phone rang. Cassie turned and reached for the phone on the nightstand. She looked at the clock as she answered, "Hello . . . Okay, I'm on my way. I'll be there in ten."

She jumped up, threw on her clothes and said, "That was Kelly. I gotta pick up the kids. I'll be back. Don't go anywhere."

About twenty minutes later, Cassie and the kids pulled up to the house. Nick's car was nowhere to be seen.

CHAPTER 14

The Hangover

Nick Greer's head felt like it was in pieces and he couldn't find them all as he sat on the edge of the bed with his face in his hands. He looked at his watch: 9:12 a.m. He didn't remember coming back to the room. The last thing he remembered was sitting at the casino bar. He realized he still had his clothes on. I must have really been toasted to sleep in my clothes, he thought. He fell back down onto the bed, rolled over onto his stomach and felt something lumpy under him. Nick rolled over onto his back, reached into his jeans pocket and removed a bunch of casino chips. They were all black chips. He looked and saw they read one hundred dollars. He counted them, thirty-seven.

He put his hand on his aching forehead, closed his eyes, and foggily remembered rolling the dice at the crap table. As his mind slowly began to clear, he remembered the dice in his hand and a bunch of people cheering. Then he remembered Cassie and what had happened in her parents' house.

He rolled over and picked up the hotel room phone. "Front desk," was the answer on the other end.

"What do you have for a headache?"

"Good morning, Mr. Greer. This is Melanie. I checked you in. Do you remember?"

"Yes, I do."

"You should be calling room service, but I'll send something up for you. I hear you had a good time last night. They tell me you were the life of the party."

"Uhhh . . . okay, if you say so."

She chuckled. "Help is on its way."

Nick hung up the phone, rolled over, and fell out of the bed and onto the floor. Flat on his back, he looked up at the ceiling and said, "Shit!" He lay there for a couple of minutes until he heard a knock at the door. He got up, walked to the door, and opened it.

A smiling Melanie Steele was standing there with a tray in her hand. "Papa's personal cure for a hangover," she said, as she handed him the tray. "Warm water, Alka-Seltzer, and two Tylenol. Wash the Tylenol down with the Alka-Seltzer. Papa said it works every time."

"Hold on, let me get your tip," he said.

"No worry, Mr. Greer. This is on me." She stepped into the room and set the tray on the table. "Hurry, the water needs to be warm to work its magic. Have a nice day." She turned and left the room.

Nick opened the packet, plopped the two Alka-Seltzer tablets into the glass, opened the pack of Tylenol, tossed them into his mouth, and gulped down the fizzy liquid. He put the glass back onto the tray and headed for the shower.

Nick was standing at the sink, shaving. His hand was steady, and the headache was gone. His stomach was still a little queasy, but he was feeling somewhat better. Monica was right. He washed the last of the shaving cream from his face, and dried it off with a towel. He looked into the mirror and stared at the image looking back at him. "What's wrong with you?" he said out loud. "You love Sue Kim. How could you be so fucking stupid?" He looked himself in the eyes and said, "Greer, you're a dumb ass!"

After he had a hearty breakfast, he dropped by the cashier's cage and cashed in his chips. Then he got into his car and drove to the Metzler home. Cassie answered the door and reached up to kiss him as he entered. He shook his head and said, "No, Cassie, no."

"The kids are in the kitchen," she said as she stepped back to let him pass.

The kids were sitting at the kitchen table eating cereal as he walked in and sat down with them. "How are my girls this morning?"

"Mommy said we don't have to go to church today," Kasey said.

"Okay," Nick answered. "Your mom is the boss."

Kelly asked, "What happened to you last night? Mom said you were sick, and you went back to your hotel."

"I'm feeling better now, sweetie. What do you want to do today?"

"Movie, Daddy!" Kaitlin yelled. "Let's go see a movie."

Kasey said, "Yeah, I wanna go to the movies, too."

Nick looked at Kelly. She nodded. "Okay, the movies, it is!" Nick said.

CHAPTER 15

The Breakup

The drive home seemed to take forever. Thoughts of his little fling with Cassie controlled his mind all the way home. What was he going to do? He had to tell Sue Kim. What would she say? He loved her, for Christ sake. He should have never let Cassie seduce him. It was her fault. All her fault! Bullshit, he thought, it's my own fucking fault!

Sue Kim's Prius was parked in its usual spot, and Nick pulled his Taurus next to it. He killed the engine and sat there for a while, running the events of the last two days through his mind. Should he tell her? There was a good possibility she would leave him if he did. And, what about Cassie? Why did she seduce him in the first place? Had she had an epiphany and wanted him back? That was never going to happen! Could she be jealous of the kids' relationship with Sue Kim and have concocted a sinister plan to break them apart? He knew she was very capable of doing something like that. He knew he had to tell Sue Kim, but not tonight. He figured he would wait for the right time and tell her what had happened in Prescott. Though he hoped she would understand, he had doubts it would turn out well.

He opened the car door, got out, and opened the trunk. He reached in and retrieved his service Glock, his ankle gun, and his badge and shoved them into the overnight bag. He slammed the trunk shut and turned toward the door of his townhouse. The door was unlocked. Sue Kim was sitting at the kitchen table. She looked up at him, and he could see she was crying. "What's the matter, baby?" he asked.

She swiped her finger across her Android and held it up for him to see. "Explain this!"

It was a text from Cassie, it read: *How does it feel to know your boyfriend is fucking his ex-wife while you're out of town?*

Tears ran down her cheeks as she looked up at him. "Tell me this isn't true?"

"I can explain—"

"That's what I thought. If you have to explain, then it is true. Explanations are not necessary. I'll be staying at Carol's until I find my own place. I'll send her for the rest of my stuff."

"Sue, no." He dropped his bag on the floor and walked over to her. "We can talk about this."

"Don't you touch me! Don't you dare come near me! There is nothing to talk about. You and me are no longer." Sue Kim took a step back; her pretty face was swollen from crying. He looked down and saw the bag sitting on the floor next to her. With tears still streaming down her face, she stood up, put her purse over her shoulder, picked up the bag and headed toward the door.

Nick stood in front of her and said, "You're not going anywhere. We need to talk about—"

That was all the words he got out as she pushed him hard. He tried to take a step back but lost his balance and fell backward over the bag he had dropped on the floor only a few moments ago.

A tear dripped from her face onto his hand as she stepped over him and headed for the door. She opened it, stopped, turned around, and looked at him lying on the floor. Tears were rolling down her oval cheeks. "You know, I really loved you! I really did!" She closed the door behind her.

Nick pulled himself up from the floor, sat at the table, put his face in his hands, and cried. His mind traveled back to the first day they had met and how lovely she had looked.

She'd been a new employee and worked in the morgue as an assistant to Nick's friend, Jack Konesky. Nick had gone to the morgue to see Jack about a corpse he was working on and ran into her. She didn't know who Nick was, and she tried to stop him from bothering her boss. Nick's attitude with her was, to say the least, arrogant and condescending. She became defensive and stood up to him. A few days later, he saw her again and apologized to her. They went out on a date and they had been together ever since.

He yelled, "That bitch!" As he thought about what his ex-wife had done, he picked up his Android and called Cassie.

"Hello, Metzler residence." Nick recognized the voice of his ex-father-in-law. "I need to speak with your daughter," Nick said.

"Nick, my boy, did you have a good weekend?"

"Ask your fucking daughter!"

"Uhhh . . . you don't need—"

Nick interrupted, speaking slowly and emphatically, "Rod, put Cassie on the phone, now!"

There was silence except for the sound of the phone being dropped onto the table. Then he heard Rod say: "It's Nick. He's pissed about something. What happened? What did you do?"

"Hello, Nick, what can I do for you?" Cassie asked in a nonchalant manner.

"Why did you do it, Cassie? What did she ever do to you?"

"You should thank me. She's not your type." There was silence as the call was disconnected.

Nick hit redial and the phone rang busy. He knew she had taken it off the hook. He called her cell phone. It went straight to voice mail. Obviously, she had shut it off. What he didn't know is that when she hung up the phone, she looked at her father, smiled, took a deep breath and said, "Ahhh, life is good!"

CHAPTER 16

New Jobs

It was Monday morning. Both Sonny Madison and Nick Greer were sitting in the outer office of the chief of detectives, wondering why they were there. Both men assumed it had something to do with Sonny's suspension.

Nick was unusually quiet. It looked to Sonny as though his friend's mind was somewhere far away. "What do you think he wants with us?" Sonny asked. Nick shrugged. Sonny added, "You're awfully quiet this morning."

Nick shrugged again. The phone on Tricia's desk buzzed. She picked it up and said, "This is Tricia. Yes, sir, they are. I will. Right away."

She hung up the phone, looked at the two detectives, and said, "Chief Mannion will see you now." The clock on the wall showed the time was ten o'clock, straight up.

Both detectives stood and went into the chief's office. "Good morning, gentlemen. Please have a seat," he said without looking up. The two detectives sat down.

Deputy Chief Bruce Mannion was known to be a no-bull person. He was one who got right to the point, and today was no exception. His face was still buried in the file he was reading when he said, "How are things going with Captain Lovett?"

Before either one could speak, the chief looked up. "You don't need to answer that. I already know. Sergeant Madison, I understand you're on suspension. Lieutenant Greer, I believe you are considering turning in your badge."

Sonny looked at Nick. "You didn't tell me."

Nick shrugged. "I want to find Pete's killer first, then I'll decide."

Sonny laid his head on Nick's shoulder and grinned. "I didn't know you cared."

A look of shock was on Nick's face, but Chief Mannion shook his head and smiled. "Nick, Sonny, I've known both of you a long time. Nick, I remember when you were a rookie and how you tried to work from that lone bottom locker. All the other cops had full-sized lockers, but you had the half-one sitting right on the floor. I thought it would be fun watching you bend your six-and-a-half-foot self down to that locker every day. After a couple of months, it wasn't fun anymore. And you never said a word, so we got you a regular one, remember?"

"That was your idea?"

"Yep. Guilty as charged! Anyway, that's not why I called you in here." He reached into his desk drawer, pulled out a badge and a gun, and slid them across his desk to Sonny. "Pick them up, they're yours. Put them on. You're back to work." The chief could see the puzzled look on Sonny's face. "Lovett's an ass. He would fuck up the whole place just to hear the words 'yes, sir' every time he barked out an order. The only reason he ever got that position is he's the mayor's wife's cousin, or nephew or something like that. The mayor doesn't like him either. This is his third command in as many years, and his last if I have anything to do with it. He needs to realize this is the Phoenix Police Department, not the U. S. Marine Corps."

Sonny said, "I appreciate this, Chief, but it's not going to be easy working under him again, after what happened."

"Don't worry, you're not." He looked at Nick. "And neither are you, Lieutenant."

Now, he had the attention of both detectives who had puzzled looks on their faces. Mannion stood up and said, "Follow me." They followed him out of his office, as he turned left and led them to the second door. The black painted letters on the door glass read: Special Investigations Unit. The chief pointed to the lettering. "Be careful, the paint may still be wet." He opened the door, stood to the side, and waved his arm and hand across his body in the direction of the interior of the room. "Behold, your new digs!"

The two detectives walked into the room. Their eyes scanned the entire room. It was furnished with four gray desks. Each one had a chair behind it and one beside it. Two of the desks had a computer and a phone on them. There was a filing cabinet against the back wall. Each desk had a nameplate setting on the front; one read, Sgt. S. Madison, the other, Lt. N. Greer. In the center of Nick's new desk were two cardboard boxes.

Chief Mannion said, "Nick, I had your desk cleaned out and all the stuff moved here. Sonny, you can bring your stuff back as soon as you are ready."

"Chief, what's this all about?" Nick asked.

"You two can drop the chief stuff. We're going to be seeing a lot of each other. Sit down, get comfortable, and I'll explain."

The detectives sat behind their respective desks and looked at their boss, wondering what was going on. Mannion cleared his throat and said, "Detectives, as of today, the Phoenix Police Department has a new unit. It will be a special investigations unit, just like it says on the door. You two will handle it for now. You will be assigned high-priority and special cases. Depending on how things go, you may get added staff. For right now, Tricia will be your clerical help. I've already arranged for your calls to be routed through her during regular hours, and she'll handle your messages for you. She says I don't keep her busy enough, anyway. Your first case is already assigned. Find Pete Mendoza's killer!"

"Uhh . . . should I ask where the funding came from?" Nick asked, remembering Rosa was let go due to department budget constraints.

"And what about the mayor?" Sonny added. "Murphy doesn't like to spend money, you know. And what about the chief? Is he on board with this?"

"Don't worry about the funding," the deputy chief answered. "The office was already here and empty. We brought your computers from your old desks, that's all. The geeks hooked them up this morning. As for the chief? It was his idea, and, yes, Murphy is on board. The mayor, the chief, and I have been talking about this for a couple of months. We were just waiting for the right time and the right persons. You two were my first choice. I wanted you both, but it would have been hard to pull both of you out of homicide at the same time. Fortunately, Lovett made it easy, the dumb ass!

"Greer, Madison, this is your gig. Run it as you see fit. You will report to me, and only to me. Now, find the bastard who killed Pete Mendoza." They both stood up as he turned and left the room.

Sonny and Nick looked at each other and shrugged. They sat at their new desks. Nick began unpacking the boxes on his desk. Everything that had been in and on his desk was in the boxes. "My desk was locked. How did they—"

Sonny said, "What, do you think you're the only one who knows how to pick a lock?" Nick barely smiled.

Sonny looked around the room, then back at his partner and remarked, "Ya know, I think I'm gonna like this."

Nick was silent as he continued unpacking.

"What's wrong, buddy? You don't seem to be yourself today. Don't you like this new idea? I think it's great! No Lovett." Sonny grinned. "Now, the only pain in the ass I gotta put up with is you."

"Uhhmm, yeah, it's fine."

"Wow, don't be so excited! Hold in some of your enthusiasm. You're gonna have a stroke with all the excitement."

"Just leave me alone, Sonny. I'm not in the mood for your shit."

Sonny Madison was silent. Nick had never spoken to him that way. There had not been a harsh word between the two of them since they had become partners.

* * *

Sonny's mind traveled back to that day eight years ago. He had been without a partner for over a month. Jay Fisher had retired after thirty years with the department, the last four of which were as Sonny Madison's partner. He had been Sonny's only partner since he joined the homicide division.

When Sergeant Nick Greer was transferred from the robbery division and first introduced to Sonny, the elder detective thought, who is this guy? He was intimidated at first by his new partner's height. Sonny Madison was five-ten and about twenty pounds overweight. This new guy reminded him of "Gumby."

It didn't take long for the two detectives to mesh. The placement turned out to be brilliant. Each one's talents complemented the other. They solved some tough cases and soon became the most respected team in the department. Nick Greer's special instincts and Sonny Madison's knowledge and relentless use of the information highway were a perfect match. It wasn't long before they became friends.

Their personalities were like day and night. Nick was serious and almost always acted respectful to his superiors. Sonny was jovial and not afraid to get in the boss's face. He had the reputation of being a maverick, but his ability to solve crimes overshadowed his rebelliousness.

Even though Nick was promoted over Sonny, he never used his rank on his partner. When Nick made lieutenant, Sonny had a big celebration party at his home.

Several times in the past, Sonny thought about taking the lieutenant's exam, but he never did. He liked working in the field and bringing in the bad guys. He was afraid he would be pulled in, as often happened with lieutenants. His fear was that Nick would be given a supervisory position and leave the squad. What Sonny didn't know was that Nick had been offered a supervisory position on two different occasions and had turned them down.

It was shortly after that when the department, due to financial restraints, split the partners up, and they began working their own cases. At times, they worked together on cases, but for the most part they did their own thing. Still, Sonny and Nick found time to talk, have a beer together, or go to lunch. The families would get together for barbecues and pool parties at either Sonny's or Nick's home. It was a friendship destined to last forever.

* * *

Nick finished putting his stuff in his desk, turned, and without a word went out the door. Sonny sat there with a stunned look on his face. He turned on his computer. Everything was fine. His password still worked, but he changed it. He looked around the empty room. He was worried about his friend.

It was about an hour later when Nick Greer returned to his new office. Sonny was working on the computer and didn't acknowledge him. It was a while before the silence was broken.

"Hhmmm . . . Sue Kim left last night." Nick said.

"Uh, left? Like you two had a fight and she needed some air?" Sonny asked without looking up.

Nick shook his head. "I wish."

"You don't mean she left, like in gone?'

Nick nodded. "She left last night. I just went back there. She must have come back this morning and got the rest of her stuff. She left her key on the kitchen table."

Sonny looked over at his friend. "She loves you," Sonny stated. "Why would she leave? What the hell happened?"

Nick sighed. "It's my fault. I went to Prescott this weekend to see the kids. Cassie and I were alone in the house while the kids were at a birthday party. We were getting along extremely well and, well—"

"Oh, shit!" Sonny's eyes got as wide as golf balls. "Tell me you didn't!"

Nick looked at his friend in silence, then looked away. Sonny shook his head and said, "What in the name of Christ would cause you to do something so stupid? And how did Sue Kim find out anyway?"

"Cassie sent her a text and told her. She sent it while I was driving back to Phoenix. I never had a chance to explain."

"What?" Sonny was mortified. "What?"

"I think I was set up. I think it was Cassie's plan from the day they talked in the hospital. It explains how all of a sudden she turned from bitch to angel."

"Damn, Nick, that's low, even for Cassie," Sonny commented. "How could you let that happen?"

"We were alone. I needed to take a leak. She said to use the bathroom in her bedroom. When I came out, the bedroom door was shut, and she was standing there in sexy lingerie. She kissed me. I tried to push her away, but she wanted more, and, well, old passions surfaced. Then, well, she always was hard to say no to. The next thing I knew we were, well, you know."

"Yeah." Sonny nodded. "I can imagine. I understand, I guess. Cassie's a good-looking woman, and she's got quite a rack on her."

Nick's eyes widened and he stared at Sonny, who grinned. "Well, it's true. So, what are you gonna do?"

"I'm going to give her some time to cool down, then I'll try to talk with her. I'm going to try to explain it. Maybe she'll understand."

"Good luck," Sonny said. "I hope it works. I really like Sue Kim. I thought she was a keeper, but you know as well as I do how proud she can be. You gotta break through that."

"Oh, yeah!" Nick took in a deep breath, shook his head, and again said, "Oh, yeah!"

"If you need some time," Sonny said, "I can handle things here."

"No, we gotta find Pete's killer. That's the number one priority."

Sonny nodded. "Okay then, let's get to it. Come on over here. I want to show you something."

Nick walked over to his partner who was now staring at the computer screen. "Whatcha got?"

"Do you remember I was about to tell you something when Lovett called us in? Do you remember the obit I was showing you?"

"Yeah, what about it?" Greer asked.

"He was Catholic."

"Okay," Nick said. "So what does that have to do with anything?"

Sonny looked at his partner and said, "They all were."

"Who all were what?" Nick asked.

"Catholic." Sonny answered. "All of them. Even the ones back east."

Lieutenant Nick Greer's face turned white as he groaned, took a deep breath and exhaled. "You gotta be shittin' me!"

"I wish I was." Sonny looked at his friend. "I wish I was."

A little over a year ago, Nick had been the lead detective on a case of a murdered priest that led to the arrest and conviction of a high-profile lawyer. The investigation uncovered fraud and corruption among some of the priests and some of the bishop's own staff. The bishop's people did everything they could to hinder the investigation. Even the mayor got involved. Lieutenant Nick Greer didn't ever want to go through dealing with Bishop O'Malley and his staff again. He hoped he wouldn't have to this time.

"Are you sure?" asked Nick.

"Positive," Sonny affirmed. "I checked the obituaries of the two back east and our lady in the lake, Madeline Meade. They were all buried in the Catholic church. She went to St. John's in Scottsdale. The guy in the wash belonged to St. Michael's in north Phoenix, and we know Pete went to St. Raphael's."

Nick said, "They all were stabbed in the heart, ring fingers chopped off, dumped in water, married, and Catholic, but none of them went to the same church. There has to be something else, something that gives us a place to start."

"As far as I can tell, except for Perrotta, they all were in stable marriages. Our Tempe lady was five years into her second marriage, and Pete was married forever."

Nick looked at Sonny. "See what you can dig up on the Tempe vic and our guy in the wash. I want to know everything about them. Everything!" Then he walked to his desk and picked up his car keys.

"Where are you going?" asked Sonny.

"First, to see Chief Mannion, then to Four Hundred East Monroe."

"You're going to the bishop's office?" Sonny asked. Nick nodded. "If they see you coming, they'll change it to nine commandments and shoot you on sight."

* * *

Lieutenant Nick Greer walked into his new boss's office. Tricia greeted him with a smile. "Back already, Lieutenant?"

"I need to see the chief."

Tricia reached for the phone to announce him but heard a voice: "Come on in, Nick."

Chief Mannion was standing by his door.

The lieutenant followed his boss into his office. Mannion sat and said, "Have a seat. What can I do for you?"

Nick sat down. "Chief, I'm going to the Phoenix diocesan office. I'm not the most popular person who ever graced their presence, but I need some information. Can you open a door for me?"

"Sure, I'll call right now. Do you want to tell me why?"

"All the vics were Catholic. I just want to see if there is any connection. Maybe they all went on a retreat together or something. Perhaps the diocese will have some sort of record, anything that might help."

"How can that relate to the vics back east?"

"I don't know, but we gotta start somewhere. Right now, that's all I got."

"I'll make the call," the chief said. "Good luck."

The detective nodded and left the building.

Mannion knew what his detective meant by his popularity within the diocese. His past investigation of the death of one of their priests had opened up a Pandora's box that devastated the bishop, one which would never leave him. Rumor had it that Bishop O'Malley had been called to the archdiocese and had gotten his ass reamed. Sonny Madison, a practicing Catholic, had said he heard O'Malley was being forced into retirement, and a new bishop was going to be appointed soon.

Just as Nick pulled into the diocesan parking lot, his phone rang through his car's speakers. He pushed the phone button on the steering wheel. "Nick Greer."

"Bruce Mannion, Nick. Sorry it took so long but I called the mayor. I figured if anyone could pave the way for you, it would be him." Both Nick and Mannion knew Mayor Murphy and the bishop were friends. "You are to see a Diane Harding. Her title is Director of Christian Formation. They said she would have access to all the records you should need."

"Thanks, Chief."

"It's Bruce. And, Nick, do me a favor. Try not to piss them off any more than you have to, okay?"

"Got it."

CHAPTER 17

Off To See The Bishop

Nick followed the sidewalk to the front door, opened it, and walked across the lobby to the reception desk. He remembered the receptionist from his previous visits. "Welcome, Lieutenant Greer. How are you today?" She smiled and before he could answer said, "Mrs. Harding is waiting for you. It's the last office on the left. I'll buzz you in. Have a blessed day."

Nick didn't expect such a cordial welcome after all the trouble he had stirred up the last couple of times he was here. He had shakened up the place so much that he figured the bishop had a dartboard with Nick's picture on it behind his office door. He pictured him throwing darts at it and laughed.

He passed some offices and noticed a couple of names had changed, names involved in the scam he had unearthed. As he approached the end of the hall, a lady came out of the last office and said, "You must be the police officer." She held out her hand. "Diane Harding."

"Lieutenant Nick Greer," he said as he shook her hand.

"Please come in and have a seat."

Nick sat as she seated herself behind her desk and said, "I understand you need some information. Please know I will cooperate as much as I can, but there may be some information I am unable to release. By the way, I heard about the retired policeman who was pulled from the canal. Does this have anything to do with him?"

"Uhh, it might. I assume you heard it on the news?"

"Yes, sir, I did, plus I live only a block away. I saw the lights, so I went to see what was going on. I got there just as they were pulling the body out of the canal. I thought I heard someone say a part of his hand was missing. Is that correct?"

"He probably got it caught on something," the detective lied.

"How can I help you, Officer?"

"It's Lieutenant, ma'am." He continued, "First of all, I must ask you not to share any of our conversation. It has to do with an ongoing investigation. Is that okay?"

"Uhm . . . I'll try, but please know I have responsibilities here that may overrule that."

"If I give you three names, can you tell me if your records show if there is anything they have in common? Like maybe they went on a retreat together, or to a seminar, or attended a church-related event of some sort? Would that be something you could share?" The detective chose his words carefully.

Diane slid the center drawer of her desk out, revealing a keyboard, and looked at the detective. "Oh, that's no problem at all. What are their names, please?"

"Madeline Meade—"

With a look of concern in her eyes, she cut in, "Maddy? What does she have to do with this?"

Nick was caught off guard by her sudden comment. "Did you know her, Mrs. Harding?"

"Yes, she was my friend. She used to go to the cathedral until she moved to Scottsdale. She was a nice lady."

"When was the last time you saw her?" the detective questioned.

"About a week before she was killed. We made it a point to have lunch once a month. What does she have to do with the man in the canal?"

"Probably nothing," Nick lied. "How about Richard Joseph Perrotta and Agapito Mendoza?"

Nick's ears heard the clicking of her keyboard as she typed. "Uhmm . . . Mr. Perrotta is registered at St. Michael's, and Mr. Mendoza at St. Raphael's."

"Can you find any time they could have all been in the same place?" She looked up at her visitor with a puzzled look on her face. "I just wondered if they had ever met, that's all," he added.

Again, she began typing. After about a minute, she looked back to the detective and shook her head. "I'm sorry, but I can't find anything to show they ever attended a registered function at the same time. Mr. and Mrs. Mendoza and Maddy were Eucharistic ministers, and Mr. Perrotta wasn't registered in any lay ministry I can find." She added, "Lieutenant Greer, may I ask you a question."

"Go ahead; I'll answer it if I can."

"I never put it together until now, but when Maddy's body was found, she had a finger missing, her ring finger. They said the killer couldn't get her rings off so he stabbed her and cut her whole finger off to get her rings. I know the man in the canal had part of his hand missing. What about Mr. Perrotta? What does he have to do with this?"

"I thought you knew," Nick said, surprised by her question. "You don't know?"

"Know what?"

"Mr. Perrotta's body was found in the desert last week."

She took a breath and said, "I didn't know that. I didn't know him. I saw something on the news last week, but the name wasn't given. Did he have a digit missing, too?"

"Ma'am, I really can't comment on an ongoing case, but I will tell you that the Tempe Police Department thinks your friend's finger was eaten by a fish." He hoped his words would appease her. They did not.

She leaned back in her chair, folded her hands across her chest, and looked at her guest as if she had just been insulted. "Lieutenant, I'm not stupid. Maddy's whole left ring finger was missing. That wasn't done by a lake fish nibbling at her hand. Can you tell me what's going on here? Why are you looking for a connection between them? Since you won't answer my question about Mr. Perrotta, I assume his situation was the same. To me, this has all the signs of a serial killer. Please tell me, are we in danger? Do we have a serial killer in our city?"

Nick was temporarily stunned. His eyes widened, and his mouth opened, and his loss for words was obvious to his hostess, who said, "Lieutenant Greer, I am an avid reader of mysteries, and I've seen every episode of *Criminal Minds* as least once. There's something going on here you aren't telling me, yet you ask me to help you. Don't you think a little quid pro quo should apply here?"

The detective thought for a moment. She was still leaning back with her arms folded, looking at him with accusing eyes. "Mrs. Harding, it's too early to tell. I'm hoping not, but I must ask you to keep this discussion between us. I don't want to alert the public to something that may not be."

"Excuse me, Lieutenant, and with all due respect, doesn't the public have a right to know if there is a danger out there?"

"Ma'am, if and when we are certain there is a danger to the citizens, the information will be made public. In the meantime, if there is someone out there perpetrating crimes, we need to catch him. The less publicity there is, the better chance we have. Please, I ask you, do not share this conversation."

"I will take your request under advisement," Harding said as she unfolded her arms, pushed her keyboard drawer shut and leaned forward. "Is there anything else I can help you with, Lieutenant?" Her words were more of a dismissal than a question. She stood and extended her hand.

Nick shook her hand. "No, ma'am. I thank you for your help. I'll find my way out."

As he stood up and turned to leave, she said, "Lieutenant, have a blessed day and find the person who killed my friend."

Nick turned around. She was holding out a business card. "Call me if you need anything else. My cell phone number is on the back."

He took her card, thanked her and left.

Lieutenant Nick Greer mentally kicked himself in the ass as he drove back to the police department. She's gonna blow it, he thought. I shouldn't have gone there in the first place. I found out what I knew before I went there—nothing!

CHAPTER 18

The Word Is Out

Nick Greer arrived back at the police department and headed for his old squad room until he remembered he didn't work there anymore. He turned and went to his new home. Sonny was sitting at his computer, still typing away. "What did you find, Gumby? Anything we can use?"

"Actually, no, and it may have done more harm than good."

Madison looked up. "Why? What happened? Did you piss off the bishop again?" He grinned.

"No, actually they were all very cordial. Whatever Mannion did, they were surprisingly welcoming. The only thing missing was the red carpet."

"Okay, then what's wrong?"

"The lady I spoke with was the Director of Foundation, or something like that—"

"Director of Christian Formation," Sonny corrected. "She's a lay employee. She doesn't wear a habit or a collar. She would be in charge of religious education throughout the diocese."

"Yeah, whatever," Nick said. "Do you know her?"

"I know of her, but I've never met her personally. Why?"

"She knew the Tempe vic, and about her finger. She also lives by the canal where Pete's body was found. She heard one of the medics talking about his finger. She was probably there at the same time we were. She's a smart cookie. She figured out we're looking for a serial killer."

"That ain't good. Do you think she'll go to the media?"

Nick said, "I don't know. She might. We need to tell Mannion."

"Right behind you," Sonny said as he logged off his computer and shut it down.

"Have you had lunch?" Nick asked.

Sonny lifted his hand and cupped it around his ear. "Ahhh, I hear the deli a calling my name."

"Let's go eat. We'll give the chief the bad news after lunch."

* * *

Nick Greer and Sonny Madison came back from lunch and went straight to the chief's office. "Hello, Detectives. I suppose you're here to see Chief Mannion," Tricia said. Without waiting for an answer, she buzzed her boss. "They're here." She smiled as she nodded her head toward Mannion's office. "He's waiting for you."

"Good afternoon, Detectives. Have a seat. How was lunch?"

"Uhh, okay, I guess. "Sonny answered.

"I'm glad you were able to chow down. I haven't had the time. Would you like to know why?"

Nick answered, "I assume you're going to tell us."

"What happened at the diocese, Nick?" Mannion asked. "I thought you were going to take it easy on them this time."

"Uhh . . . I did. There was no problem. I spoke to a Diane Harding, Director of . . . of . . ."

"Christian Formation," Sonny added.

"Oh, yeah," Nick said. "The meeting went well I thought. She checked her files and said she couldn't find any connection. I was surprised to find out she knew the Tempe vic pretty well, and she was at the scene when they fished Pete out of the canal. She lives close to the canal. She seems to have a passion for murder mysteries. She figured out right away I was chasing a serial killer. When she asked me, I told her it was too early to tell. But I don't think she bought it. I asked her to keep our discussion confidential. I hope she will."

"Well, I guess that explains why I have a press conference at two o'clock this afternoon."

"You're going to a press conference?" Sonny asked. "Where and why? Who's holding it?"

Bruce Mannion answered, "Here, because the mayor said I would, and me."

"Huh?" Sonny was confused. He looked at his partner who shrugged.

Bruce Mannion continued, "Apparently your lady blabbed, or somebody did. The mayor's office has been flooded with calls from radio and TV stations wanting to know if the Phoenix Police Department is hiding information from the public about a serial killer. He called Chief Morris, and as shit always does, it rolled down hill and stopped right here." He pointed to the center of his desk. "Chief Morris told me there was a news conference at two, and I should get a statement ready because I was going to be the guest speaker."

"I'm sorry, Bruce. I was blindsided by her. It never occurred to me that the first vic and she would be close friends, or that she would know about the missing finger, or Pete." The detective described his meeting with Diane Harding almost as if it were a video-tape replay.

"I don't know what else you could have done," said Mannion. "She doesn't know about the vics back east, does she?"

"No, and that's our saving grace, if they're related."

Mannion looked at Nick. "You sound as though you have doubts."

"Oh, no. It's not that at all. I just don't know how to connect them, that's all."

Mannion looked at Madison. "Sonny, you've been unusually silent. What's your take on this whole thing?"

"I was just thinking," Sonny answered. "I realize she lives near where Pete was found, but she also knew the first vic, too. The feds said the perp was a male, but why not a female?"

"Serial killers are almost never women," Nick answered.

"You're right, almost never. But what about Aileen Wournos? Or Nannie Doss?" Sonny responded.

"Wournos was a hooker who liked to kill her johns, and Doss thought it was easier to kill her husbands than divorce them," Nick said.

Sonny laughed. "Yeah, all five of them."

"You guys should see this lady." Nick laughed. "She is barely over five foot, and I'll bet she doesn't weigh much over one hundred pounds. There's no way she could have lifted Pete, not without help."

"Check her out anyway," Mannion said. "I got a press conference to go to."

"Do you want us to come along, Boss?" Sonny asked.

"First of all, knock off the boss crap. Chief, or Bruce, will do fine. I prefer Bruce. Second, you two stay as far away from the TV cameras as possible. I don't want them seeing your faces or knowing your names. Or the bastards will be going to your homes and knocking on your doors."

"Yes, Boss, Bruce." Sonny grinned as both detectives got up and went back to their office.

* * *

Lieutenant Nick Greer and Sergeant Sonny Madison were watching the news conference on their computers as Bruce Mannion walked up to the podium. He looked out at the crowd of about twenty reporters and their support crews. He was flanked by Mayor Murphy and Police Chief Morris.

Mannion began: "I have a prepared statement." He reached into his pocket and removed a pair of reading glasses, put them on, and began to read. "There has been a series of homicides within the past few months in Maricopa County that have similar characteristics." He looked up and saw that all eyes were on him in anticipation of his next words. "All of them died due to a stab wound in the chest." He looked up again at the crowd before continuing, "Each victim was also missing a finger." He waited for the oohs and ahs of the crowd to subside.

"One of the bodies was found in the Tempe Town Lake a few months ago. The other two were found last week, one in a canal, and the other in the desert in North Phoenix. We have reason to believe they were all killed by the same person. Please know that we are doing our best to find the perpetrator and bring him or her to justice."

One of the reporters yelled out, "Which fingers were missing? Was it the same one on all of them?"

"I'm not at liberty to say at this time," Mannion answered.

Another reporter spoke loudly, "Is it true it was the ring finger on each person?"

"I cannot comment any more since this is an ongoing investigation."

Another reporter asked, "You said him or her. Could it be a woman?"

"We seldom find a situation like this involves a female, but it would be imprudent to rule it out completely."

"I understand the FBI has been called in. Can you confirm that?"

"We have no need for the FBI. We are perfectly capable of handling it ourselves," Mannion answered.

A young woman raised her hand. Bruce Mannion pointed to her. "I understand all three victims were Catholic. Is there any correlation there?"

"They were? What would that have to do with anything? There are over eight hundred thousand Catholics in the diocese." He looked out at the crowd of reporters and said, "That is all I have for you at this time." He left the podium and walked away, followed by the mayor and the chief. The crowd of reporters tried to follow them, yelling out questions, but the uniformed police were able to hold them back.

"Good field," Sonny exclaimed. He made expressions with his eyes and moved his head around as he continued, "They were? What would that have to do with anything? There are over eight hundred thousand Catholics in the diocese. Did you hear him? He danced around that one like a pro. He should be on *Dancing With The Stars.* A ten from Len! Hell, he missed his calling. He should have been a politician."

Nick shook his head and smiled. "Find anything on Harding?"

"Nada. Clean as a whistle. She's been with the Diocese of Phoenix for three years. She came up here from Tucson."

"Check and see if there were any murders with the same MO in Tucson."

"I already did. Nada."

"Any connection to Pete?"

"Negative."

"Perrotta?"

"Nope."

Just then both of the detective's phones rang. Each read the same text from their new boss: *See me.*

They looked at each other and shrugged. "His master's text," Sonny said, grinning.

CHAPTER 19

Travel Orders

Lieutenant Nick Greer and Sergeant Sonny Madison walked into the lobby of Deputy Chief Bruce Mannion's office and were greeted by Tricia. "Welcome back again."

"Yeah," Sonny replied. "Maybe they should have put the SIU in here."

Tricia smiled. "I imagine that could be arranged. Chief Mannion is waiting for you."

The two detectives went into their boss's office. "Have a seat, Detectives. This won't take long." Nick and Sonny sat down.

"How would you guys like to take a little trip, all expenses paid?"

The two detectives looked at each other. Sonny said, "Uh, Tahiti would be nice."

Mannion smiled as he pressed the intercom and asked, "Are they here yet?"

"The courier just arrived. I'm signing for them now," Tricia answered.

"Fine. Bring them in, please."

A few seconds later, Tricia came into the office and handed her boss an envelope. She turned around and smiled to the two cops as she left.

Chief Mannion reached into the envelope and pulled out two smaller ones. He opened each one and inspected them. When he was finished he tossed one to Nick and one to Sonny. "They're airline tickets, but not to Tahiti. Nick, your flight leaves at seven-ten a.m. for Pittsburgh. Sonny, yours leaves at five-twenty-five a.m. for Baltimore. Sorry it's so early, but it's the only nonstop we could get on such short notice. You can sleep on the plane. Gather all the info you have and take it with you." He handed another envelope to each of them. "In there is a department credit card and info on who to see. There will be rental cars waiting for you at the airports. Find out all you can on the two vics. There has to be something pointing to Phoenix. Find it. When you come back here, I want something that will lead us to our killer."

The detectives looked at their boss. “You got it, Bruce,” Nick said.

“Take what’s left of the day and go home. Spend the rest of the day with your family, Sonny, and that little cutie in the lab, Nick.”

Nick looked at Sonny and back to Mannion. “Uhhh, I’ll see what I can do.”

Bruce Mannion was puzzled.

“Uhh . . . we’re not . . .” Nick stammered.

“She left him,” Sonny stated. “He fucked up big time.” He looked at his friend who stared at him. Sonny’s eyes widened. “Well, you did!”

The chief looked at his lieutenant. “Goddamn it, Greer. What did you do? You better fix it. Half the department adores that girl, and the other half hasn’t met her yet.”

“I’ll see what I can do, Chief.”

“Good luck, gentlemen. Bring me back some good news.”

CHAPTER 20

The Harbor

Sonny left Baltimore-Washington International Airport in his rental car and followed Route 95 into Baltimore. His watch read ten minutes before one, when he pulled up to 500 East Baltimore Street. The sign told him he was at his destination: the City of Baltimore Police Department. He parked his car around the corner, walked up the steps to the front door, and went in. He told the officer at the front desk who he was, showed her his badge, and said, "I'm here to see Detective Petrosky. I called earlier. He's expecting me."

She picked up a clipboard from her desk, looked at it, and flipped the page. "Hold on." She picked up the phone on her desk and punched in some numbers. After a few moments she handed him a visitor's badge, pointed to the security screening area, and said, "Over there, and then you'll take the elevator to the third floor. I'll let Detective Petrosky know you're coming."

"No need," came a voice from behind her. The man reached out his hand. "Joe Petrosky. Welcome to Baltimore."

"Sonny Madison. Thank you."

"Follow me, Sergeant. I've been waiting for you." As they rode up in the elevator, Petrosky said, "You're not how I pictured you."

"Let me see," Sonny said. "You were expecting cowboy boots, a bolo tie, a six-gun, and a ten-gallon hat, I'll bet."

"Uh, what's a bolo tie?"

Sonny laughed. The elevator opened, and he followed Petrosky to the squad room where he sat behind his desk and gestured for Sonny to have a seat. He handed his visitor a file and said, "It's all in here. Everything we got. I could have faxed it all to you and saved you the cost of the trip."

"We had some money left in the donut fund, so we used that," Sonny said. Petrosky laughed.

Sonny read over the file. When he was finished, he said, "It says the vic was James Pennington. What about the wife? Uuhh, Janice Pennington? It says she was working when this all went down?"

"Yeah, her alibi checked out. You'll see she was working at Target. She's clean."

"Is there anything you can remember that might not be in here?"

"No clue. It wasn't my case."

Sonny looked up at his host. "Uhh . . . it says you were the investigating officer."

"No, sir. If you look close, it says, Sergeant J. Petrosky. That was my father."

"Is he available? Can I speak with him?"

"I'd give anything to be able to do that for you, but we lost him last year. Coronary."

Sonny's tone went from anticipation to somber as he remembered his own father's shocking death, also of a coronary only two years ago. Petrosky could see the sincerity in his guest's eyes. "I'm sorry for your loss. I really mean it. I didn't know."

"It's okay. Thank you. He was a great cop. Just like his father, my grandpa. They were both married to the job. Pop could have made lieutenant, but he wouldn't take the test. He said he was afraid they would make him a supervisor. He loved what he did, and he wanted to stay in the field. That's what killed him. I truly think if he had slowed down, he would be here talking with you instead of me. My wife and I had our first child a few weeks ago. His first grandchild. Joseph Petrosky the Third. I wish he could have seen him. I wish Joey could have known his grandpa." He reached up and rubbed one eye. "Sorry, allergies."

"I'd like to see where the body was found, if I can." Sonny said.

Petrosky picked up his car keys from his desk and looked at his guest. "Let's go."

The view of the Baltimore inner harbor was fascinating to Sonny. It seemed peaceful, though there was a lot of activity. Petrosky could see the look on his face, and said, "Most new folks are awed when they see this for the first time. Wait until tonight. This place sure livens up at night. There are great restaurants here, and weekends can get rowdy at times."

"Where was the body found?" Sonny asked.

Petrosky opened the file and looked at the pictures. He pointed to some piers with boats docked next to them. "Over there." Sonny followed him about two hundred feet until he stopped. He pointed to a spot under one of the piers. "A couple in a small boat said they felt like they had hit something, so they stopped. They saw a body floating next to the pier support. There were a couple of bicycle officers pedaling by. They responded. It's all in the report." He handed the file to Sonny. "It's all yours, Arizona."

"Thanks," Sonny said. "How about the boaters? Could they be any help?"

"Nah, they were clueless. Both of their names, contact information, and addresses are in the file. Trust me; you'd be wasting your time with them."

"What about the two bike patrolmen? Are they available?"

"Let's see." Petrosky looked at their names. "Morgan was killed a couple of years ago. I'll check on Jesky and let you know."

Sonny wrote his cell phone number on the back of his card and handed it to the detective. "Call me when you find out?"

Petrosky nodded, wrote his cell number on the back of his card and handed it to his visitor. "Here is mine if you need anything."

"How did he die?" Sonny asked.

"Who?"

"Officer Morgan?"

"He was off duty and tried to take down an armed robber at a convenience store. The perp saw him reach for his ankle piece and took him out before he could pull it."

"What happened to the perp?"

"He got death, but the state recently passed a bill abolishing the death penalty. It didn't make any difference though, 'cause two weeks ago he was found with his throat cut. Even the politicians couldn't change his fate. He got what was coming to him, if you ask me."

They returned to the police station. Sonny got into his car, checked in at a motel, grabbed some KFC, and went back to his room. He called the numbers in the file but, as he expected, neither one was any good. Both were cell phones. Thomas Thatcher's phone number had been assigned to another person who never heard of the guy. The other, Rebecca Thatcher, was a bogus number. Sonny double-checked the file. It didn't say if, or how they were related, but he assumed they were husband and wife.

Sonny pulled his notebook from his pocket and wrote: send Petrosky a bolo.

He looked at his watch: 4:00, Arizona time. He pulled his cell phone from his belt and called April.

"It's about time you called," she said.

"Sorry, I've been busy. I'm here safe and sound. Anything going on there?"

"Nope, the same stuff. I went to see Elena today. We talked a little, but she seemed to be preoccupied with something. Sonny, you knew Pete well. Just between you and me, do you know if he ever cheated on Elena?"

"Who, Pete? Fool around? No way. He was as straight as an arrow. Why would you even ask?"

"Something Elena said didn't make sense."

"What? What did she say?"

"She said something like she would be watching for a strange woman at the funeral. When I asked her what she meant, she changed the subject. It made no sense to me."

"Or me," her husband answered.

April said, "I remember about a month ago, we were playing cards. She asked me what I would do if I ever found you cheating on me."

"Uhh, and you said?"

"Oh, I said, do you mean before or after I gelded him? The girls all thought it was funny." She continued, "What are we going to do about Nick and Sue Kim?"

"We're going to stay out of it," Sonny stated.

They talked about her day and the kids, and finally they said goodbye. Sonny looked out from his second-floor window. He marveled at some of the older buildings that made up the Baltimore landscape. There's a lot of history here, he thought. Too bad I don't have time to enjoy it.

He reached for the envelope Detective Petrosky had given him, removed the contents, and scattered them out on the small, round writing table. He started with the reports. His eyes scoured each page, looking for something, anything, that would help. He shook his head in disappointment. He picked up the pictures and looked at them one by one. There were several pictures: a couple of the body, the rest of the surrounding area. He put them down and began to shake his head, but stopped, and picked up one of the pictures and looked at it again, carefully. It was a shot of the body next to a pier post, but in the corner of the picture was a boat. There was something on the side of it. What is it? he wondered. He looked closely, but couldn't tell what it was. He peered out the window and saw a drugstore across the street. Perfect, he thought. They'll have it. After grabbing his cell phone, Sonny locked the motel room door behind him and marched across the street like he was on a mission.

Sonny returned to his room, sat back down at the table, reached into the plastic bag, and removed its contents: a magnifying glass. He carefully ran it over the picture and whistled when he saw the results. He picked up Detective Petrosky's card and dialed his cell phone.

"Joe Petrosky," the answer came through Sonny's phone.

"Joe, it's Madison. Sorry to bother you, but I have a couple of questions."

"Fire away," said Joe.

"Do you know if the boaters were interviewed? I mean, really interviewed?"

"I don't think so. Nothing in the report about it. If they were just a couple of innocent boaters, there would be no reason to—"

"Maybe they weren't so innocent," Sonny cut in.

"What do you mean?" Petrosky asked.

"I want to show you something. You got some time in the morning?"

"Where are you?"

"The Home Town Inn. A couple of miles from—"

"I know where it is," the detective said. "There's a KCF across the street. I'll be there in a half hour." He hung up before Sonny could respond. Back to KFC, he thought. At least I have time to take a quick shower. The humidity here is like a steam room.

Detective Petrosky was sitting in a corner, sipping a coke, and eating some chicken wings as Sonny walked in. "Want some wings?" The detective held up the box.

Sonny shook his head. "Once today is enough."

Petrosky looked at the manila envelope in Sonny's hand. "Whatcha got?"

Madison reached into the envelope, pulled out the picture, handed it to Petrosky, and laid the magnifying glass on the table.

Petrosky looked at the picture, took a sip of his drink, wiped his fingers on a napkin, and asked, "Would you like to tell me what I'm looking for?"

Sonny answered, "Take a gander at the boat at the edge of the picture." He picked up the magnifying glass and handed it to the detective. "You'll need this." He waited a moment as Petrosky examined the picture. "Well, do you see it?"

"See what? What am I supposed to see?"

"Look at the boat. Look at the edge of the boat. What do you see?"

Detective Petrosky studied the picture closely and looked up to Sonny. "It looks like a stain of some sort. Might be blood. So?"

"So?" Sonny responded. "So? Don't you think that's important?"

"It could be red paint, too."

"That's not paint!" Sonny was beginning to wonder how this guy ever made detective. "The mark is consistent with a body being dragged over it. What do you know about the boaters?"

"Sergeant Madison, I wasn't even a detective then. I have no idea. What does the report say?"

"All it lists are their names, phone numbers, and an address. The phone numbers aren't any good, and I'm willing to bet they don't live at that address anymore."

"Uhh, they never did," Petrosky said as he looked at the file. "I recognize the address. It's a video store; well, I mean, it was."

"Was?"

"They tore it down about three years ago. It's a Wendy's now."

"You gotta be shitting me!" Sonny exclaimed. "Didn't anyone check them out? Are there any pictures of them? What kind of police work is this, anyway?"

"I don't know the answers, Sergeant, but my father was an excellent detective. If he didn't check it out, then he didn't think it was important. All they did was bump into the body."

His defensive manner did not intimidate Sonny, who leaned toward the detective and said, "But it would be important if they killed him and dumped him into the water, wouldn't it!" He took the picture and pointed to the stain on the boat.

Petrosky's eyes widened. "What?"

Sonny pointed to the report. "Look, Joe, it says the body had only been in the water for a short time. What if the two boaters dumped the body at the end of the pier and were heading back to tie up but saw the two bicycle cops close by? What if they thought they would get caught so they called out to the cops, thinking it was a good way to cover their tracks and make it look like they innocently found the body?"

Petrosky put both of his elbows on the table, folded his hands, and rested his chin on them. He took a breath, closed his eyes, and thought for a moment before he spoke. "First thing in the morning, I'll see if I can track down Officer Jesky. I'll call you as soon as I know."

Sonny thanked him and went back to his motel room where he plugged in his laptop and began searching. A little over four hours later, he closed the laptop. He decided to turn in. He had found nothing. He would make one call before he called it a night. He picked up his cell phone and called Nick Greer.

* * *

Lieutenant Nick Greer pulled his rental car into the Beaver Valley Motel. He went into the office, registered, and went to his room. He had phoned the Beaver County Sheriff's Department and had arranged a meeting for tomorrow morning. It was two-thirty in Arizona, and three hours later here in the east, so it was too late to meet today. Nick was hungry. He had skipped breakfast, and the bag of peanuts he had on the plane didn't offer much in the way of nutrition. The motel manager had suggested a restaurant a couple of miles down the road.

Nick returned to his motel room, unpacked, showered, and sat on the end of the bed. His eyes caught his Android lying on the bed where he had dropped it. He reached for it and dialed Sue Kim's number. It rang several times and went to voice mail. She's still ignoring me, he thought. I'll bet she'll read a text. He wrote: *Sue, I'm stupid. I shouldn't have let it happen. Never again, I promise. I'm in PA on assignment. Should be back in a couple days. Let's talk. I do love you.* He hit send.

He finished dressing, turned on the television, scanned the channels, but found nothing that interested him. Remembering a tavern he had seen while on his way to the restaurant, he decided to go sample a few of the local beers. He returned a couple hours later, put his cell phone on the nightstand, grabbed the remote and turned on the television. He picked up the file and read it once again. He soon nodded off to sleep and didn't hear the text come in.

It was shortly after ten p.m. mountain time when Nick's cell phone rang and woke him. He looked at the screen, it read: Sonny. Nick sat up in the bed. "What's up in Baltimore?" The television was still on, so he picked up the remote and shut it off.

"I wonder how these cops function," Sonny said.

"Huh?" Nick was puzzled.

"I'll explain later. There may be two perps."

"Two? How—"

Sonny cut in, "I'm not sure yet, just a hunch."

Nick listened as his partner brought him up to date on his visit to Baltimore. After he was finished, they both hung up. Nick plugged his phone into its charger and went back to sleep.

CHAPTER 21

The Dam

The new morning sun blasted its rays directly into Nick Greer's face. He had fallen back to sleep last night, without completely closing the motel room curtain, and the light announcing the new day found its way through. He reached to the nightstand and looked at his watch: 2:57. He mentally added three hours: six a.m. He sat on the edge of the bed, stretched his long arms, and yawned. Though he slept through the night, his dreams had been haunted by the look on Sue Kim's face and the tears in her eyes when he'd arrived home from his visit to Prescott last Sunday.

He showered and turned on the television. The news was saturated with coverage of a tornado in Oklahoma. A school had been leveled, and several small children were killed. He wondered how God would allow innocent children to die in such a way. He was thankful for his daughters. He thought about calling them, just to tell them he loved them. But he was reminded it was still early in Prescott; they would all be sleeping. I'll call later, he thought. He disconnected his cell phone from its charger. It was then he saw the text. It was Sue Kim's answer to his text from the night before. It said: *How could you?* At least she answered, he thought.

He was hungry and remembered the restaurant he had visited yesterday. A good breakfast would be welcome before he set out on today's mission. Though by now the file was mostly committed to his memory, he read it over once more as he consumed the ham, eggs, and home-fried potatoes. When he was finished, he got into his rental car and set its GPS to his destination: the Beaver County Courthouse. The sheriff's office was located inside.

Deputy Sheriff Jason Marshall was waiting for him when he arrived. He greeted Nick with a handshake. "I'm Deputy Sheriff Marshall. Welcome to Beaver, Pennsylvania."

Nick grinned. "Thank you. I'm Lieutenant Nick Greer from Phoenix, Arizona. Please accept my apology if I appear amused, but the name and title, well."

"Yeah, I know. I get it all the time. Sheriff Marshall, Marshall Sheriff. One of my colleagues calls me Corporal Captain. I'm used to it. I figure it's a good thing I'm not a U.S. Marshal; I'd be Marshal Marshall." He grinned as he motioned for his guest to have a seat. "Lieutenant, I understand there are some similarities in a couple of your cases and one of our cold ones, a James R. Widmann."

Nick liked the fact that the deputy got right to the point. "Yes, we have three victims who were stabbed in the chest. And, like your guy, had the ring finger severed, and we believe were dumped in water post-mortem."

"You believe? You're not sure?"

"Oh, I'm sure. Have you ever been out west?" Nick asked.

"I've been to Vegas a couple of times."

"The desert is full of natural dry washes where the water channels when there is a large rainstorm. It happens mostly during the late summer when we get the monsoons. One of the bodies was found in a dry wash. I believe it was dumped during a storm and was washed about a half-mile. That would make it consistent with the other three. One of them was found in a canal and the other one in a lake."

"You got lakes there? In the desert?"

"Yeah, we got streetlights, too. Put 'em in last year. The horses don't like 'em at night, though."

Marshall laughed. "Okay, it's just that Phoenix is in the des . . . Never mind. I understand one of the victims was a police officer."

"Yes, sir. He was not only a police officer. He had been my captain and a close friend. Pete had recently retired from the force."

"Your deputy chief, uhhh." He opened a file on his desk. "Mannion says you're the best there is. Is that true?"

Nick was caught off guard by the question. "Uhhh, I don't know about that. I can hold my own, I guess."

The deputy sat up straight and looked his guest in the eyes. "Do you think just because you come from a big city that makes you smarter than us small town cops? Do you think you're better than us?"

Nick didn't know what to say. His eyes widened as he looked at the deputy. "Deputy, I have no feelings of superiority or inferiority. I'm sure you are good at what you do, or you wouldn't be doing it. All I want to do is find out who killed my friend before the feds get involved and screw it up. It is not my intention to offend you or your office."

The deputy leaned back in his chair, put his hands behind his head and locked his fingers. A huge grin came upon his face. "Lieutenant, I'm just messin' with ya, just tuggin' on your pant leg. I'm glad to have you here. This case has been bugging me ever since I first saw the body. I want it solved, too. If you can help, I'm all for it." He slid the file across the desk. "Here's everything we have on it. Perhaps a fresh set of eyes can find something we didn't."

Nick was not happy that he had been duped by the deputy, but he knew the prudent thing to do was to let it go. He took the file, opened it, and read through it thoroughly. He looked at the deputy and asked, "It says here the responding department was, uh, Patterson Township, but didn't you say you saw the body?"

"Brady's Run Park is one of the main recreational spots in the county," Marshall answered. "It covers a little over two thousand acres of forest, streams, and a lake. It is situated partly in Brighton Township and partly in Patterson Township. We were called so there would be no jurisdictional problems, so they said. But I think the responding cop had no idea what to do."

Nick nodded. "That makes sense. Is there anything you can tell me that might not be in the report? Even a gut feeling would be welcome."

"Not a clue. I hoped something from your vics would help."

Nick tossed the file he had brought along onto the desk. "Here, knock yourself out. Maybe something will click."

Deputy Marshall read the file carefully, then closed it, shrugged, and said, "I got nothing."

"What do you make of the finger?" Nick asked.

"The whole damned thing was gone," the deputy responded. "Sliced off clean, so that ruled out anything that lived in the lake. There's nothing in that water that could have done that. Some sort of instrument was used. It's all in the coroner's report."

"You ruled out robbery, I take it?" Nick questioned.

"At first I thought it was a robbery, but his wallet was still in his pants, and there were eighty water-soaked dollars in it. His watch was on his wrist, too, and a gold cross around his neck. It wasn't a robbery, no, sir. I figured it was a jealous husband or boyfriend."

"Why do you say that?" Nick asked.

"Well, this guy was married, but during my investigation, I found out he had wandering eyes. He lived in Rochester. That's the next town over. He owned a small construction company. We checked as best we could, any contacts he may have had, especially of the female persuasion. But no one would admit being with him, of course. You should have heard his wife scream at me when I asked her if he might have been seeing another woman. I thought for a minute I was going to have to restrain her."

"It sounds like she had quite a temper. Did you consider her? She wouldn't be the first to bury a sharp object into the chest of a cheating husband."

Marshall shook his head. "She's clean. She wasn't even in town. The medical examiner said the body had been bobbing around the lake for about a week. It finally surfaced near the dam. A guy saw something hanging over the dam that looked like a body and called it in. She was in Philly the whole time, visiting family. The family confirmed that she was there for two weeks. We checked the airlines. She flew out from Pittsburgh a week before he was killed, and didn't return until two weeks later. She didn't even know he was dead until she got back. He didn't come home that night, so she called the Rochester police. They called me, and we went to her house. She ID'd the body the next day. I felt sorry for the little thing."

"Did she have any contact with him while she was gone?"

"She said she didn't speak with him the whole time she was gone," the deputy answered.

"Didn't you think it odd she would be gone for two weeks and not at least phone her husband?"

"A little, but sometimes the old lady and I don't talk to each other for days, and we're in the same house." He grinned. "It depends on how pissed she gets at me."

Nick nodded and thought about Sue Kim. "Yeah, I know." His mind returned to the task at hand. "I assume you checked his associates and his employees. What about business contacts? Sometimes contractors can piss off clients, and sometimes they get involved with the wrong people."

"He owned a small construction company. He worked it mostly himself. He did small remodels, windows, bathrooms, roofs and the sort. He had a good reputation as far as I was able to find. It looks as though he was quite a charmer, though. Folks said he was good looking, and he liked the ladies. But no one would say who any of the ladies were. That's why I still think it was a jealous husband or a boyfriend, or perhaps even a girlfriend. Maybe that's why the ring finger was cut off. Maybe he was banging some chick, and she found out he was married."

"What about life insurance?" Nick asked.

"None."

"Children?"

"None. They were newlyweds. They'd only been married a little over a year," the deputy stated. "Her maiden name was Ayers."

Nick nodded and cupped his chin with his hand. "Any chance I could see where the body was found?"

"Sure. We can jump into the cruiser, and I'll give you a tour of the countryside."

While they were in the car, Nick asked, "Do you know the fable about why the wedding ring is placed on that particular finger?"

"Of course. Doesn't everybody? The ancient Romans thought the vein in that finger ran straight to the heart. That's why they called it vena amoris. Latin for the vein of love, the vein to the heart."

Nick shook his head. How come everybody knows that but me? he wondered.

Nick got out of the cruiser and followed his host to the shore of the lake. He took a deep breath and let the clean air fill his lungs. As he exhaled, he thought, I could handle it here. This is a nice place. The statuesque, green trees, the clear water. I'll bet the fishing is great. He remembered looking out of the window as his plane was descending into the Pittsburgh International Airport, and seeing the spot where the Allegheny and Monongahela rivers meet to form the Ohio. How cool, he thought.

Deputy Marshall pointed to a dam. "The body was there. It surfaced and floated toward the dam, but it was too heavy to go over, so it just hung there."

The water gently lapped along the shore as Nick stood at the edge of the peaceful, recreational lake and looked across to the other side and back to the dam. "Do you know where the body was dumped?"

The deputy shook his head. "It could have been anywhere. Probably upstream a ways where it wouldn't be noticed.

"Okay," Nick said. "I guess that's all here."

Their ride back to the courthouse was silent for a while as Nick again read over the sheriff's report. Finally he spoke, "It says he was stabbed in the heart, the upper aortic arch."

"Yeah, dead center. Used an ice pick, I think."

"How is the reception here?" Nick asked, as he retrieved his cell phone from his belt.

"It's spotty. Lots of hills and valleys around here."

Nick searched his phone for his contacts and dialed the Maricopa County Medical Examiner.

"Medical Examiner's office," came a voice from the other end.

"This is Lieutenant Greer. Can you run me through to Doctor Konesky, please. It's important, and I'm calling from Pennsylvania."

"Yes, Lieutenant, right away."

He heard a couple of clicks and then a familiar voice: "Maricopa County Morgue."

"Uhhh, hello, . . . it's me, Nick."

"What do you want? Why are you calling me here? Can't you tell I want you to leave me alone?"

"I didn't know you would answer. I thought you'd be upstairs. I called to talk with Jack." He heard the phone drop and he waited.

"Doctor Konesky."

"Jack, it's Nick."

"I thought you were back east somewhere."

"I am. I'm in Pennsylvania. I need to know something about our latest victim."

"Fire away!"

"The stab wound. What can you tell me about it?" Nick asked.

"It went directly into the aorta."

"Uhh, would that be the upper aortic arch?"

"Uhhh, yes, 'Doctor' Greer. Why do you ask?"

"It seems all of our vics were poked in the same exact spot, including the guy here."

"They weren't poked, at least not this one, or Pete."

"Talk to me," Nick said.

"First of all, both of these victims had a clean, but fatal wound. It looks like the killer held the weapon in the exact spot he wanted and shoved it into their chests. The weapon was pushed in all the way to the handle, and then pulled straight out. I think it was held in until the perp was sure they were dead, and then he pulled it out."

"How much power would it take to do that? How strong would he have to be?"

"Oh, I don't know. Average, or above, I guess for a male, anyway. You'd have to go through cartilage, and would have to be strong enough, or know how to do it. It could have been someone with some sort of medical knowledge. Like I said, both of the wounds were precise."

"How much?" Nick questioned.

"How much what? Knowledge?"

"No, power. How strong would a person need to be to bury an ice pick through the sternum in that manner and hit the same exact spot every time?"

"Depends on how sharp the weapon was. I guess you or I could do it with no problem, but I don't know about the little one here." He looked at Sue Kim.

"I could if it was him!" she said. It was then Nick realized they were on speaker. "I could turn it a few times, too," Sue Kim added.

Konesky reached down to the phone and shut off the speaker.

"Thanks, Jack," Nick said. "That helps. By the way, how is she doing?"

The medical examiner saw the look on Sue Kim's face and whispered, "Uhhh, let's just say you're not her favorite person right now." He moved out of her earshot and added, "She acts like she caught you fucking your ex-wife or something."

"She told you?" Nick was shocked.

"Uhh, no! I was just kidding. I didn't . . . I mean, I didn't know what happened. Honest!"

"What is she doing there, anyway? I thought she was back upstairs," Nick questioned.

"The feds want a copy of our reports on both vics. She came down to see if it was all right."

"Do me a favor," Nick answered. "Stall them until I get back. Just a day or two. I'm not quite done here yet."

"I'll see what I can do." The phone disconnected.

Nick looked at the deputy. "What do you make of it being dead center?"

"Huh?"

"The wound. What do you think about it being a perfect bull's eye?"

"I never gave it any thought. A lucky shot, I guess."

"They all were," Nick stated.

"What all were what?"

"Lucky shots. Dead center. Bull's eye. Balls-on-perfect. All of the vics were stabbed in exactly the same place."

The deputy looked over at his passenger. "That's odd. What do you make of it?"

"Someone knew what they were doing. The perp, at least one of them, must have had a proficient knowledge of anatomy."

"Uhhh, at least one? What are you saying? Are you thinking there may have been more than one perp?"

"I'm starting to wonder." Nick put his cell phone back into its case. He looked out the window as their cruiser pulled into the Beaver County Courthouse parking lot. "Did you find any possible suspects, any at all?" he asked the deputy.

"Nada. All dead ends." As he was about to shut off the engine, Deputy Marshall's cell phone rang. "Jason Marshall . . . uh-huh . . . okay. I'm right outside."

He looked at Nick. "You said something earlier about the feds screwing it up?"

"Yeah, they want to work it. I'm trying to keep a step or two ahead of them."

"Yeah, well, you had better pick up the pace. They're on their way here. They're coming up from Pittsburgh. They wanna see me. I figure they're about fifteen minutes out, maybe less."

"F-u-u-u-ck!" Nick moaned.

"Hey, I can't tell them anything I haven't told you. And if it's not much help to you, it sure as hell won't be to them, either."

"I just don't like them getting in the way, that's all," Nick said.

"Yeah, I know. The last time they were here, I almost got suspended. They pissed me off so much I told one of them to go fuck off!"

The corners of Nick's mouth turned upward in a smile. "It's a good thing Sonny isn't here."

"Sonny? Who's Sonny?"

Nick grinned. "My partner. You two would get along fine."

"You wanna sit in on this?" Marshall asked.

"Oh, you bet!" Nick nodded.

"Okay, good, but let's go across the street and get a cup of coffee and a sandwich first," the deputy suggested.

"Uh, what if they come while we're gone? Aren't they on their way?" Nick asked.

"Yeah, I figure they'll be here pretty soon. They can wait! I'm hungry."

Wait, they did. Two men in blue suits were sitting in Deputy Marshall's office when he and Nick Greer arrived. They had taken their time with lunch and talked about each other's families, etc. Nick liked this guy. He kind of reminded him of Sonny, in a way. Though this guy was huge compared to Sonny, their personalities were the same. Deputy Marshall stood just over six feet. His massive shoulders and long arms looked like he could reach out and squeeze a bus like an accordion. His bushy, red mustache was just beginning to curl at the ends. He kind of reminded Nick of Yosemite Sam, and he had the voice to go with it.

They had spent almost an hour in the restaurant before they finally returned to the sheriff's office.

"Well, you must be the gentlemen from the government," the deputy said, as he walked into his office and saw the two men in blue suits sitting in front of his desk. "How was the drive? I hope you haven't been waiting too long."

"One of the men stood up, extended his hand to the deputy, and said, "I'm Special Agent Anthony, and this is Special Agent Biggerstaff."

The deputy shook both of his guests' hands and looked at Nick. "This is Lieutenant Greer. He's here visiting us from the Phoenix Arizona Police Department." The two agents gave each other puzzled looks and shook hands with him.

"Deputy," Biggerstaff began, "please explain to me why we have been waiting here for almost an hour. I understand you were right here when you were told we were only a few minutes away."

"I'm sorry, sir, but I was out in the cruiser with the lieutenant here when the call came in. Isn't that right, Lieutenant? Weren't we out in the cruiser?"

Nick looked at the two agents, nodded, and said, "Yep, we were in the cruiser."

"I don't know how you got the idea I was here," Marshall said.

"Your office called you several times. Why didn't you answer?" one of the agents asked.

"I've been having trouble with the two-way on my rig. Sometimes it works and sometimes not. I think there might be a short in it. I mean to take it in as soon as I get a chance. I figure as long as I have my cell phone, it's okay."

The special agent was getting angrier and leaned forward as he spoke, "They called your cell phone. I suppose you're going to tell me it has a short, too?"

"Oh, no, sir. It works fine," the deputy stated, as he reached for his cell phone and pulled it from his belt. He held it out in front of himself. "Aw, shit! It looks like I forgot to turn it on. Damn! Sorry about that. Anyway, what can we do for our friends from the Federal Bureau of In–ves–tee–gay–tion?"

It was all Nick could do to keep from laughing out loud. He wished Sonny was here. He would've finally met his match.

"You know why we're here, I assume," Biggerstaff said. "We show that you were the investigating officer on a case that has recently come under our jurisdiction: the murder of a James Robert Widmann. Is that correct?"

"Oh, yeah. That was me all right," Marshall stated. "He was found decorating the dam at one of our lakes. We just came back from there, didn't we, Lieutenant Greer?" Nick nodded.

"By the way, how does it come under your jurisdiction, all of a sudden?"

Ignoring the deputy's question, Special Agent Anthony looked at Nick. "Lieutenant Greer, may I ask why you are here?"

"I think you know quite well why I'm here," Nick responded. "You know there are three cases in Phoenix. You know my partner and I are investigating them. And you know that I and my partner spoke with one of your agents in Phoenix about the case. Why would you even ask? Perhaps I should ask why you are here?"

"Correct me if I'm wrong, Lieutenant, but were you not told that this case is under federal jurisdiction? So I ask again, why are you here?"

"Agent, let me put it this way." Nick was still standing, but he bent down and looked the agent in the eyes as he stated, "One of the victims was a retired Phoenix police officer. He was my captain and my friend. I don't give a rat's ass about your jurisdiction. I will work this case until someone is in jail for the crimes. Neither you nor anyone else will prevent that. And furthermore, I will be here, or I will go to Baltimore, or to bum-fuck China if I have to. Now, are we clear on that?"

Agent Biggerstaff began to rise from his seat, but his partner held up his hand with the palm out toward him. "Please, take it easy, Lieutenant. I understand your concern for your friend. Let's just try not to get in each other's way, that's all."

Agent Anthony was not happy when he saw the amusement in Deputy Marshall's face. "Do you have the file we requested?"

Marshall reached for the phone, punched in a couple of numbers, and said, "Betty, did you copy that file for these gentlemen?"

"It's on your desk. In your top bin where you asked me to put it," she answered.

He put down the phone and looked at the file sitting on top of his top bin. "Oh, yeah, here it is." He retrieved the file and slid it across his desk to Agent Biggerstaff who took it, opened it, and began reading. They all sat silent for about two minutes as he turned the pages.

"Deputy," Biggerstaff said, "is there anything you can remember that might not be in the report. Is there anything you can add?"

Marshall shook his head. "Nope, it's been eight years. I've been over it all with the lieutenant here. There's nothing I can remember that ain't in the file."

"Are you sure?" the agent probed.

The deputy leaned forward, put his elbows on his desk, folded his hands, and rested his chin on them as he stared into the agent's eyes. "I'll have you know that Lieutenant Greer and I have been through this entire file together. We just got back from the scene where the body was found. He asked me every question imaginable. Everything I have is right there." He pointed to the file. "It's all yours. Do with it as you will."

"Well, with all due respect, Deputy, with your apparent disdain for our presence here, I just wondered if you were holding anything back, that's all."

Deputy Marshall stood up. The anger inside him was like a bomb ready to explode from his massive frame. Nick was surprised to see how calmly he began: "Agent Biggerstaff, this case is not about who gets the collar. It's about one of my citizens getting murdered and the murder of a cop." His voice began rising. "If you ever say anything again to even insinuate that I'm trying to torpedo this case, or any other, I'll personally take you out to the parking lot and kick your ass!" He was now yelling. "Now take the file and get out of my office!"

The two agents simultaneously got out of their seats and headed for the door. Just as they were about to leave, Marshall yelled, "Hey, Biggerstaff!"

The agent turned around and looked at the deputy. Marshall was holding a manila folder in his left hand, and his right hand was hiding behind it. "Guess how many fingers I'm holding up!"

After they left, the deputy sat down, leaned back in his chair, and smiled.

Nick asked, "You aren't worried they'll call your boss?"

"Let 'em. The sheriff is my uncle. He hates them more than I do. If he were here"—he pointed to the folder he had covered his hand with—"he wouldn't have used this thing. He would have held up one finger on both hands and told Agent Teeny Weeny to pick a side!"

Nick laughed, and then came back to the subject at hand. "Where's the wife? I want to talk with her."

"Gone. She moved away a couple of months later. She moved back to Philly, I guess. Haven't heard from her."

"You've had no contact from her since? She must have called, or emailed about the status of the case. She must have at least inquired about her husband's killer," Nick stated.

The deputy looked at the file, then typed something into the computer. "Uhhh, not that I know of. There's nothing on record." He looked at his visitor. "Not even a phone call that I can find."

"Don't you think that's a little strange?" the detective asked.

"Uhhh, I do now."

"Do you have an address in Philly?"

"It's in the file, I believe," Marshall answered.

"Yeah, I see it," Nick said. "How long does it take to get to Philly from here?"

"Oh, about eight hours by the turnpike," Marshall answered.

"How about from Baltimore?"

The deputy typed MapQuest into his computer, entered Baltimore MD as the starting point and Philadelphia PA as the destination. He waited a moment and said, "Uhhh, it says here about two and a half hours."

Nick pulled his cell phone from his belt and dialed. "Chief Mannion's office," was the answer on the other end.

"Hi, Tricia. Is the chief available? It's Lieutenant Greer."

"He's been waiting to hear from one of you. I'll put you through."

"Well, hello, Lieutenant. How are things going in Pennsylvania?"

"Not as well as I would like, but I need permission to spend some more money."

"Uhhh, okay, what's going on?"

"Either I, or Sonny, need to go to Philly. There's something that needs to be checked out there." He explained his reasoning.

"Who's closest?" the chief asked.

"It's an eight-hour drive for me, two-and-a-half for Sonny. I haven't checked the airlines."

'Okay, have Madison change his return ticket to leave from Philly instead of Baltimore. He can drive there when he is finished in Baltimore. Will that work?"

"Perfect. I'll call him right away."

"Do you have anything, anything at all?"

"Not much, but we'll see how Sonny makes out. Oh, by the way, a couple of feds were here today. I guess Phoenix has turned up the fire."

"I'm not surprised. I'll bet Butch wasn't happy."

"Butch? Who's Butch?" Nick asked.

"Sheriff William 'Butch' Hensen."

"Do you know him?" The confusion in Nick's voice was obvious.

"We went to school together," Mannion said. "I'm from that neck of the woods. We used to go swimming right there where their body was found. Butch and Sonny both have one thing in common. They both hate the feds!"

"I guess it runs in the family," Nick commented.

"Huh?" The chief wondered what his detective meant.

"I'll explain it when I get back."

"And when should that be?"

"Maybe tomorrow, maybe Friday. I want to snoop around a little. I should be back by the weekend, anyway."

"Bring me something."

"I'll try." He disconnected the call.

Nick put his phone back on his belt and turned his attention back to the deputy. "What about the construction company? Whatever happened to it?"

"I don't know. Closed up, I guess," the deputy responded. "Hold on, let me check something."

Nick's ears listened to the click-clack of the keyboard as the deputy typed, then waited a moment as he studied the screen in front of him. "Widmann Construction is no longer in business. It says here, he didn't file his annual corporate minutes, and his certification was pulled. It makes sense, him being dead and all." He smiled.

"Anything about a forwarding address? The wife may have filed something."

"Nope. Nothing! According to this, she wasn't on the corporation. He's the only one listed."

Nick Greer looked at his watch. It read: 11:37, Arizona time. He stood up, shook hands with the deputy, and said, "Thank you for all your help, Deputy Marshall. I appreciate you taking the time to show me around."

"Any time, Lieutenant. I hope you find the perp, and something tells me you will. Keep me informed, okay?"

"Will do, sir." Nick left the sheriff's office, got back into his rental car and drove to his motel. He unlocked the room, shut the door behind him, and sat on the edge of the bed. Pulling his Android from his belt, he hit speed dial four. He hoped Sonny was where there was good reception.

CHAPTER 22

The Detour

There was a Denny's restaurant a block down from his motel. Sonny figured it was as good a place as any to start the day. After he finished breakfast, he drove to the address where the file said the victim had lived. He hoped someone would remember him or his widow. It was a row house in Reisterstown. No one remembered them, so he returned to the Baltimore Police Department where he again met with Detective Petrosky.

"I found Officer Jesky," the detective told Sonny. "He's running his father's fishing business out of Sarasota, tourist stuff. He likes it there."

Sonny got to the point. "What about the two boaters? Does he remember either of them?"

"He said he remembers they were a young couple. She was blonde and small, and her husband had light brown hair and was pretty well built. He said he looked like he worked out."

"Did he remember anything that might not be in the report? Anything at all?" Sonny questioned.

"Nothing. He said they looked more scared than anything. It isn't everyday someone finds a body, ya know."

"I'm not so sure they found it."

"What?" Petrosky said.

"Never mind," Sonny said. "Does he remember what they looked like? He was a cop, maybe he could describe them to a sketch artist."

"It's been six years. I doubt it. But we can call him."

"I'd like to speak with him, if you don't mind," Sonny said.

Petrosky nodded and picked up the phone. He looked at a number he had written on a piece of paper and dialed. "May I speak to Mike Jesky, please. It's Detective Petrosky from the Baltimore PD again." He pushed the speaker button, and the voice came through for Sonny to hear.

"He's out launching one of the boats. Can I have him call you?"

"How long do you think he'll be? It's important."

"Hold on. I'll call his cell." She put the phone on hold. A few moments later she came back on the line. "He said, if you want to hold on a couple of minutes, he'll be back in."

"Thank you," Petrosky said. He leaned back in his chair.

Sonny looked at his host. Joe Petrosky was small for a cop. He was about five feet seven and thin. Sonny remembered the first time he saw him, how the nine-millimeter on his side looked like a cannon hanging there.

"Hey, Joe, did you forget something?" the voice came through the speaker.

"Mike, I have Sergeant Madison from the Phoenix PD here with me. He has a couple of questions for you, if you don't mind."

"Sure, go ahead. Hello, Sergeant."

"It's Sonny. I'm sorry to take you away from your work, but I need to ask you something about the case the detective was talking to you about earlier. How well do you remember the boaters? Can you picture their faces?"

"She was a nice-looking girl, long blonde hair. He had light brown hair, but I told all that to Detective Petrosky."

"How about any unusual mannerisms? Can you remember anything that can help us?"

"I didn't pay that much attention to them. We were involved in pulling the body out of the drink. I didn't interview them; my partner did, but he's gone now."

"Yes, I'm sorry. Detective Petrosky told me what happened to him."

"Yeah, he was a good guy. When he got it, I decided to get out. I have kids, and I didn't want them to grow up without a father."

"Tell me, could you describe either one of them well enough for a sketch artist?" Sonny asked.

"Oh, wow. It's been a long time, you know. I doubt it, but I'll give it a shot if you want."

"Okay, you know the drill. I'll have my super give your department a call. Sarasota, right?"

"That be it."

"Is there anyone we should speak to? Does anyone know you there?"

"Nope. I came here as a civilian and I stay here as a civilian."

"Thank you, sir. I appreciate your time and your help. And good fishin'."

"If you're ever down this way, drop by. I'll give you a discount." The dial tone told both cops that the call had been disconnected.

Sonny thanked Detective Petrosky for his help and left the building. As he was about to get into his rental car, his cell phone rang. It was Nick. "Sonny," he answered.

"Hey, buddy, what do you think of the City of Brotherly Love?"

"Uhhh, that's Philadelphia. It's in another state. Don't you remember your history, Mister Master's Degree?"

"Oh, I remember it well. I'm glad you do, too, 'cause that's where you're heading."

"Huh? What are you talking about?"

"Are you close to done there?"

"Yeah, I'm more than close. I'm gonna head back."

"I need you to make a small detour. I need you to go to Philly."

"Uhhh, why? What would interest me in Philly besides a cheese steak?"

"An address," Nick answered. "I spoke to the chief. He's okayed a little side trip for you."

"Why me?"

"You're closer, and I'm not quite finished here yet. You're to drive to Philly. I need you to check out an address and talk with the family. I'll text you the address. You can turn in the rental car and fly home from there, okay?"

"I guess so. I can use the miles when I go fishing."

"Fishing?"

"I'll explain later," Sonny said. "Why am I going to Philly? What's going on?"

Nick filled his partner in on his visit to Pennsylvania and the need to check out where Catherine Ayers Widmann was staying when her husband was killed. Sonny knew to talk with the relatives and friends and extract all the information he could. He hoped he could get it all done and be home for the weekend.

"How are things with you and Sue Kim? Any better?"

"Uhh, she answered when I called the ME's office."

"I take it she wasn't thrilled it was you."

"Well, she didn't hang up on me when I asked for Jack."

"What did you call him for? Did you find something?"

"I don't know. We'll talk about it when you get back. By the way, see if you can find out if Catherine Widmann had any medical training."

"Why?"

"I'm not sure. Just see what you can find."

* * *

The next morning, Detective Lieutenant Nick Greer got up, showered, and went to the restaurant for breakfast. Last night he had made airline reservations to fly back to Phoenix. The next direct flight he could get left at six-thirty tonight. He figured he had the day to snoop around and maybe find something that could help the case. Even though it had been eight years, Nick went to the apartment the couple had lived in. He didn't figure he would find any help there, and he was right. He checked out Widmann's place of business. It was a small warehouse with offices on the top floor. One of the tenants remembered him. He told Nick that Widmann was a nice guy and never caused anyone there any trouble.

Nick went back to his motel room. He studied the Beaver County file again, and compared it to the Phoenix file. Nothing stood out. He looked at his watch. It was time to check out and head for Pittsburgh International Airport.

Nick was about to board the aircraft when his cell phone rang. He pulled it from his belt. It read: Sonny. "Hey, partner, what did you find?"

"Why did you send me to a church?"

"Huh?" Nick didn't understand.

"The address you sent me to is a church. Saint Luke's Catholic Church. No one there ever heard of your lady. I'm sitting in front of the church now."

He heard the call to board the plane. "Sonny, I gotta get on the plane. We'll talk when you get back, I guess."

"I'm catching the first plane out of here."

"Okay, I'll see you when you get back." Nick shut off his phone.

Sonny immediately dialed the airline. He got lucky and booked a seat on a flight leaving in a couple of hours. He called April and told her his flight number and when to pick him up at Phoenix Sky Harbor Airport.

CHAPTER 23

The Pool

It was eight-twenty a.m. when April Madison answered the telephone. "Hello. Madisons."

"Good morning, April. Where's the love of your life? I need to talk with him."

"Assuming you're talking about Sonny," she said, giggling, "he's still asleep. His plane was two hours late, and he has a case of jet lag. Can I have him call you, Nick?"

"Uhmm, it's important," Nick answered.

"I'm here," Sonny's groggy voice came through the extension. He yawned as he said, "What the hell do you want? If it's Armageddon, don't bother me. I'll meet you in the afterlife, somewhere in hell I suppose."

Nick heard the phone click as April hung up her end. "You didn't answer your cell."

"That's because I shut it off. I do that when I don't want to be disturbed. It's in the charger—not being disturbed—unlike me!"

Nick said, "Sorry, buddy, but it's time to get back to work. We got another one."

All of a sudden the sleepiness left him as he sat straight up in the bed. "Another body? Where?"

"Yeah, off of Thirty-Fifth Avenue and Thunderbird. I'm heading there now. It looks like the wife found him floating in the backyard pool. I just got the call."

"Text me the address. I'll grab a shower and meet you there. You better have coffee." Sonny hung up the phone.

* * *

When Detective Sonny Madison arrived, the coroner's wagon was already backed into the driveway of the residence. A Phoenix crime unit van, a fire department rescue truck, and three police cars were parked in the street, as was Nick Greer's Taurus. Sonny's eyes saw the side gate was open, so he went through it into the backyard. Nick was talking with one of the uniformed officers. He handed Sonny a Styrofoam cup of coffee and said, "Ask and you shall receive."

Sonny opened the coffee and took a sip. "What do we have?"

Nick pointed to the covered body lying on the cool decking next to the pool. "I just got here, but it looks like the wife came home and found him in the pool. It looks like the same MO as the others. Chest wound, finger gone."

"Have you talked with her yet?" Sonny asked.

"I'm getting ready to."

Sonny looked over at the body and saw two CSIs bent over it. "You talked with them? What did they say?"

"Uhhmm, one of them will talk with me. But the other one, well, I think she'd probably rather talk with you."

Sonny shook his head and walked over to the body. Sue Kim looked up and saw him approaching. "Hello, Sergeant Sonny."

"What do we have?" he asked.

Sue Kim lifted the sheet covering the victim and showed him the severed left ring finger, then pointed to the chest. "He's been dead for about twelve hours, I'd say. He's in full rigor."

"You know what to look for when you get back. This one's fresh enough," said the detective.

"Yep. First thing when we get the body back."

"Good." Sonny turned to leave, stopped, turned back to her, and squatted down beside her. "He's hurting, you know."

"Your point?" She kept looking at the body.

"I just thought you should know, that's all."

She looked at Sonny. "And you think I'm not?"

He put his hand on her shoulder. "Honey, I know you're hurting. You both are. That's why you two need to talk."

She turned her head away in silence. Sonny got up and walked over to his partner.

"How is she?" Nick asked.

"Uhhh, she didn't say to tell you to drop dead or anything like that."

"Hmmm!" Nick scratched his head. I guess that's good, he thought.

His thoughts were interrupted as a uniformed officer came up to them. "Excuse me, Detectives, but the wife is in the living room. Did you want to talk with her? She's pretty messed up."

"Did you talk with her at all?" asked Nick.

"A little. It seems she came home from work and found him in the pool. She said she tried to pull him out but she couldn't, so she called nine-one-one. The paramedics pulled him out and called us." He ripped a page from his notebook and handed it to the detective.

Just then another uniformed officer came up to them. "Excuse me, Detectives, we're trying to rope this place off, but there are a couple of news crews trying to push their way in. I called for more backup. I just thought you should know."

"Great!" Nick said. "Get it cordoned off, and keep the damn cameras out of here. Push them down the block a ways. Hell. Push them to Tucson if you can!" Nick looked at his partner. "Let's go talk with the wife."

Sonny heard his name called and looked back to where the body lay. Sue Kim was standing up and pointing to the six-foot block fence behind her. A news reporter was leaning over the top of the wall, filming the scene from the alley behind the house.

Lieutenant Greer's eyes widened. He said to the uniformed officer, "Get them the hell out of there, now." He and Sonny went into the house.

They walked through the kitchen and into the living room where they saw a lady sitting on a sofa. The two detectives approached her. Nick spoke first, "Mrs. Marquez?"

She held a tissue to her nose as she nodded.

"Ma'am, I'm Lieutenant Nick Greer." He looked toward Sonny. "This is Sergeant Sonny Madison. I know this is hard for you, but do you mind if we ask you a few questions?" She nodded in assent.

"First of all, we're both sorry for your loss." Again she nodded. Her eyes were flooded with tears.

"I understand you found your husband in the pool when you got home. What time was that?"

"Around six-thirty. I'd just gotten home from the hospital."

"The hospital?" Nick asked.

"Yes, Arrowhead Hospital in Glendale. I work there. I'm a surgical nurse."

"Can you tell me what happened when you got home?"

She dabbed her eyes and said, "I put the car in the garage, then I came into the house. Cam wasn't in bed, and it looked like the bed hadn't been slept in. I called him and looked all through the house, but he wasn't here. I went out on the patio and that's when"—she took a deep breath and exhaled—"that's when I saw him. He was in the pool, facedown. I ran to him and tried to pull him out, I really did, but I couldn't lift him. I knew he was dead. His body was rigid." She began to sob uncontrollably.

Nick waited until she regained control of herself before asking, "Ma'am, when was the last time you saw him?"

"I left here at three-thirty yesterday afternoon. I'm on swing this week."

"But you didn't get home until six-thirty this morning, is that correct?"

"Yeah, we had two emergencies. The last one was a gunshot. The surgery lasted until after five. We lost him."

"I see," Nick said. "Mrs. Marquez, what kind of work did your husband do?"

"He is a salesman for Smitty's Appliance and TV Center. He's been there for seven years."

"Ma'am, I'm sorry, but I have to ask, do you know anyone who would want to hurt him?"

She looked at the detective, shook her head, and began sobbing again.

Sonny asked, "Do you have someone who can be with you? Someone who can help you? Some place you can go? You really shouldn't be alone."

"Our daughter is on her way. She should be here any minute. She can stay with me."

Nick said, "Ma'am, I'm sorry, but this is a crime scene. You won't be able to stay here tonight."

Just then one of the uniformed officers came in and said, "Excuse me, Detectives, but there is a young lady outside. She says she's the vic . . . , uh"—he looked at lady sitting on the sofa—"the man's daughter."

"It's okay, Officer." Nick said as he looked at Sonny, who got up and left.

A few seconds later Sonny came back into the room, along with a female who looked to be about thirty. She sat down and embraced her mother. They both cried as they spoke back and forth in Spanish.

The two detectives gave them time to collect themselves before Nick spoke to the younger one, "I'm Lieutenant Greer, and this is Sergeant Madison. May I ask your name, please?"

"Serena . . . Serena Mitchell. This is my mom and . . ." She looked out in the direction of the backyard.

"We're sorry for your loss," Sonny said. She nodded. "May I ask where you live?"

"Anthem. We live in Anthem. My husband and our two children."

He knew Anthem was about a thirty-minute drive from the Marquez home. Sonny looked at Mrs. Marquez. "Ma'am, I'm sorry, but we're going to have a crime team go over this entire house. Is there somewhere you can stay for the night?"

"I'm not going—"

"It's okay, Mama. The police need to find out who did this to Papa. You can stay with Todd and me until they're done, longer if you need to."

Marquez nodded. "I need to get some things."

Sonny remembered he'd seen a female uniformed officer outside so he went to get her. When he returned with the police officer, he introduced her to Mrs. Marquez and her daughter. The officer accompanied them as they packed a small bag and then escorted them out of the house.

The two detectives walked around the house and began looking for clues. Nick was out by the pool when he heard Sonny call out to him: "Take a look at this."

Sonny was squatted down on the patio. The floor was covered with green indoor-outdoor carpeting. He pointed to two small drops of what he was sure was blood, then he pointed to another spot. "Looks like drag marks."

A second crime scene crew had arrived while the two detectives had been interviewing the victim's wife. Nick motioned to one of them, who came and took pictures and cut out a piece of the carpet containing the blood drops.

"How is it going, Detectives? Got anything?" They heard the voice behind them.

"Ahhhh, his master's voice," said Sonny.

Nick answered, "It's still early, Chief. It'll take a while, but it doesn't take a genius to see where it's heading. It follows the pattern."

"That's why you two were called. Do what you need to do here, and meet me back at my office. Our perp is picking up speed. We gotta get this shit stopped. Those fucking reporters were all over me coming in here. They remembered me from the press conference."

"Ahhhhh, the price of fame," Sonny said.

Deputy Chief Mannion chuckled and said, "You guys are going to have to leave here, too. Have fun getting though the crowd. See ya." He turned and left.

The chief was right. The two detectives left about a half hour later, and even though the street was blocked off and yellow police tape was strewn all over the place, they still had to get to their cars. The news crews were waiting for them, reaching out and trying to stick microphones in the detectives' faces and yelling out questions like, "Is this the work of the serial killer? Why haven't you caught him yet? Are the people of Phoenix safe? What are the Phoenix police doing to protect us?"

All Nick or Sonny said was, "No comment."

The two detectives got into their cars and headed toward the police station. About halfway there, Sonny called Nick from his cell phone.

"Yeah, Sonny, what's up?"

"The widow is a surgical nurse," Sonny said.

"And your point?"

"She knows anatomy."

"Okay, we'll check out her alibi."

"Did you notice anything else?" Sonny asked.

"Like what?"

"Like a cross on the wall? Looks like another Catholic."

"Yeah, I did. I saw something else, too."

"What?"

Nick smiled. "Detective Madison, I'm surprised. Did you see the calendar on the fridge?"

"Uhh, nooo. Why?"

"It looks like they went to St. Michael's."

CHAPTER 24

The Philadelphia Connection

It was shortly before noon when Lieutenant Nick Greer and Sergeant Sonny Madison arrived at their office. They decided to compare notes on their recent treks before reporting to the deputy chief.

"Okay, Sonny. Whatcha got?"

"First of all, the detective who investigated that case is gone."

"Gone? Where?" Nick asked.

"Uh, wherever you go when you're dead. That big precinct in the sky, I guess." Sonny grinned and added, "Heart attack, I'm told. It was his kid whom I spoke—"

"His kid?"

"He's not a kid anymore. He followed in his old man's footsteps. He's a homicide detective. And guess what? So was the grandfather. A real dedicated family of blue bloods."

Nick nodded and Sonny continued, "The report says the body was accidentally found by a couple of boaters, but I'm not so sure about that, the 'accidentally' part, that is." He pulled some pictures from an envelope, and handed them to his partner. "Take a look at these pics and tell me what you think."

Nick studied each picture carefully, then looked at them again. He looked up at his partner and shrugged his shoulders.

Sonny reached into the envelope and pulled out the magnifying glass. He retrieved one of the pictures, and handed it along with the magnifying glass to Nick. "Now, look and tell me what you see."

The lieutenant ran the magnifying glass over the picture. He looked at Sonny and shook his head.

"Look at the boat! Look at the damn boat!" Sonny said as he pointed to the boat in the picture.

Nick moved the magnifying glass to the right edge of the photo. The left side of the boat was barely in the picture, but he could see what Sonny was talking about. Nick whistled and said, "It looks like blood, doesn't it? Good eyes, Detective Madison, good eyes."

"Yep, the idiot in Baltimore thought it was paint." Sonny proceeded to tell his partner everything he had discovered in Baltimore.

When he was finished, Nick filled Sonny in on his findings in Pennsylvania, including the deputy's demeanor with the feds.

"I like that deputy." Sonny grinned.

"Yeah, I figured you would," Nick said. "Let's go see the boss."

Deputy Chief Mannion was waiting for them. They sat in front of his desk, and he got right to the point. "Okay, gentlemen. What do you have for me? Tell me the funds I okayed for your trips were well spent."

Nick began, "Well, like we figured, they all followed the same pattern. Stabbed in the chest, looks like an ice pick. The left ring fingers were all missing, they were all dumped in water, and none of them appear to have been robberies. They all were married, and they all were Catholic."

"What about our vic this morning? Catholic?"

Nick looked at Sonny, who said, "Yeah, I think so. St. Michael's."

"What else?" Mannion asked.

"Well, I'm thinking there may be two perps, at least in Baltimore," Sonny stated. "There were two people in that boat and both of them seem to have disappeared." He handed his boss the pictures and the magnifying glass. "What do you think of this, Chief?" Sonny pointed to the boat at the edge of the photo.

"You made me hunt for it," Nick stated.

"Rank has its privileges," Sonny commented.

Nick chuckled. "Kiss ass!"

Mannion laughed, then began studying the picture. He looked up to Sonny. "Damn, Madison, you've got good eyes. I understand how they could have missed it. What did the Baltimore cop say about it?"

"He thought it might be paint."

Mannion ran the magnifying glass over the picture again, looked closely at the boat, shook his head and said, "It could be, but I don't think so. The pattern is smeared. It looks like something bloody was either pushed, or pulled over the side."

"Yeah, the same side as the body was found," Sonny added. "I'm thinking we may have two perps, or at least one of them is an accessory."

Mannion looked at Nick. "Anything in PA to substantiate that?"

"Nothing at all, but there is something strange."

"I'm listening," the chief said.

"The victim's wife is missing, and much of the info they have on her is bogus." He explained his findings and the results of Sonny's trip to Philadelphia.

"How about her driver's license?" Mannion asked.

"It looks like she didn't have one. Not in Pennsylvania, anyway. I checked under Ayers and Widmann. No hit."

"How about her social security number?"

"They didn't get it, I guess. It wasn't anywhere in the file."

The chief looked at Sonny, who replied, "The information in the Baltimore file was bogus."

"Pretty sloppy," Mannion said. "Did you check out the church?"

"Yeah, no one there ever heard of her," Sonny responded. "But we might have some help on the Baltimore case. One of the original two responding officers has moved to Florida. I talked with him and he's agreed to get us a sketch, as best he can remember. Oh, yeah, could you call Sarasota and arrange it? You have more clout than I do?"

"Got it." He looked at Nick. "What do you think? Should we have the PA sheriff do the same?"

Greer nodded. "It's been eight years, but it can't do any harm."

"I'll call Butch. He's gotta have a sketch artist. Let's see what happens," the chief said.

"There are two things that stick out for me," Nick said. "It appears the victim was a player. He liked the ladies. The deputy sheriff said the wife had quite a temper. Maybe she caught him boning some other woman and took him out."

"Then she moved to Baltimore, and then out here?" Mannion questioned as he looked at the notes in the file. "There's a phone number here. It says it's the number they called to verify her alibi. Did you check it out?"

He didn't wait for an answer. He picked up the phone and dialed. After the eighth ring, he was about to hang up when he heard, "St. Luke's Parish."

"Uhh, this is Deputy Chief Bruce Mannion of the Phoenix Arizona Police Department. May I ask to whom I am speaking, please?"

"This is Father Crandall. I'm the pastor. Can I help you?"

"Yes, Father, please. I'm sorry to bother you, but we found this phone number among some notes in an old file. We were wondering where it went, so I've just called it."

"It's one of the back lines here at our parish office. We have five lines coming in, and it's the last one in the system. It usually only rings when the rest are busy, but it rang by itself just now. I figured it was a wrong number, but when it kept ringing I answered it."

"How long have you had that number, Father?"

"Oh, I don't know. I've been here for four years. It was here before I got here. Hold on while I ask someone." He put the phone on hold.

After about three minutes he came back on the line. "I just spoke with our secretary. She's been here for over twenty years. She says that number has been here as long as she has."

"So it was there eight years ago?" Mannion asked.

"Apparently. Tell me, does this have anything to do with those two men who were here earlier today?"

"I'm not real sure. What men?"

"They were G-men from the FBI," the priest answered.

"What did they want?"

"They wanted to know if a Catherine Ayers or a Catherine Widmann ever worked here or was registered here. I checked the computer, and I couldn't find any Widmann. We have a family named Ayers, but none of them ever worked here, and none of their names were Catherine. They've only been in the parish for four years. I told that to the FBI men, but they wanted their address and phone number anyway."

"Did you give it to them?"

"I don't know if I should have, but I did," the priest answered. "After all, they were G-men, and I figured they'd find it anyway."

"Could you share that information with me, please?"

"Uh, I don't know. These men were from the federal government. They had identification. I don't know for sure who you are."

"Father, I understand your apprehension, but we could really use your help. You see, we have someone out here, in our city, who is killing people. The only clues we have is this phone number and the names I gave you. If you would like, I'll be glad to give you the phone number of the department switchboard. You can call and ask for Deputy Chief Bruce Mannion. They'll ring you through to my office. That way, you'll know I'm really who I say I am."

"I guess that won't be necessary," the priest said. He gave the chief the address and the phone number. Mannion wrote it down.

"Thank you, Father. You have a nice day." Mannion hung up the phone.

The chief looked at his detectives and said, "At least the phone number matches the church address, for whatever that's worth. It's a back line at St. Luke's church, and the feds just left. They're right behind us. I'd sure like to know who answered that phone eight years ago."

"Wouldn't we all?" Sonny commented. "It's a big church. It could have been anybody. It could have been an employee, or even a volunteer. It's the proverbial needle in a haystack."

"Yeah, but whoever it was had to have been waiting for the call, so he had to have worked there, or at least volunteer there. He would've had to have been someone who was inconspicuous, but someone who knew their system. Someone had to have seen him hanging around. According to the file, he claimed to be her brother," Mannion said. "Whoever it was gave an alibi for the wife. If you find out who it was, you've got the killer. Or at least an accomplice."

He slid the file across his desk. Nick picked it up and answered, "We'll see what we can find." He and Sonny got up and returned to their office.

Bruce Mannion picked up his phone. Tricia answered, "Yes, Chief."

"Get me the mayor."

CHAPTER 25

The Deli

The two detectives entered the Special Investigations Unit room. Nick said, "I'm kind of hungry. Wanna go to the deli?"

Sonny pulled out his wallet, retrieved a ten-dollar bill and handed it to his partner. "Would you mind bringing me something back? I want to do some research."

Nick took the money. "What do you want?"

"Uh, pastrami on rye will work," Sonny answered. "I'll get a soda or something from the machine in the hall."

* * *

As soon as Nick walked into the deli, his eyes saw Sue Kim sitting in the back corner, alone. He thought for a moment, then decided to go over to her. What's the worst that could happen?

She didn't see him coming until he sat across from her. She looked at him with surprise, turned her head, and looked out the window. Just then, a waitress came over with a glass of ice water and said, "Well, hello, Lieutenant Greer. What can I get for you today?"

Sue Kim looked at the waitress. "He was just leaving." She turned her head to the window again.

Nick looked at the waitress and said, "Hi, Melanie. How about a ham and cheese on white for here, and a pastrami on rye to go for Sonny?"

"Anything to drink?"

"A coke will work," Nick responded.

Sue Kim looked toward the waitress. "May I have my check, please?" She looked at her half-eaten sandwich and said, "I'll take the rest of this to go." She looked across the table and back to the waitress. "I suddenly lost my appetite."

Melanie turned and began to walk away. Sue Kim looked around the room. "Melanie," she called out. The waitress turned around and saw Sue Kim pointing to an empty table. "I'll be over there." She reached for her plate and her drink.

"No, she won't," Nick said to the waitress. "She'll be right here."

Melanie knew both of her customers from the many times they had come into the deli together. She had noticed Sue Kim coming in alone the last few days. One day she'd asked her where Nick was, and Sue Kim had answered, "In hell, I hope!"

Melanie liked them both and had been glad when they became a couple. She could tell Nick wanted to talk with Sue Kim, so she decided to take her time getting the to-go box.

Nick looked at his ex-girlfriend. "We can't keep doing this. We have to talk."

"I'll call the cops. I'll say you're stalking me!"

Nick leaned back, folded his arms across his chest, and smiled. "Really?" He reached to his belt, retrieved his cell phone, set it on the table, and slid it toward Sue Kim. "Here, go ahead, call the cops. But it might be easier just to scream 'cause this place is loaded with them."

She looked around at the patrol and plainclothes officers dining there, and unsuccessfully tried to hide a smile. "You're an ass!"

Nick nodded. "Yes, I am. And I'm sorry. All I ask is that you let me explain. Let me tell you what happened . . ."

She looked at him, pursed her lips, squinted, and said, "I already know what happened!"

"Okay, but at least let me explain how. Give me a chance to convince you it will never happen again."

Her eyes began to well up with tears. "You broke my heart!"

"And mine," he stated.

The look in his eyes told her that he was suffering, too. "Okay, but this isn't the place."

"I have an idea. How about we go to Rusty's for dinner tonight? It's quiet and we can talk. I can pick you up—"

"No! I'll meet you there. I'll take my own car."

"Seven?"

She nodded. "Now, leave me alone!"

Nick looked across the room and saw Melanie looking at them. He nodded to her, and she came over to the table with his to-go order. He handed her his plate and said, "Make mine to-go, too."

The waitress looked at Sue Kim as Nick said, "I'll let her finish her lunch quietly." He got up and went to the counter where Melanie bagged his sandwiches. He thanked her and left.

Melanie waited until he was out the door before she went over to Sue Kim. She sat down in the chair where Nick had sat and said, "Honey, I don't know what happened between the two of you, and it isn't any of my business. But I do know this. That guy loves you, and whether or not you want to admit it, you love him, too. Listen to Melanie; don't throw it away. A love like that doesn't come along every day." She got up and left Sue Kim sitting alone.

* * *

Nick returned to the SIU with the sandwiches. "You decided to eat in? Did you miss me that much?" Sonny said, grinning.

"I ran into someone there. It was a little awkward, so I decided it was best to come back here."

"Uhh, I'll bet it was female, short, and the cutest little thing the crime lab has ever seen."

"Something like that," Nick responded as he tossed Sonny's sandwich on his desk. "Your change is in the bag." He turned toward his own desk.

Sonny unwrapped his sandwich, opened the mustard packet, and squeezed its contents onto the sandwich. He got up and walked down the hallway to the soda machine. When he returned, Nick was standing at the back of the room, staring out the window. "You okay, buddy?" Sonny asked.

"Yeah," Nick said, as he turned and went back to his desk.

"What did she do? Tell you to eat shit and die?"

"Uhh, in not so many words, I think, but she did agree to have dinner tonight."

"With you?" Sonny asked.

Nick looked over to his partner and said, "Duuhh, not with you!"

"Good!" Sonny said.

"We're going to Rusty's. She's meeting me there."

"Well, it's a start," Sonny stated.

"I hope she shows."

"She will," Sonny assured his friend. "She will."

Sonny changed the subject. "I checked on the Marquez woman. I spoke with one of the supervisors. It appears she was at the hospital from four p.m. yesterday, until five-thirty this morning."

"Is all of her time accounted for?"

"All but about an hour and a half between surgeries."

That's plenty of time to go home, whack the old man and come back," Nick stated.

"Huh-uh," Sonny said. "Her break was between twelve-fifteen and one-forty-five. Sue Kim said the body was in full rigor. He would've had to have been dead eleven to twelve hours. The timing doesn't work."

The door opened and Deputy Chief Mannion came into the room. "Gentlemen, I spoke with Mayor Murphy. He's calling the bishop. It's a long shot, but he's asking O'Malley to call his counterpart in Philly and see if he can get us a list of all personnel attached to St. Luke's from seven to nine years ago. If he agrees, I can pull in a couple of investigators to help, if you want."

"Let's see what we get from them," Sonny said.

"I'll let you know," Mannion said. He looked at Nick. "Good luck tonight."

Nick Greer's mouth flew open. "You got this place bugged or something? How the hell did you know?"

Mannion laughed. "Boy, some detective you are. Maybe I should rethink this whole SIU thing. You're supposed to be observant, but you didn't even see me sitting at the table next to you? I heard it all." He smiled and left the room.

Sonny was busy typing away at the computer and chomping on his sandwich. He looked over to his partner, took a sip of soda, and grinned. "Big department, small deli."

CHAPTER 26

Dinner

The restaurant was packed. Though Nick Greer had made reservations for seven o'clock, he arrived fifteen minutes early. He had asked for a quiet table by the window that looked out over the city. The view from this mountainside resort was breathtaking, especially when the city lights were sparkling on a clear night. He knew the dinner would be expensive, probably around a hundred and fifty dollars. But this was Sue Kim's favorite restaurant, and he needed to win her back.

A waiter came to Nick's table. "Good evening, sir. My name is Robert. I'll be your server. Would you like to see our wine list?"

"Thank you, Robert, but I'm waiting for someone. I'd rather wait until she gets here."

"I'll leave a menu for you, sir. Would you like an appetizer while you're waiting? Our bloomin' onions are legendary."

Rusty's Mountainside Steakhouse was famous for its bloomin' onions, and Nick loved them, but he wanted to wait for Sue Kim. "My friend should be here in a few minutes, thank you."

It was seven-ten. He was still sitting alone when the waiter came back to the table, topped off Nick's glass of water and left.

He looked at his watch. Seven-twenty-one. She's not coming, he thought. He shook his head and began to get up when he saw her coming toward him. He stood and held the chair for her. She sat down. "I was wondering if you were going to come."

"I wasn't." She looked at him. "Carol made me do it."

"Thank her for me," he said.

Sue Kim was about to speak when the waiter returned to the table. "I see your lady has arrived, sir, and may I say you are a lucky man." He handed Nick the wine list and poured her a glass of water.

Nick looked at Sue Kim as he responded, "Yeah, I know."

"I really am not in the mood for wine tonight," she said. "I'll have a glass of tea, please."

Nick looked at her and then to the waiter. "I'll have the same. Do you have raspberry?" The waited nodded.

Nick looked at his date as the waiter walked away. "So how have things been with you?"

"Good, I guess. Carol wants me to stay with her, but that wouldn't work out. I'm going to get an apartment. I thought about going to the old place. I liked it there."

"Are you and Carol not getting along?" he asked.

"Oh yeah, we get along well. Too well."

"Huh? I don't get it."

Her face reddened as she whispered, "She likes women. She's a lesbian."

His mouth flew open, and he couldn't hide the surprise on his face. "You're kidding! Really? No!" She nodded. "I'd have never known," he said.

"Boy, some detective you are." She smiled for the first time since she arrived. He realized how much he had missed that smile. "I thought you were supposed to be able to read people."

"Uh, she doesn't look like a lesbian. She's an attractive woman, and definitely feminine looking."

"You know, all lesbians don't have short hair and wear clodhoppers." She giggled. "She made it clear to me she prefers women. Very clear. A little too clear."

"Uhh, you didn't . . ."

"Of course not! I would think you'd know better than that." She giggled and her face turned red.

Robert came back with their drinks. Nick ordered for both of them and the waiter left. Neither of them spoke for a minute until Sue Kim broke the silence. "Anything more on our serial killer?"

"Sonny and I have a new position. We are now the Phoenix PD Special Investigations Unit. We will be assigned special high-priority cases. We have our own squad room, and no, we're working on it."

"Yeah, I heard. The word is you two have special status. We're to give you priority. Which reminds me, have you seen the report from our victim in the pool?" she asked.

"Not yet. Anything I should know?"

"Oh, I'm not supposed to share any information until its official. You know that, Detective."

"Uh, but didn't you say we have special privileges?"

He looked at her and she smiled. "Rohypnol."

"I thought so."

"There's more," she teased.

"Enlighten me," he said.

"The blood on the carpet?"

"Yeah, what about it?"

"Not the victim's."

"Are you sure?"

"The blood is from a female. The victim was a male; so yeah, I'm sure."

"Maybe his wife?" Nick asked.

"We typed her, not a match."

"Daughter?"

"Nope. Not family."

"You ran it through CODIS, I assume."

"Yep. Nothing. No match."

Robert came to the table with their steaks sizzling on hot plates. He sat one in front of Sue Kim and one in front of Nick. "Will there be anything more for you or your lady?"

"That'll be all for now, Robert. Thank you."

As the waiter left, Sue Kim said, "I'm not, you know."

Nick looked at her, puzzled. "Uhh, you're not what?"

"Your lady! Not anymore!"

Nick was silent for a moment, then he laid his fork on the table, looked at her and said, "Sue, I know I messed up. I can't even begin to tell you how sorry I am. I should have never let it happen, but it did. It will never happen again. Just give me the chance to prove it."

She looked at him, then she looked out the window at the city lights and said, "It's such a clear night. I love the view from here."

CHAPTER 27

The Hacker

Lieutenant Nick Greer and Sergeant Sonny Madison had been working all morning. They decided to go through all the names published under personnel on the diocesan website. They had split the list and hoped one of them would get lucky. Nick had been unusually silent through it all.

"You didn't tell me about your weekend," Sonny said. "You've been mopey all morning, so I assume it didn't go as well as you had hoped."

"It went okay, I guess. At least we got to talk a bit, and she was civil. She was late, though, and it was beginning to look like she wasn't going to show up. That girl is never late for anything. She admitted she wasn't going to come, but she changed her mind."

"Hey, at least she came. That's a step in the right direction. So, tell me what happened."

Nick described the evening to his friend. He told him that when he tried to kiss her good night in the parking lot, she turned away. And when he asked her if he could see her Saturday, she said no; it was too early, that she had to work some things out. He said he would call her. She said okay, but when he called a couple of times over the weekend, she didn't answer and the phone went to voice mail.

"Work some things out, huh?" Sonny said. "That sounds like a positive sign. At least she didn't tell you to drop dead, or anything like that. What kind of things?"

"I don't know. Me, I guess."

"Maybe she's been hanging around the lesbo too long." Sonny grinned.

"Huh? What the hell are you talking about?"

"Uh, that Carol? Her flute player friend? You know she's a lesbian, don't you?"

"Yeah, I guess I do." Why does everyone know this stuff before I do? he thought. "That's why she wants to get an apartment. I think the chick might be coming on to her and she doesn't like it."

"Are you sure she doesn't like it?" Sonny grinned again. "Maybe she's turning to the other side."

Nick shook his head, grabbed the inside of his thigh, and said, "Bite me, Madison."

Sonny laughed and looked back at his computer. "I got nothing! I've been through the whole list. I checked and cross-checked. Nothing!" Sonny's tone was a mixture of disappointment and anger.

"Yeah, me, too. At least nothing useful. The backgrounds I was able to check were negative except for a couple of minor charges, one drunk and disorderly, a couple of DUIs and one assault. One of the DUIs was a priest."

"I guess he takes after his boss."

Nick knew what Sonny was referring to. Recently, the bishop had been charged with hit and run. He had hit a man while driving home one night. The man was dead at the scene. Folks figured he was so smashed he didn't remember hitting the guy.

"And they got all that altar wine lying around. Can't let it go sour," Sonny joked. "What about the assault case? That might connect."

"I don't think so. According to the report, he got into a shoving match with a neighbor. They both were arrested, pled to a lower charge of trespassing, and ordered to attend anger management classes. He paid a fine and was released."

"The chief had the mayor call the bishop, you know," Sonny said.

"What for?"

"To see if he would call his compadre in Philly and get us a list of personnel for St. Luke's seven to nine years ago."

"Let me guess. He said no."

"Good guess, Detective," Sonny responded. "According to the chief, the bish cited confidentiality issues. He wouldn't even make the call."

Nick recalled his previous experience while investigating the murder of one of the priests. Bishop O'Malley was less than cooperative. "Some things never change."

Sonny shook his head. "It looks like the only thing our victims seem to have had in common before they were killed, was religion and marital status. There doesn't appear to be any other connection: different professions, different lifestyles. It's like they all lived in different worlds."

Nick looked over to his partner. "You know, you're right," he commented as he stroked his chin. "What if it did have something to do with marriage?"

"Huh?" Sonny wondered where Nick was going.

"What if they were all seeking marriage counseling? You know the Catholic church's position on divorce. What if all of our vics were seeing a counselor? Maybe the same counselor? What if the skull jockey they saw was a nut case himself? You know, it wouldn't be the first time."

"You don't really think Pete and Elena were having troubles, do you? Do you think they were going to a marriage counselor?" Then Sonny remembered what April had said on the phone the other day: "Elena asked me what I would do if I ever found you cheating on me."

"I don't know. It's unlikely. They appeared to have had a model marriage, but sometimes things aren't what they seem. Can you check and see if any counselors who moved here in the last couple of years could've also lived or gone to school in Pennsylvania or Baltimore?"

Sonny began typing: Arizona Board of Psychologist Examiners. "You gotta be shittin' me!" he exclaimed.

"What?" Nick went over to Sonny and looked at his computer screen.

"Look at how many there are," Sonny said. "Do you realize there are over two thousand people in their registry? Wow, there must be a helluva lot of crazies in this state to keep all these shrinks busy."

Nick laughed. "Start with those whose addresses are in Phoenix. Maybe we'll take Bruce up on the extra help." He thought for a moment. "Hey, wait a minute. I got a better idea. Let's start with the Catholic Social Services. The list should be shorter, and that's most likely where a Catholic would go, or where they'd be referred to."

"That makes sense," Sonny answered. He typed and searched. "There's nothing I can find on their site that lists the names of their counselors."

"We can go there. We can subpoena their records if we have to," Nick said.

"You don't think that might tip off our perp?" Sonny asked. "If he's one of them, and he gets wind we're looking, he might bolt. And besides, what judge do you think would agree to sign the warrant?"

"Yeah, you got a point. Got any ideas? You're pretty good with computers. Work your magic."

"Uhhhm, I'm good, but I'm not good enough to hack into their system. I was hoping there'd be a list, someplace to start. But unless you know the name, you can't get any information. We need a list of their counselors, and that would take someone who can do things I can't." Sonny's eyes widened. "Uhhh, I may need to solicit some help."

"Help? From whom?"

Sonny looked at his partner and squinted. "Uhhhm," he said as he stroked his chin. "I'll let you know." He shut down his computer, cleared off his desk, and left the Special Investigations Unit.

* * *

It was a couple of hours later when Sonny returned accompanied by a young man in his mid to late teens. He introduced him to Nick, "This is Jake, a friend of mine. He's going to help out with our little project."

Nick shook his hand. "Lieutenant Nick Greer." He thought for a moment, looked at Sonny, then looked back at the visitor. "How do you know Sergeant Madison?"

"Uhhh . . ." He looked at Sonny.

"He's just a friend who is better at computers than I am," Sonny stated and turned away from Nick. He logged on to his computer, pointed to his chair, and said, "It's all yours, Jake. Do your thing."

The young man began typing. Nick had seen some fast typists in his day, but this kid was a pro. His fingers flew over the keys like they were in warp drive. He watched the kid in awe, then he motioned for Sonny to follow him. They went out into the hall, and Nick looked at his partner. "You brought in a hacker? Are you nuts? You know that's against policy. Where the hell did you find him?"

Sonny tried to conjure up an innocent look, but to no avail. "Okay, you remember a couple of years ago when I left homicide on assignment to the cyber unit?"

"Yeah?"

"Do you remember the kid I arrested for hacking into the PPD and the sheriff's personnel records?"

"Uhhh, yeah."

Sonny pointed through the open door to the young man typing away at the computer, looked back to his partner, and grinned.

"You brought a hacker, an ex-con, into the SIU? Are you trying to see how quick this unit gets shut down?" Nick said.

"Hey." Sonny shrugged. "You asked for magic. David Copperfield was booked, so I got the next best thing. Besides, he's not an ex-con. He got probation."

Nick shook his head. "What if his PO finds out?"

"Uhh, he's off probation, I think."

"You think?"

Sonny shrugged. "If you wanna go get some coffee or something, I can call you when he's done. That way you can plead innocent."

"No, I guess I'll stick around." He looked into the room at Jake's flying fingers. "The kid can type; I'll give you that."

It was a little over a half hour later when Jake sat back and smiled. Sonny looked at the young man as he pointed proudly at the computer screen. "Detective Madison, we're in!"

Sonny Madison looked at the screen. "Good work, Jake. Go ahead and have a seat over there." He pointed to one of the empty desks. "I might still need you." Jake sat down at the desk as directed. "Do you want something to eat or drink?" Sonny asked Jake.

"Some chips and a soda would work."

Sonny pulled his wallet out and gave the boy four one-dollar bills. "There's a machine across the hall. Knock yourself out."

It wasn't long before Nick heard the sound of the printer coming to life. He walked over to it, removed the papers from the tray, and handed them to Sonny. Jake had returned and was enjoying a bag of Fritos and a Coke.

"Do you know how to use a copier?" Sonny asked the boy.

"Duhhh, yeah," Jake answered.

Sonny chuckled as he handed the boy the papers. "How about making me two more copies of each of these?"

Jake fed the papers into the copy machine, made two sets as requested, and gave them to Sonny, who gave one set to his partner.

"Uh, who's the other list for?" Nick asked.

"Me, I hope," Deputy Chief Bruce Mannion said as he came in through the open door. He looked at the young man at the computer and said, "How's it going, Jake? Are you staying out of trouble?"

"Uhh, yes, sir. I'm doing my best."

"How's school?"

"Four-point-zero grade point average," Jake said proudly.

Mannion grinned. "It looks like you still got the touch." The young man smiled.

Chief Mannion looked at Nick who had a questioning look on his face. "What? You got a problem with this, Lieutenant Greer?"

"Uhh, I think, uhh, I don't know, should I? Well, I guess not," Nick said.

Mannion laughed and said to Sonny, "Go ahead and take him home."

Sonny handed the chief a copy of the paperwork, nodded to Jake, and left with him.

Chief Mannion looked at Nick and smiled. "Don't be such a tight-ass, Lieutenant. Sometimes you gotta bend the rules; sometimes you gotta make your own. That's why I created this unit." He pointed to the papers in his detective's hand. "Let's hope there's something in there to help find Pete Mendoza's killer."

The deputy chief turned and walked toward the door, but he stopped and turned back toward his detective. "By the way, that special ops case where Sonny arrested the kid?" Nick nodded. "I was lead. It was me who talked the ADA into recommending probation. They wanted to send him to juvy."

"Why?"

"You know the DDAs. They wanted to make an example out of him."

"No," Nick said. "Why did you go to bat for him?"

"He seemed like a good kid. There wasn't any malice there; he was just fooling around. He didn't even know what he had done."

"Yeah, but all that information was compromised."

"True, but we learned about our vulnerabilities and sealed them. Besides, I thought it was amusing watching the animation he created of Sheriff Joe jumping around the screen, laughing, and wearing nothing but pink underwear and a bolo tie."

Nick laughed as he remembered. One of the things their sheriff was famous for was making the inmates, male and female, wear pink underwear. "That it was. That it was."

Mannion left the room, and Nick sat at his desk and began looking at the lists. Wow, he thought, as he thumbed through the pages, that kid is good.

Nick was reading and taking notes when Sonny returned carrying an easel and a whiteboard. He took the easel from Sonny, looked around the room, and set it up in the corner where it was easily visible from both detectives' desks. Sonny set the whiteboard on the easel, reached into his pocket, and pulled out a pack of colored dry-erase markers.

"You need me to do anything?" Nick asked.

"Yeah, I do," Sonny said.

"Name it."

"Get out!"

"Get out? Why?"

"I need to concentrate. Come back in an hour or two."

"I'm crushed." Nick grinned.

"Yeah, I'm sure you are," Sonny said as he reached into his desk, pulled out the files, and sat down. "I mean it. Can't you find somewhere to go?"

"Now that you mention it, yeah. There is something I want to check out."

CHAPTER 28

The Question

Nick dialed the Mendoza home. After the third ring he heard: "Mendozas."

He recognized the voice on the other end. "Jordana, it's Nick Greer."

"Hi, Nick. What's up?"

"How is your mom?"

"Still the same. She doesn't want to talk about it. She is not grieving, Nick. That worries me. She's angry, but not grieving."

"May I speak with her?"

"Sure. Hold on."

A few moments later he heard, "Hello, Nick. What can I do for you?"

"Elena, I need to speak with you in private. Just you, Elena. Can I come over?"

"Sure."

"I'm in my car. I'll be there in about twenty minutes." His cell phone went silent as she hung up the phone.

* * *

Nick Greer pulled his Taurus in front of the Mendoza home, got out of the car, and pushed the button on his clicker. The lights flashed, and the horn honked lightly in response to the signal.

A large saguaro cactus stood tall and proud in the center of the mature front lawn. Green ivy covered part of the white slump block exterior and climbed its way up the front of the house behind a statue of Our Lady of Guadalupe.

He walked onto the driveway to the sidewalk that led to the front double doors and rang the doorbell. Elena was waiting and opened it immediately. "Come in, Nick."

He entered the foyer, closed the door behind him, gave her a hug and said, "How are you holding up, Elena? I'm worried about you."

She broke the embrace, looked at him and said, "I'm fine. What do you want to talk about? You're not here to tell me you found Pete's killer, or you wouldn't have asked to meet me alone." He could sense the anger in her voice, just like Jordana had said.

"Where are the kids?" Nick questioned.

"Jordy just left for the gym, and Petey is running some errands. You said this was a private matter?"

"Can we sit down and talk?" Nick asked.

"Let's go into the living room. Go ahead and have a seat. I just brewed some tea. Would you like some?"

"Your tea? You bet!" he answered with a smile as he went into the living room and sat on the sofa. On his way here, he had thought about what he would say to Elena. He knew he would need to choose his words carefully.

Soon she came into the room balancing a silver tray holding a pitcher of freshly brewed tea, a bowl of ice cubes, several sweetener packets, a bowl of freshly sliced lemons, two spoons, and two glasses. She set the tray on the coffee table and said, "Help yourself, Nick."

"Thank you, Elena." He scooped some ice and dropped it into his glass. She reached for the pitcher and poured its contents into Nick's glass. He lifted the glass to his lips and took a long drink.

"Ahhh! I needed that. Thank you. Tell me, what is there about your tea that is different? It has a special tang to it."

"It's a secret family recipe," she whispered. Then she added, "You said you wanted to talk in private, so talk."

"Yes, Elena." He looked at her and continued, "This is very delicate. But I have to ask you something personal."

"Go ahead."

"How were you and Pete getting along? Was everything good between you?"

"Nick Greer! Where are you going with this? How could you even think I would harm my husband? I thought you knew me better than that."

"Oh, Elena, I do." He was surprised at her answer. "I know you wouldn't harm Pete. That's not what I meant, not at all."

"Then what did you mean? Why would you ask me such a question?"

"Romantically, Elena. How were things there?"

She turned her head and looked away. She was silent. Nick reached out and touched her hand. "It's okay, Elena. You can talk to me."

She turned back toward her guest and said, "I think he, well, maybe he, uh . . . , might've been seeing someone." Tears ran down her cheeks.

"What would make you think that?" Nick asked.

"A wife knows, especially when you're married as long as we were. He hadn't been in, well, you know, in the mood. I didn't know what was wrong. I thought I wasn't attractive to him anymore."

"Elena, you're still an attractive woman. I'm sure that wasn't the problem."

Though she had recently turned fifty and was about twenty pounds overweight, Elena Vasquez-Mendoza looked younger than her years. Her skin was smooth, and the bangs from her shoulder-length black hair framed her face perfectly.

"I thought maybe it was his age, but then there were the texts," she added.

"What texts?" Nick questioned.

"Several times I saw him receive a text message and go out of the room. He didn't even do that when he was on the force. I asked him one time who it was, and he said just one of the guys on the force. But the smile on his face and the gleam in his eye said something different."

"How long had this been going on?"

"Oh, a few months, I guess. It seemed to get worse the last couple of months. I only recently started to wonder what was going on." She looked into her guest's eyes. "Nick, you knew him. You worked with him. You ate and drank with him. Please, tell me. Was he having an affair? I need to know."

"I don't know," he answered. "If he was, I wasn't aware of it. I know he loved you, Elena. Of that, I am certain. By the way, were you two going to counseling, by any chance?"

"No," she answered. "Nick, I want you to promise me something."

"If I can."

Elena looked into his eyes and said, "If you find out he was seeing someone, I want you to tell me. But I do not want the kids to know. They adored their dad."

"No problem, I promise," Nick responded. "I'll let you know." He gave her a hug. "Thank you. I'll see my way out." He turned and walked toward the front door.

"Cinnamon," Elena said.

He turned and looked at her. "Huh?"

"Cinnamon." She smiled. "In the tea. Cinnamon."

CHAPTER 29

Enlightenment

Lieutenant Nick Greer left the Mendoza home, but he didn't go directly back to the station. He decided to make a detour, reached for his cell phone, and made a call. "Carmen Cruz," was the answer on the other end.

"Lieutenant Nick Greer. Do you remember me? Phoenix PD?"

"Oh, yes, you're the tall one. How can I help you, Lieutenant? Are you having any luck finding our killer?"

"Are you available to meet? I need to talk with you."

"Okay, same place?"

"I'm on the one-o-one. I should be there in about thirty minutes."

"I'll see you then." She disconnected the call.

* * *

Detective Carmen Cruz was seated in the same booth as before, waiting for him. As he slid into the seat across from her, a waitress came over with a pot of coffee in one hand and a cup in the other. "Coffee?" she asked Nick.

"Sure. Black, please," he answered. Steam rose from the pot as she poured the coffee. She then topped off Carmen's cup and walked away.

"So how is the investigation going?" Carmen asked. "What is so important that you would drive all the way here from Phoenix instead of just using the phone?"

Nick kept looking down at his coffee as he asked gently, "Carmen, how well did you know Pete Mendoza?"

"Like I said the other day, he spoke at a seminar once. That's where I met him. Why do you ask?"

He looked at her and said, "Carmen, I didn't ask you where you met him. I asked how well you knew him."

A look of shock came across her face as she answered, "Why would you ask me that? I attended a seminar. He was the speaker. We talked afterwards. That's it."

Nick Greer earned his spending money while in college by playing poker due to his uncanny ability to read faces, and he could see clearly that she was lying. "Detective, I think Pete was having an affair, and I think you know, because you were the one he was seeing."

"How dare you!" Coffee splattered from their cups as she tried to jump up from her seat but bumped the table hard.

Nick held up his cell phone and snapped her picture.

"Why did you do that?" she asked. Her face was red with anger.

"I need your picture to show to the motel manager when I find out where Pete went on Wednesday afternoons. I'm sure when my partner goes through his credit card receipts he'll find out where. Even if he paid cash, they would have his license number. My partner, you remember Detective Madison, is known as the department digger. He's the best there is, and he's a whiz at computers. He'll find out where your little love nest was; I'll bet my badge on it."

Carmen Cruz hung her head as she sat back down. Her face took on a look of humility as she asked, "How did you know?"

"I didn't. Until now it was just a guess. You see, the last time we were here, you referred to him as Pete. It made me wonder why, if you only heard him speak once, you would refer to him by his first name instead of 'Captain.' And also why you said he was a good guy, if you didn't know him."

"If it's any help, I was in love with him." Her eyes began to tear up as she told the story: "I was really impressed by his presentation. After the seminar, I asked him if we could sit somewhere and talk because I had some questions. We went into the hotel restaurant and had coffee. We talked for over an hour. He explained some things to me I had never thought of. I wanted to learn more, so we met at a restaurant in Scottsdale a couple of times. He knew more about criminology than I ever learned in college, and he explained it better than anyone. He could have been an excellent teacher. I don't know when I started to have feelings for him. But one day when we were leaving, I kissed him and, well, I guess you can fill in the rest."

"When was the last time you saw him?"

"The last time I saw him? It was two weeks before he was killed. He said he was having problems dealing with the infidelity. He said he loved his wife, and the guilt was getting to him. He said he felt he needed to go to confession. I don't believe in that stuff, but to each his own."

"Did he break it off with you?" Nick questioned.

"Well, not really. At least he didn't say so."

The lieutenant stood and said, "Thank you, Detective. I appreciate your time."

"I'm sorry," she said. "I guess I should have told you."

"Yes, you should have." Nick left, got into his car and headed back to Phoenix.

* * *

Sonny was staring at the whiteboard when Nick returned to the SIU. The names of the victims were written in a time line from left to right beginning with the Pennsylvania victim. Notes were written in a column underneath each one. "Anything new, Detective Madison?"

Sonny held up his right index finger as a sign he was thinking. He stood back, scratched his head, and stared at the board for about a minute. Then he turned around, went to his desk and reviewed each of the victim's files. "No kids," he said. He looked up at his partner. "No kids! None of the vics had any small kids at home. They either had no kids at all, or they were grown."

Sonny handed the file to his partner and pointed as he spoke, "Look, Montgomery was a grandmother. The two vics back east were childless. Perrotta had two, but they were both in college. Marquez only had one. You met her at the house. And Pete had Jordana at home, but she ain't no kid." Sonny got up, went back to the whiteboard, and wrote under each column: 0 kids.

"What do you think that means?" Nick questioned.

"I don't know. Maybe nothing. Maybe the killer has a conscience."

Nick went over to the board and stared at it. He stroked his chin, looked at his partner, then back to the board, and said, "Perhaps our perp lost a parent when he was a child. Maybe he doesn't want to leave some other kid in the same situation. Maybe that's how he chooses his victims."

Sonny squinted. "A serial killer with a conscience? What the hell were you smoking while you were gone? And where were you anyway?"

"I went to see Elena. I had a hunch and she verified it, well, almost. I wondered if Pete was having an affair." He filled his partner in on his visit to the Mendoza home.

"Then I remembered something. Do you remember our visit with the Tempe detective?"

"Oh, yeah, how could I forget her?" Sonny grinned.

"Do you remember she said she only saw him once, at a lecture Pete gave?" Sonny nodded. "Well, I remembered something about the conversation. It didn't hit me at the time, but she referred to him as Pete, and later she said he was a nice guy. Didn't you think that a little odd?" Nick asked.

"Uhh, I do now."

"Well, I went to see her. Carmen Cruz and Pete Mendoza were having an affair."

Sonny whistled. "Wow! Pete was banging that pretty young thing? Holy shit!"

"Yep. I promised Elena I would tell her if I found out anything, but she doesn't want the kids to know. Got it?"

"Got it! Were they going to counseling?"

"I asked Elena about that. She said no."

"So that blows our marriage counselor theory."

Just then the phone on Nick's desk rang. He looked at Sonny. "Uh . . . how are we supposed to answer it?"

"Why don't you try hello?" Sonny grinned.

Nick picked up the phone. "SIU, Lieutenant Greer speaking, how may I help you?"

"Good God, Greer! You have to take a breath to get all that out," said Deputy Chief Mannion. "This isn't Walmart."

"Okay, Bruce, how do you want us to answer it?"

"Uhm, let's see, you could say SIU, or a simple hello would suffice."

Sonny was laughing so hard he almost fell out of his chair. Unknown to Nick, when he reached for the phone, he had accidentally put it on speaker and his partner heard it all.

"Your sketches? The ones you asked for?" Mannion said.

"Yeah. Are they in?"

"Your cop in Florida didn't remember the male at all, and what he gave the sketch artist on the girl should come through your fax momentarily. The deputy in Pennsylvania should have something soon. Keep me posted." He hung up the phone.

About twenty seconds later, the phone rang again. Nick answered, "SIU, Lieutenant Greer."

"That's better." Bruce Mannion laughed and hung up the phone.

"Who was that?" Sonny asked.

"Wrong number," Nick answered.

The fax rang, and Sonny went and pulled the paper from the tray and studied it for a moment. "Shit!"

"Shit what?" Nick asked.

Sonny handed the fax to his partner. "The picture. It's shit. It could be any one. Talk about generic! Shit!"

Nick shook his head. "A bad memory, or a lousy sketch artist?"

"It's so bad, it has to be both. The girl looks like a guy. Fuck!"

"There's always the deputy in Pennsylvania. He's pretty sharp."

No sooner were the words spoken than the fax rang, and Sonny went over to it. He waited impatiently for the print to drop into the tray, then he grabbed it. He went to his desk and compared it with the one from Florida.

"How is that one?" Nick asked.

"Better, but—"

"But what?"

Sonny handed the picture to his partner. "See for yourself."

Nick Greer looked at the picture, then picked up the other one. He compared them and looked at Sonny. "Unbelievable! Other than the hair, they look like two different people. What do you make of it?"

"I think the cop in Florida is confused. Look at the features. The nose, the eyes look more masculine, don't you think?" He didn't wait for an answer. "I think he got a better look at the male than he thought and he has them confused. We may have them both here and not know it."

"Let's talk to Ted," Nick said.

Ted Zajak was the precinct sketch artist. His talent was known throughout Maricopa County and beyond. It was his detailed sketch that helped bring in the Baseline killer a few years ago. He came into the SIU and sat down with the two detectives. "Congratulations to you both. I heard about this new venture. The word around the department is give them whatever they ask for. You guys are becoming real celebrities, you know."

"Really?" Sonny said.

"Well, we won't be signing autographs quite yet," Nick said as he handed the Florida sketch to Ted. "Though it doesn't look like it, this is supposed to be a female."

Zajak looked at the sketch and said, "I don't think so; the features look more male. It could be female, or it could be a lousy sketch, but it looks male to me."

"Remember, this is extracted from a six-year memory. The cop who did this was a rookie, and he's no longer on the force. There were two people involved, a male and a female. I think he has them mixed up." He handed Ted the other picture. "We think this is the female. This one is a couple years older. It happened eight years ago, the other, six. Can you do anything with them?"

Ted looked at the picture and shook his head. "You guys are asking a lot. My name is Ted, not Leonardo, but I'll give it a shot." He took the sketches with him as he left the SIU.

Sonny asked, "What's next?"

"Two of our vics were from St. Michael's. I think I'm going to take a shot in the dark and talk with their pastor. Maybe he'll know if they knew each other."

"I didn't think you would ever want to go near that place again," Sonny stated.

Nick grunted. He remembered St. Michael's and the priest who was murdered there about a year ago.

Sonny googled St. Michael's, retrieved the phone number, and gave it to his partner. Nick dialed. "St. Michael's Church," came the answer on the other end.

"Yes, ma'am. My name is Lieutenant Nick Greer. I'm with the Phoenix Police Department. I would like to see your pastor, but I don't know his name."

"Oh, Father Frank is our pastor, but he is incapacitated."

"Uhh, incapacitated?"

"Yes, sir. Father Frank had a heart attack last weekend. He won't be back for a while. Father Brett is his associate. Today is his day off, but he'll be back tomorrow."

"Thank you, ma'am." He hung up the phone.

Sonny asked, "Do you want me to come along?"

"No, I got it. I'm going home. I'll see you tomorrow."

CHAPTER 30

The Shower

Nick got into his car and headed home. About halfway there, he decided to drop into Charlie's tavern and have a cold beer. He liked to talk with Charlie, but he wasn't there, so he had a draught and left. He went next door to the China Den where he picked up some takeout and went home.

He turned on the television. The news was partly over, but he heard the newscaster say: "We're telling it like it is." The scene changed to a reporter standing in front of the Phoenix Police Station holding a microphone. She said, "There is a serial killer on the loose in our city, and the police are clueless as to his identity. Are we safe in our own city?"

"Shit!" he said out loud and hit the up button on the remote. He found the Arizona Diamondbacks game, and stopped there. He thought he'd watch the game for a while and eat his dinner. He was about to open the bag containing his takeout when his cell phone rang. He looked at it and saw there was a text from Sue Kim. All it said was: *Hi.*

He texted back: *Hi U at the game?* He knew Sue Kim was an avid Diamondbacks fan and that she and her friend Carol had season tickets.

Uh, they R in LA

He looked at the television and texted back: *Oh right I just turned it on*

What R U doing?

Watching game eating moo goo, thinking of you. What R U doing?

Watching game eating PPJ

You don't like PPJ

I know

Where's Carol

Shower

She waiting 4 U?

Not funny!

You want some moo goo? Got plenty

K

I don't deliver

I know lol

Door unlocked

Nick put the food in the microwave. He would heat it up when Sue Kim arrived, but first he had just enough time to shower and change before she got there. He went into the bedroom, and stowed his Glock in the gun safe. Then he reached down to his ankle and removed the thirty-two that was strapped there. He put it next to the Glock, and he closed and locked the safe.

He began to undress when his cell phone rang. He hesitated on answering it. He thought it might be Sue Kim calling to say she wasn't coming after all. When he looked at the readout, he saw it was Cassie. His first thought was to ignore it, but he changed his mind. "Yes, Cassie. What do you want?"

It was Kasey. She was crying. She told him she was having trouble in school. It seems his middle daughter was being bullied. They talked a while, and he was able to calm her down. He told her to talk to her teacher or to her principal about it. She said she was afraid the kids would call her a snitch if she did that. "If I was there in Phoenix, they would leave me alone because my dad is a cop!"

He thought for a moment as his mind searched for the right words to send to his tongue. "I know, princess, but you're not here. Let me talk to your mother."

"Yes?" The voice on the other end was his ex-wife.

"Go to the school tomorrow. Talk with the principal."

"She doesn't—"

"Go to the school. Talk with the principal. Get it stopped! Put Kasey back on."

"Yes, Daddy," Kasey answered.

"Your mother is going to talk with your principal tomorrow. Everything will be all right, princess. I promise."

"Okay, Daddy."

"I love you," Nick said.

"I love you, too, Daddy." She seemed happier.

Nick finished undressing and headed for the shower. He needed to hurry. She would be here soon. He was glad he left the door unlocked.

He was just about to shut the water off when he heard the sound of the shower door sliding open. He had company. She came to him, and he took her into his arms. They were oblivious to the water as it cascaded over them. All of their attention was directed to each other.

CHAPTER 31

The Ninja Priest

Nick Greer pulled into St. Michael's parking lot, killed the engine, and got out of his Taurus. He heard the car's horn answer as he aimed the clicker and set the alarm. It was almost ten o'clock. He hoped Father Brett would be there.

As he entered the lobby, he was reminded of his last visit. The picture of their previous pastor had been replaced by the new one. He was older and had a kind look. The picture of Pope Benedict was still on the wall. It looks like they haven't gotten around to replacing it with the new guy yet, he thought.

"Can I help you, sir?" came a welcoming voice from behind a glassless window.

He held out his gold badge for her to see. "I'm Lieutenant Greer, Phoenix Police Department. I'd like to see Father Brett, please."

"Hold on, sir, I'll be right back," she said as she got up and disappeared through a side door.

A few seconds later, a young priest appeared and greeted Nick, "Father Brett Masters. It's nice to see you again, Lieutenant. Come on into my office and have a seat."

Nick remembered the young priest. He had interviewed him while working the case of the death of the previous St. Michael's pastor. As he sat down, he said, "Yes, Father Brett. I thought the name was familiar. I see you're not in Scottsdale anymore."

"Yes, I've been here for a few months. Shortly after Father Frank came here, Father Roman took ill, and I was transferred here on a temporary basis. When he passed away, the bishop made it permanent. It's a nice community. I like it here."

"You say Father Roman died? What happened?" Nick remembered the priest from his past dealings involving the previous pastor's death. He had been the associate pastor at that time. Nick liked him.

"He had liver cancer. When the doctors opened him up, they said he was too far gone. There was nothing they could do. He left the diocese and went back to his home in North Carolina, I think. It was about a month later when we got the news he had passed."

"He was a nice guy," Nick stated.

"You knew him?"

"I met him a couple of times," Nick responded.

"May I ask if you are Catholic?"

"I used to be, but that's not why I'm here. I'm checking into a couple of deaths. You lost two parishioners recently. Both were victims of, shall we say, unnatural deaths."

"Yes, Mr. Perrotta and Mr. Marquez. They both were good men, I understand. I was with Marcella Saturday. She's having a rough time. Mrs. Perrotta hasn't returned my calls. I have left several messages. I'm concerned about services. I must go see her."

"Actually, Father, I'm investigating their deaths, and that of others."

"Others?" He looked surprised. "You know, I've seen on the news that there may be a serial killer. Is that true? Is that why you're here?" The priest's eyes widened.

"The news isn't always accurate, Father, but I was wondering if you could answer a couple of questions."

"I confess!" He leaned forward, held his hands out, and grinned. "Take me in."

"Funny, Father, but be careful. That kind of thing can get you in trouble, even if you are a priest."

His demeanor became serious. "I'm sorry, Lieutenant. I guess that wasn't as funny as I thought. How can I help you?"

"If I were you, I'd stay away from airport terminals. The TSA would not be as understanding as I."

"Your point is well taken, Lieutenant. Again, my apologies."

"I'm looking for anything the two victims might have had in common," the detective said. "Are there any places they may have gone together, perhaps a retreat, a seminar, or maybe even a meeting? I'd be interested in knowing if they knew each other."

"Let me look and see if they shared any ministries." The priest pulled his computer keyboard in front of him and began to type. After a few keystrokes, he looked at his visitor and said, "There's nothing I can find in here. Mr. Marquez was a Eucharistic minister. It appears Mr. Perrotta was an usher at one time, but he is not on any ministry roster at the present."

"How about a women's group? All churches have a women's group. Perhaps the ladies may have met there?"

"Our records do not show Mrs. Perrotta, only Richard."

"How about the Knights of Columbus?" Nick asked. "Maybe they were—"

"Our Knights have been disbanded. The previous pastor didn't want them around. Father Frank was talking about resurrecting them until he took sick."

"Boy, it sounds like St. Michael's has had its share of tragedy," the detective commented.

"It keeps me busy, that's for sure," Father Brett answered.

Nick looked around the priest's office. The oak desk was aged, but functional. A bookshelf to the left was about three-quarters full, and neat. He noticed the diploma on the wall. The priest had graduated from St. Mary's School of Divinity. As his eyes scanned the room, they caught sight of something he thought rather unusual. "Father, is that really a Samurai sword on the wall there?" He pointed to a scabbard with the handle sticking out of it.

"Uhh, it's actually a ninja dragon sword. It's very old."

Nick looked at the priest with questioning eyes.

"Ahhh, yes. You're wondering why a priest would have such a weapon on his wall, I'll bet."

Nick nodded. "It does seem a little out of place."

The priest chuckled. "I have been a fan of Asian arts and warfare for most of my life. A parishioner, who knew I am a collector, gave it to me." He smiled as he continued, "I like to tell people it was the sword of an angel. I'm also a fourth-degree black belt and a karate instructor."

"Whoa, Nellie!" Nick exclaimed. "A fighting priest."

"Oh, I don't consider myself a fighter. It's the discipline and the concentration that it demands that's important. I began teaching to help some at-risk kids. You'd be surprised what something like that can do to keep them off the streets, especially when they see a priest break blocks of wood. They want to learn how to do it, so we make an agreement: I teach them, they go to church and to youth group."

"That sounds like a form of bribery. Does it work?"

"Call it what you will. It works for some, and for some, it doesn't. I feel blessed for the ones for whom it works. I pray for the others."

"An interesting approach," the detective said. "You said you are a collector. What do you collect?"

"Oh, various things, throwing stars and knives, nunchucks, chains, you know, that kind of stuff. I have a set of kamas that is believed to have been owned by a real ninja."

"Where do you get all that stuff?"

"Oh, the Internet, mostly, though sometimes people give them to me. And you'd be surprised what you can find at a yard or estate sale."

Nick patted the Glock on his side and said, "I prefer these. You know what they say, you can't outrun a bullet."

The priest shook his head. "I don't do guns. I don't like them. There's no art or discipline there. I do believe in self-defense. You're right, Lieutenant, you can't outrun a bullet. All you can do is hide from it. I believe we should face our fears, not run from them. I teach martial arts as a self-defense mechanism, not as an attack aid. Guns attack. Karate defends. Karate may break a bone at times, but it seldom kills. Can you say that about guns?" Before Nick could answer, the priest said, "Have you ever killed anyone with your gun, Lieutenant?"

Nick stood up, shook the priest's hand, and said, "Thank you, Father. I appreciate the information."

The priest looked at his visitor and said, "Would you like to pray with me before you leave, Lieutenant?'

Nick was caught off guard, and it showed. "Uhhh, thank you, Father. Maybe next time."

As the detective left the priest's office he heard: "I'll pray for you, that you never have to use your gun, if that's all right."

Nick Greer didn't answer. He left the building, got back into his car, and headed back to the SIU.

CHAPTER 32

The Sketch

Lieutenant Nick Greer walked into the SIU and saw his partner, Sonny Madison sitting at his desk, and with him was Ted Zajak, the sketch artist. "We've been waiting for you," said Sonny. "How was your visit to your favorite church?"

"Interesting. I met a Ninja."

"Huh? A real one?" Zajak asked.

"Yeah, and guess what? He wore a collar."

"A priest? A Ninja priest? You gotta be kidding!" Sonny exclaimed.

"Not exactly," said Nick. "Do you remember the young priest that was at St. John's in Scottsdale last year? Father Brett Masters?"

Sonny thought back to the case of the murdered priest they had solved last year. "Yeah, I never met him, but I remember the name."

"Well, he's at St. Michael's now. It appears Father Brett is a martial arts instructor, and he uses that to minister to kids. You know, kids at risk."

Ted said, "Yeah, I've seen these guys on television. They come out on the stage, do some karate stuff, break a couple of boards or blocks, then they pick up a Bible and start preaching. It's actually kind of neat."

"Yeah," Nick said. "I've seen that, too, but this guy is cunning. He agrees to teach the kids self-defense, if they agree to go to church and stuff." He told them about his visit to St. Michael's and the priest's fascination for Japanese weapons.

"Wow!" Sonny said. "He's got my respect."

"Hmm." Nick chuckled. "Hearing you say that made it worth the trip, even though I got jack out of it."

The detective noticed a picture lying on Sonny's desk. "What do we have here?"

Zajak said, in a preacher sort of mode, "Ask and ye shall receive, says the Lord and Ted Zajak." He looked back and forth at the detectives who were looking at him strangely. He smiled and said, "I thought that might be appropriate since you just came from church, you know."

Nick looked at him, then at Sonny, shook his head, and said, "Sonny's rubbing off on you." He picked up the sketch and looked at it. "That's better, I guess. At least it looks like a female." He looked at his partner. "What do you think, Sonny?"

Sonny Madison shook his head. "They look a lot alike. I don't know if we have one or two."

Nick Greer stroked his bushy mustache with his thumb and forefinger as he thought about what his partner had said. "What if there are two of them and what if they're related?"

"You mean like brother and sister?" Madison asked. "That would explain the resemblance."

"I don't know. Let's not rule it out," Nick stated. "It could just be the way the cop remembered it after six years; and yet, they could be related."

The lieutenant thanked Ted for his work, and the artist left the SIU.

Nick sat down, put his elbows on his desk, put his head in his hands, exhaled heavily, and said, "This sucks!"

"Yeah, I know," said Sonny. "We owe Pete better than this. We've been working this case for over two weeks and what do we have? Nothing!"

"We have more than nothing, partner," Nick said.

"Yeah, but we can't tell Elena we have anyone locked up."

"We will, buddy. We will."

Sonny changed the subject. "Any headway in your love life?"

Nick smiled. "She came over last night."

Sonny looked at his friend's head from side to side like he was looking for something. "What are you looking for?" Nick asked.

"Bruises. I don't see any bruises on you." Sonny grinned.

Nick laughed. "Yeah, she kind of surprised me. She stayed." What he didn't tell his friend was when he woke up, Sue Kim was gone, and she hadn't returned his calls this morning.

CHAPTER 33

Discovery

"Hey, Nick, check this out!" Sonny said.

Nick Greer got up and walked over to his partner's desk. "Whatcha got?"

"Take a look at this guy! He fits our profile. He's originally from Pennsylvania. Wow, he's an Iraq vet, uhh, two tours, and he was stationed at Walter Reed in Bethesda, Maryland. That's not far from Baltimore. His name is Alex Murray."

"Walter Reed. Isn't that where they send soldiers who get wounded? He must have gotten hurt."

Sonny shook his head. "Huh-uh. I don't think so. It says here he was a corpsman, a medic. And from what I can see, he was at Reed before he went on his second tour."

"Where at in Pennsylvania?"

"Uhhh, it says, New Brighton, and that's innnnn, Beaver County!" Sonny looked up at his partner. "Isn't that where your guy was found?"

"Yep, it sure is. Where was he when each murder occurred?" Nick asked.

Sonny typed and said, "It looks like he was still in Pennsylvania eight years ago, aaaaand, yep, he was in Bethesda when the Baltimore vic was killed." He looked at his partner. "He fits the profile, age, gender, and he was near enough at the time of all the killings."

"A medic would certainly know anatomy," Nick said. "When did he come to Phoenix?"

"Uhhhh," Sonny said as he typed some more. He picked up one of the files, looked inside, then back to the computer. "About six weeks before the Tempe vic was fished out of the lake."

"Where does he work out of? Where is his office?" Nick asked.

"It looks like he's independent. I think he works out of his home. The address is—let's see." The room echoed the sound of fingers stroking computer keys. "According to the Maricopa County assessor's website, the address on file is owned by a Marcia Marie Meyers, so he must rent it."

"Put her into the system. See what you get," said Nick.

"I'm on it," Sonny said, as his fingers swiftly maneuvered over the keyboard. "She's a widow. And guess what her maiden name was?"

"Tell me it was Ayers."

"No," Sonny answered. "Murray. It looks like she's his sister."

"How did her husband die?" Nick asked.

Sonny searched, and after a few minutes said, "Bryson Meyers was a long-haul trucker. His truck ran off the road just outside of Indianapolis three years ago. A kid was texting while driving and crossed into his lane. He swerved and went through a guardrail and into a ravine. The truck caught fire. He must have been thrown, because his body was found in a small river at the bottom of the ravine."

"Can you get their pictures?"

Sonny checked the motor vehicle records, pulled their driver's licenses, and pushed print.

Nick pulled two pages from the printer and compared the pictures on them with the sketches. He handed them to his partner. "What do you think?"

Sonny Madison compared them, shook his head, and sighed. "I don't know, Nick. Maybe, maybe not. These composites are pretty shaky."

"What do you say we go for a ride?" Nick said.

Sonny shut down his computer, and Nick asked, "You'll need to get back in that thing, won't you?"

"Yeah."

"How are you going to do that without your teenage friend?"

Sonny looked at his partner and smiled. "Oh, you of so little faith." He held up a sheet of paper with handwritten notes on it. "Behold, the road map through cyberspace."

* * *

It was about a thirty-minute drive from the station. They turned right from Beardsley Road onto Pontiac Drive. The house was on the corner in a nice area of tract homes in the city of Peoria. The detectives left their vehicle and rang the doorbell. A few moments later, a man opened the door. His face matched the picture on the driver's license Sonny had pulled from the MVD.

"Alex Murray?" Sonny asked.

"Who wants to know?" he answered.

Sonny pointed to the badge hanging from his belt and said, "I'm Sergeant Madison, and this is my partner, Lieutenant Greer. We're from the Phoenix Police Department. We'd like to ask you a few questions, if you don't mind."

"About what?"

"Sir, would you mind if we came in?" Sonny asked. "It's kind of private." He nodded his head toward the neighbor across the street, who had been trimming bushes in his front yard when the two detectives pulled up. The neighbor had stopped his work and was now looking at them. It was obvious they were police officers as each wore a blue shirt with the Phoenix police insignia. If that weren't enough, the metal handcuffs, the shiny badges, and the nine-millimeter Glocks that hung from their belts would surely have done the trick.

Murray looked across the street at his neighbor, and back to Sonny. "Yeah, I guess it's okay. Come on in." He stood back as the two detectives walked into the house. "Come into my office." He pointed to a set of double doors directly to the right of the entrance. "Have a seat, gentlemen. Would you like a glass of water?"

"No, thank you, Mr. Murray," Nick said, as he and Sonny sat down.

"What can I help you with?" Murray asked.

The office was professional looking. Directly behind their host, was a certificate indicating a degree in social work from the University of Pittsburgh. On the left wall hung three pictures of Alex Murray and various soldiers, all dressed in camouflage.

"I can't help but notice the pictures. Where were they taken?" Nick asked.

"Iraq. Two tours."

"Thank you for your service," Nick replied. "What did you do over there?"

"I was a medic."

"I'll bet you saw some gruesome stuff," Nick said.

"Yeah, I did, but I doubt that's why you're here."

"Mr. Murray, we understand you are a counselor. Is that correct?" Nick asked.

"Yes, sir. Family counseling, mostly," he answered. "I like to work with veterans with Post Traumatic Stress Disorders. If you're here about a patient, I'm sure you are aware that my communications with my patients are confidential. I cannot divulge any information."

"Yes, we understand," Nick responded. "We were wondering if you do any marriage counseling."

"Oh, yes. Especially when the PTSD affects the marriage."

"Do you just do marriage counseling for those with PTSD, or do you do it for others as well?" Nick probed.

"I mostly work through the Catholic Social Services in Phoenix. Whomever they refer me to, I try to help. Why do you ask?"

Nick didn't answer. He continued on his planned track. "Do you mind if we show you some pictures?"

"Uh, I guess not."

Sonny reached into a manila envelope and pulled out a picture of the Pennsylvania victim and set it on the desk in front of the counselor. "Mr. Murray, do you recognize this man?"

Murray looked at the picture and shook his head. "No, sir, I can't say that I do. Should I?"

Sonny didn't answer as he laid the photo of the Baltimore victim next to the other one. "How about this one?"

Again, the counselor shook his head. "No, sir. I've never seen him before. What's this all about, anyway?"

"Please bear with us, sir," Sonny said. He showed Alex Murray each of the other four pictures and received the same negative response.

Nick took over. "Mr. Murray, you're from Pennsylvania, I take it?"

"Yes."

"Uh, New Brighton. That's in Beaver County, is that correct?"

Alex Murray leaned forward and looked into the detective's face. "Will you please tell me what's going on here? You seem to know a lot about me. How do you know where I'm from? What do you really want with me? Why are you really here?"

Nick held his composure and continued, "You were in Baltimore, Maryland, for a while about six years ago. Is that correct?"

"Yes, I was working at Walter Reed. Look, Detectives, I've tried to be cordial to you. But I demand to know why you are here, why you are asking me these questions, and why did you show me those pictures?"

The pictures Sonny had shown him were driver's license photos. Nick reached into another envelope and removed another set of pictures, ones of the dead faces of each victim. The first set was lined up neatly in a row across the counselor's desk. Nick purposely placed each of his photos on the desk directly above the corresponding ones. Murray looked back and forth at them, and then at the lieutenant, who said, "They're all dead!"

Murray straightened up and raised his voice slightly. "And just what does that have to do with me?"

Sonny leaned forward. "Well, sir, it's like this. My partner and I here"—he looked at Nick and then back to Murray—"we were doing some research on a case, and we discovered that you lived in the area at the time when each of these murders was committed. You were in Beaver County, Pennsylvania, here, were you not?" He pointed to the first picture. "You were in the Baltimore area here, were you not?" He pointed to the second picture. "And, these?" He pointed back and forth across the remaining pictures, and looked at the man across the desk as he continued, "I believe they all occurred since your arrival here in Phoenix. We thought that was a little, let's say, coincidental, so we thought we would drop by and ask you if you could explain it."

Murray stood up as the anger raged through him like a volcano getting ready to spew its lava. "Do you have a warrant?" He didn't wait for an answer. "Get the hell out of this house, now!"

Sonny grabbed the pictures and both detectives rose from their seats and headed for the door. They knew the law. They had no warrant and no real cause. The interview was over. As they left, they heard him yell, "If you ever come back here again, you better have a fucking warrant and a SWAT team." He slammed the door behind them.

The two detectives got into Nick's Taurus. As they drove away, a car turned into the Murray driveway. The automatic garage door opened, and the car took its place inside the garage. Nick made a U-turn, and as they drove past the house, a female got out of the car and quickly disappeared as the garage door closed.

Nick asked Sonny, "Did you see her?"

"I sure did."

"What do you think?"

"She seems to fit the description."

"Did you get the plates?"

"Of course!" Sonny answered. "What's next?"

"Let's see what we can find on the sister."

CHAPTER 34

The Shrink

Sonny ran a full background check on Marcia Marie Murray and Marcia Marie Meyers. When he was finished, he said, "Hey, Gumby, take a look at this."

Nick walked over to his partner's desk. "It says Murray's sister graduated from Monaca High School, which is in Beaver County, Pennsylvania, and she went to Slippery Rock University in Butler County, Pennsylvania. Uh, she graduated with honors."

Nick looked at Sonny. "Slippery Rock? Really? What the hell is that?"

"That's what it says," Sonny answered. "She holds a master's degree in education. Her height and weight match the descriptions of both the Pennsylvania victim's wife and the boater in Baltimore."

"Yeah, and half the women I know. We need more than that," Nick commented. "Can you put her close enough to any of the murders? Perhaps we can connect her and her brother in some way."

"Let's see, she was enrolled in the college when the Pennsylvania vic was found. It looks like this Slippery Rock place is only about an hour's drive from her home, so that's a possibility."

"What about Baltimore?"

Sonny made a few more keystrokes. "I don't see where she was ever there, but it's only a five-hour drive from Pittsburgh to Baltimore. She could have driven there, and we wouldn't know it."

"Where is she teaching?"

"She's not," Sonny said. "She's selling real estate."

"Really?" Nick looked at the screen as if in disbelief.

"Yeah, she's a broker. Marcia Meyers Realty. You know, Perrotta was a realtor. He owned his own company, too. Maybe we can find a connection there. Maybe they sold a house together or something. Who knows, maybe they were banging each other. You know what Perrotta's wife said. Hell, maybe she had him whacked."

"Finding a connection won't be easy to do, but check it out," said Nick. "By the way, did you know the DNA on the Marquez carpet was not from our vic?"

"I didn't see the report," said Sonny.

"It was female, and not the wife or daughter. Not family."

"Are you sure?"

"Yeah. Sue Kim did it herself."

"Are you thinking what I'm thinking?" asked Sonny.

"Yeah, we need to get a DNA sample from Marcia Meyers."

"Uhhh, that ain't gonna to be easy," Sonny replied. "Especially after she talks with her brother. And besides, I don't know if we have enough for a warrant. Perhaps we should talk with Bruce."

"Let's talk with Missy, first. I'd like to get her take on all of this."

* * *

Melissa Webster was the department psychologist. Her office was three doors down from the SIU. She looked up and smiled when she saw the two detectives enter through the open door. "Well, Detectives Greer and Madison. To what do I owe the honor of a visit from my new neighbors? Are you here for your psych evals?"

"Yeah, sort of," Sonny said. "You see, I used to think that everyone in the world was nuts except me and Nick here. But lately, I've been having my doubts about him. We thought maybe you could help." He grinned.

She laughed. "I'm sure it's the other way around, Detective Madison, but what really causes our new SIU detectives to grace my office with their presence? Congratulations, by the way. We've been working on this for several months. I'm pleased it is finally in place."

"You were involved in the SIU set up?" Sonny asked.

"Oh, yes. You don't think the chief picked your names out of a hat, do you? We wanted a team whose combined abilities exceeded the sum total of their individual abilities added together."

The two detectives looked at each other, puzzled, then looked back at Missy.

"In other words, we wanted a good team, one whose talents and abilities complement each other."

"And he chose us?" Sonny grinned. "Maybe he should be in here talking with you."

"Cute, Detective," she answered. "But I'm sure, you're not here to pass the time. What can I do for you?"

"As you know, we're working on Pete Mendoza's case. We need some help, you know, shrink stuff." Sonny said.

She shook her head and smiled. "Yes, our serial killer. What would you like to know?"

Nick handed her the files. He and Sonny sat in silence as she read through them. After several minutes she looked up and asked, "What else can you tell me that isn't in here?"

Nick and Sonny shared with her everything they knew. They described their trips to the east and every detail they could think of.

Missy thought for a moment, then said, "The signature indicates the same killer or killers in each case. The wounds, the removal of the fingers, the water, and the drugs can't all be coincidental. Of course, you already know that. I think you may be right about it being a pair."

The two detectives looked at each other and nodded. Missy continued, "I think what we have here is a pair of sick minds that complete each other." She looked back and forth between her two guests and smiled. "Kind of like you two."

"Touché," said Sonny. "Good call."

"I have my moments," Missy answered. She continued with the evaluation, "There's a strong bond between these two, and it's that bond that keeps them together, and it's that bond that also justifies their actions. When these two minds collide, they're unstoppable. It's like a perfect storm."

"Do you agree with our theory that they're related?" Nick asked.

"There is a strong loyalty between them. Though it's highly unusual." She nodded. "I wouldn't rule out the possibility they are related."

"Remember the Hillside Strangler?" Sonny added. "You know, Bianchi and Buono were cousins."

"Point well taken, Detective," Melissa answered.

"Yeah, I have my moments, too." Sonny grinned.

"Anything else?" Nick asked.

"Yes," she answered. "A relationship like this doesn't just happen. Something in one, or both of their pasts, has triggered their psychoses. Perhaps one, or both of them, experienced a traumatic loss. Could have been a sibling, a spouse, or maybe even a parent."

Both detectives nodded. "Anything else?" asked Nick.

"That's all I can think of for now," Missy said. "But if I come up with anything else, I'll let you know. By the way, how is Elena Mendoza? I've tried to reach out to her, but she hasn't returned any of my calls."

"I don't know," Nick answered. "I spoke with her yesterday. She seems to emit more anger than grief. That worries me."

"People handle their grief in different ways," the psychologist said. "Anger is a part of the process. Though it is unusual to surface this early, it is not unheard of. Is there any news on funeral planning?"

"Nothing yet."

"If you see Elena, please ask her to call me," Missy said.

"Will do," Nick answered, as the two detectives left her office.

* * *

Tricia was not at her desk, so the two detectives went into their boss's office. Deputy Chief Bruce Mannion greeted them: "Well, Detectives Greer and Madison. You're delivering good news, I hope."

Nick got right to the point. "I need a warrant, Chief."

"So, get it. You don't need my permission to get a warrant. What's it for, anyway?"

"A DNA swab," Nick answered. He told Chief Mannion about his and Sonny's visit to Alex Murray and about their conversation with Melissa Webster.

"So you don't think she'll submit willingly?"

"Not after she talks with her brother," Nick answered. "Especially if they're the perps."

"What makes you think a judge will see enough cause to sign a warrant?"

"Uhh," Nick said, pointing to the deputy chief's nameplate, "that." He then held up his lieutenant's badge and pointed to it. "Yours trumps mine."

"Uhh, I'll need more than my title. I need to convince a judge."

Sonny spoke, "Look, the brother was a medic. He did two tours in Iraq. He knows anatomy, and he's seen plenty of blood and guts. We can place them in the areas where each murder occurred, at least him. She's the brains, I think, and he's the brawn."

"That's why we need the warrant," Nick said. "We want to compare her DNA with the DNA from the Marquez home. If it matches, we got 'em."

"And if I strike out with the judge, what's your plan B?" Mannion asked.

Nick looked at Sonny, who shrugged and said, "Uhh, we're working on that, Chief. Aren't we, Nick?" He looked at his partner.

"Uhh, yeah, we are now," Nick answered.

Mannion shook his head and chuckled. "I'll go see Judge Gallo. You two start working on plan B, 'cause I think we're going to need it." He got up and left his two detectives sitting there.

Sonny looked at Nick. "I'm hungry. You want to get something?"

"You go ahead. I have an idea."

Nick stood up and Sonny asked, "Where are you going?"

"I'm going to go talk to plan B."

* * *

Sue Kim was working in the lab when he walked in. "What are you doing up here?" she asked.

"You didn't return my calls."

"I know."

"May I ask why?" He reached for her hand, but she pulled it away.

"I have to work things out in my head."

"I thought we worked things out pretty well last night," he said.

She giggled, and her face turned red. "Yeah, I guess we sort of did." She looked at him. He could read the seriousness in her eyes. "I need some more time, Nick. I'm not saying no, but I need time."

"I understand." He touched her hand. This time she didn't pull it away. "But I do need your help with something else."

"What?"

He explained his plan to her.

* * *

When he returned to the SIU, Sonny was sitting with his elbows on his desk and his head in his hands. There was a half-eaten sandwich lying next to him. "What's the matter, Sonny?" Nick asked. "You look down."

"The chief struck out with the judge. He wants more for cause. I'm trying to figure out what to do next."

"Sonny, do you think she saw either one of us?"

"Who?"

"Marcia Meyers. When we drove by, do you think she saw our faces?"

Sonny thought for a moment as he ran the morning's scene through his mind. "I don't think so. Her back was mostly toward us, and it was only a couple of seconds until the garage door closed. Why do you ask?"

"Plan B may depend on it."

Sonny sat up straight. "Uhh, you got a plan B?"

"Yeah, I think so."

Sonny's eyes widened. "Uh, do you want to share it with your devoted partner?"

"I'll let you know." Nick locked the drawers in his desk and walked out the door.

"Where are you going?" Sonny called to him.

"I'm going home," Nick said. "See you tomorrow."

CHAPTER 35

Plan B

It was exactly seven o'clock Tuesday evening when the doorbell rang. She was right on time.

At first, Nick thought he and Sue Kim would pose as a couple looking to sell the townhouse. But then he realized, if the realtor was any good at her job, she would research the unit first and his name would come up as the owner. Just in case her brother had mentioned Nick's name to her, he decided to stay out of sight, though he was worried about Sue Kim handling this alone.

Using the phone number from the website, Sue Kim had phoned the Marcia Meyers Real Estate company and secured an appointment to discuss purchasing a condo. She had explained that her job required a lot of travel, and she would only have time to see the realtor this evening.

Nick had parked his Taurus at the far end of the townhouse complex, well out of sight from his unit. He was worried. He wanted to have Sue Kim wired in case something went wrong, but she refused.

"All I'm going to do is ask her to find me a house," she had told him. "I'm not going to try for a confession."

They agreed on a signal. He had a good view of the front window from where he would be watching. Should there be a problem, she would open and close the mini-blind.

Sue Kim answered the door and greeted her visitor, "Ms. Meyers?"

"Yes, ma'am. Marcia Meyers. You must be Miss Lee." She reached her hand out and Sue Kim shook it.

"Come on in," Sue Kim said as she pointed to the living room. "Please have a seat."

Marcia sat on the living room sofa. Sue Kim sat next to her. The realtor handed her hostess a business card, and said, "Thank you for calling me. If I may ask, how did you know about me, anyway?"

"The Internet," she answered. "I googled realtors and my zip code. Wow! Do you know how many there are?"

She smiled. "There are a bunch. Thank you. If I may ask, why you chose me over all those others."

"I chose you because I saw it was run by a female." Sue Kim smiled. "I know how hard it is to compete sometimes, so I try to patronize females in business when I can." She looked at her guest. "Oh, please, forgive me. Would you like something to drink? I just made some tea. I also have soda and water, if you would like."

"A glass of tea would be nice," Marcia answered.

"I'll be right back." Sue Kim returned with a tray containing two glasses of iced tea, a bowl of sliced lemons, two spoons, and some sugar packets. She set the tray on the table in front of them. "Is sugar all right? I'm out of sweetener."

"This is fine, thank you," the realtor said as she squeezed a lemon, dropped it into the glass, opened a sugar packet, and stirred it with the spoon into her drink. She took a deep drink and said, "Thank you, Miss Lee. Very fine. Now, you said you were looking for a townhouse. I assume you are renting this one?"

"No, actually it belongs to a friend of mine. I've been staying with him, but it's not working out, so I want to get my own place. I would like a townhouse or condo because I travel a lot, and I don't like yard work."

"Where would you like to be? What part of town?"

"Central, I guess."

"Do you have a price range?" Marcia asked.

"I'd like to keep it around a hundred thousand, maybe one-fifty if I have to. I want a nice area. Three bedrooms, if possible, and two baths."

"How about a down payment? How much do you have to work with?" the realtor asked.

"Oh, thirty to forty thousand, I guess."

"How is your credit?"

"Fine. Excellent, actually," Sue Kim answered. "I can pay cash if I need to. There's no problem there."

"What is your time frame? How soon would you like to move?"

Sue Kim smiled. "Uhh, yesterday would work."

Just then her cell phone rang. She saw the caller ID read: Nick. "Hello," she answered.

"Is everything okay there?"

"Yes," she answered. "I remember. I'll be there in a bit. I'm almost finished here. No problem."

He hung up the phone. As long as she said no problem, he was okay.

She looked at her guest. "I'm sorry. I have to run. If you can figure out how to add a couple of more hours into the day, I'll pay extra."

Marcia smiled, took another sip of tea, and said, "Thank you, ma'am. I'll check the MLS tomorrow and see what I can find. I'll call you with the results."

"I'll be waiting for your call."

Marcia Meyers handed Sue Kim another one of her cards and left. As soon as the door closed, Sue Kim went into the bedroom where she had hidden her forensics case. She prepared the glass, the utensils, and Marcia's business card for processing.

Nick impatiently waited until Marcia Meyers was out of sight, then he hurried into the townhouse. Sue Kim was closing her black case as he came through the door. "Is everything okay?" he asked.

"She seems like a nice lady. It would be hard to believe she could be a serial killer." She stood up and started for the door, but Nick reached out, pulled her to him, and kissed her. She held the forensics case in one hand and wrapped the other arm around his neck as she returned his kiss. Then she let go of him and started for the door.

"You can stay, you know," he said.

"Yeah, I know," she answered as she opened the door, closed it behind her, and left him standing there alone in his townhouse.

CHAPTER 36

The Results

It was mid-morning and Sonny Madison was nowhere to be seen. Nick had left a message on his voice mail and he texted him two times. But there had been no answer. He wanted to tell his partner about what happened before he reported to Chief Mannion. He looked at his watch: 10:10. He figured he had better report so he went to the deputy chief's office and told him what had transpired the night before. Chief Mannion said he was somewhat concerned about the way they obtained the DNA, but he would defer judgment until they received the results. If the tests were positive, he would deal with it. If they were negative, it wouldn't matter.

"Oh, by the way, we had a visit from the feds after you left yesterday," Mannion said.

"What did they want?" Nick asked.

"They wanted to know where we were on the case."

Nick looked at his boss. "And?"

"I told them what they already knew. You went to Pennsylvania, and Sonny went to Baltimore. I told them about Sonny's trip to Philly, and my phone call to the church there, and the bogus phone number. I acted surprised when they said they already knew about it. I said I thought we were supposed to share information. One of them answered, 'That's why we're here.' "

"It sounds like they want us to share our info with them, but it's a one-way street. It's a good thing Sonny wasn't here," Nick said. "So they know nothing about Murray or Meyers?"

"I don't think so. If they do, they're keeping it to themselves. Sergeant Madison was in the SIU when they came. It was a little before five. Thank God he didn't see them. I'd still be pulling the chief's teeth marks out of my ass."

"Speaking of Sonny, have you heard from him this morning?" Nick asked.

"No, I thought he was in the SIU."

"I haven't seen him. Oh, well, he'll show up." Nick left his boss's office and headed back to the SIU. As he was about to sit down, his cell phone rang. It was a text from Sue Kim: *The results are in.* That was quick, he thought, as he headed for the crime lab.

* * *

Sue Kim was looking at some papers when he walked into the crime lab. "Whatcha got for me?" The anticipation on his face reminded her of a little kid waiting to open a birthday present.

She shook her head as she handed him the results of the DNA test. The anticipated joy changed to disappointment as the detective read them over. "Shit! I thought for sure it was them. It's text book. They fit the profile perfectly."

"It still could be them," she stated. "Just because there's not a DNA match doesn't prove her innocent. It could be someone else's blood. Maybe he had a visitor."

He looked at Sue Kim. "Are you sure? Maybe there's something wrong with the equipment." He didn't ask her if there could've been something she missed. He knew better than to go down that road.

She shook her head. "I checked it twice. I'm really sorry, baby, but the blood from the Marquez home is definitely not a match to Marcia Meyers. Personally, I don't think she's our killer; she's too nice."

He shook his head and turned to leave. "I'm free for lunch," she said. "I mean, if you wanna."

He smiled. "Sure, I'll call you later." He left the crime lab. She called me baby, he thought. Things are looking up.

* * *

On his way back to the SIU, Nick dropped into the deputy chief's office. Tricia was at her desk. "Is he in?"

She said, "He'll be back shortly. You can wait in his office, if you want."

"No, thanks. Would you give him a message for me, please?"

"You don't look very happy, Lieutenant. Is there anything I can do?"

Nick shook his head. "Just tell him the test was negative. He'll know what I mean." He turned and left the office.

* * *

Marcella Marquez answered the door and invited the detective in. They sat in the living room. "How can I help you, Lieutenant? Please tell me you're here because you have caught my husband's killer." Her red and baggy eyes bore evidence of hours of sleepless crying.

"Mrs. Marquez, I wish that was the reason I came, but we're still working on it. I have a couple of questions for you, if you don't mind."

"Go ahead, Lieutenant. By the way, may I offer you something to drink?"

"No, thank you, ma'am. I'll only be here a few minutes."

Nick carefully chose his words as he continued, "As you know, we removed a piece of your patio carpet, because it contained blood droppings, fresh ones. We thought, and I still do, that it belonged to one of the people who was here that night. The problem is, we ran it through the DNA database and couldn't find a match. Do you remember anyone cutting themselves, or do you have any idea where the blood might've come from? It doesn't match the samples we have from you or your daughter, so we know it's not a family member."

She shook her head. "No, Lieutenant, I have no idea. It wasn't there the morning of the . . ."—she hesitated—". . . the morning it happened. I vacuumed the patio floor that morning, I would have noticed it, I'm sure."

Nick stood up and said, "Thank you, ma'am. I'll see myself out."

As he was about to open the door, he heard her say, "You said one of them? Do you think there was more than one?"

"Uh, what do you mean?" His back was to her as he looked out through the glass in the door.

"You said it belonged to one of the people who was here that night. Does that mean you think there were more than one?"

Nick didn't want it to get out that he thought the killers were a team, so he turned to her and said carefully, "We don't know. Anything is possible. We have to consider any and all possibilities. I guess that was a poor choice of words on my part. Thank you again." The detective turned, and left the Marquez residence, hoping his words would suffice.

CHAPTER 37

Plan B.1

Sonny Madison was at his desk when Nick Greer finally returned to the SIU. "Well, good afternoon, Sergeant Madison. I'm glad to see you could make it in today. Did you have a nice vacation?"

Sonny looked at his partner and grinned. "Be careful, Lieutenant Greer. You may be eating your words."

"I sent you two texts. How come you didn't answer?" Nick asked.

Sonny pointed to the cell phone on his desk. "I left it here. The battery died. It's charging. Tell me, how did plan B go?"

"Uh, good news and bad news. The good news, it went off without a hitch. Sue Kim did a good job and got her DNA. The bad news, it wasn't a match to the Marquez place. It doesn't look like she's our perp."

"What was plan B, anyway, and what happened?"

Nick explained to his partner the events of the previous evening.

"You know, Nick, that was really a good idea." Remembering the words of Alex Murray as they left his home, he added, "At least we didn't have to go back there with a SWAT team for nothing."

Sonny got up and walked over to the whiteboard, bent down, and picked up a roll of paper towels from the floor. He ripped off a sheet, and erased Murray and Meyer's names. He stood back, looked at the board, and said, "Okay, now. Let's see, what does that leave us? Oh, yes, only two suspects left. Jack and shit!"

Nick shook his head and sat at his desk. He put his elbows on the desk, cradled his head in his hands, and said, "Fuuuuck!"

Sonny looked over to his partner. "Why so sad, Gumby-won? Never underestimate the power of the force," he said in a Darth Vader tone of voice. "Or the ingenuity of your partner. Things may not be as bad as you think."

Nick looked up and over to Sonny, who said, "While you and Sue Kim were involved in your covert operation, I decided to try something else, you know, just in case. Let's call it plan B point one! I figured if you two hit pay dirt, maybe I could find something to help back it up. If you struck out, maybe I would get lucky."

"Annnnd?"

He looked at Nick and grinned as only Sonny Madison can. "Stand by to be impressed!"

"Go ahead," Nick said. "Impress the shit out of me. I could use it right now."

"You remember when we talked with Missy yesterday?" Sonny didn't wait for an answer. "Something she said kept eating at me, so I worked all night here, trying to figure it out."

"All night?" Nick said. "You were here all night?"

"Well, not all night," Sonny replied. "It was a little past midnight when I got home. But the quart of coffee I drank kept me up until three o'clock. That's why I was late this morning. Remind me to get some decaf for this place. Anyway, April had shut the alarm off and I slept in. If the dog hadn't jumped up on the bed and licked my face, I might still be zeeeing."

Nick smiled. "I need to get a dog. What did Missy say that bugged you so much?"

Sonny answered, "She said one or both of the perps had some traumatic experience in their lives that triggered their—whatever she called it—anyway, whatever made them go bonkers."

"Psychoses, she said psychoses," Nick stated.

"Okay, smart ass," Sonny answered. "Anyway, it made me think. So I started digging through the archives of the Beaver County and Baltimore newspapers, and guess what I found?" Again he didn't wait for an answer. "Twenty-two years ago, a woman killed her husband, in Anne Arundel County, Maryland. The story is, she found out he was banging another woman, and she stabbed him in the chest. Then, she dumped his body in the bathtub, and sliced off his ring finger."

"Wow," said Nick as he walked over to his partner. "You should work late more often."

"Oh, there's more." Sonny smiled. "The couple had two small children, a boy and a girl. They were both seven years old."

"Twins?"

"You caught that? There's hope for you yet." He grinned again.

"Let me guess. Their name was Ayers." Nick was excited.

Sonny shook his head. "You guessed wrong. It was Spivey, Monica and Richard Spivey. It looks like the kids were dumped into the system. Apparently there were no relatives, at least none that I could find. I couldn't find anything on their whereabouts, either. They seem to have disappeared into thin air. Their names were Catherine and Jason. The problem is there's no record of any Catherine or Jason Spivey fitting the age group any place. At least, none that I could find. The next stop is the Maryland child protective services, I guess."

"What about the mother? What happened to her?" Nick asked.

"Uh, it says, Monica Spivey was arrested, tried, and convicted of second-degree murder and aggravated assault. She was sentenced to twenty years to life, and was incarcerated in the Maryland State Penitentiary."

"She should be long out by now. As a convicted felon, her address would be in the system. We need to talk with her."

"Good luck, unless you can talk to ghosts," Sonny said. "Four months after her arrival as a guest of the state, Monica Spivey hung herself in her cell."

Nick thought for a moment, as his mind processed what his ears had just heard. "Twins! That would explain the sketches and why they looked so much alike. It's because they are alike. Twins!" He patted his partner on the back. "Good job, Detective Madison. Good job."

"Yeah, but what now? We gotta figure out how our Spivey twins became Ayers and whatever."

"By the way, you said she stabbed her husband. What did she stick him with?"

Sonny looked at his partner and smiled. "An ice pick, what else!"

Nick sat down at his desk and fired up his computer. "You check the adoption records in Maryland. I'll check school records. We'll check the Girl Scouts if we have to. We gotta find Catherine or Jason Ayers."

It was a couple of hours later when Nick's cell phone rang. It was a text from Sue Kim. All it said was: *lunch was good.*

"Shit!" he said out loud.

"What's the matter, Nick?" Sonny asked.

"I was supposed to meet Sue Kim for lunch. I spaced it."

Sonny shook his head. "Thank God you handle your life as a cop better than your love life, or else you'd probably be walking along Jefferson Street, sliding parking tickets under wiper blades."

Nick didn't look up. He just put his elbow on his desk, raised his hand to his partner, and gave him half of the peace sign. Sonny laughed.

CHAPTER 38

Revelation

The two detectives worked relentlessly, searching for anything they could find that might lead to the identity of either one of the twins. It was three-thirty-five when Sonny finally broke the silence. "Hey, Gumby, you're not so dumb after all." He motioned with his hand. "Come on over here. Take a gander at this."

Nick walked over to his partner's desk and leaned down to see the computer screen. "Whatcha got?"

"It seems that Richard Spivey had a half-sister. Her name was Lisa Powell. She lived in Pennsylvania. Though there is no record of her ever having any children, about six months after the murder, she enrolled a young boy, age seven, in a Catholic School in Beaver, Pennsylvania, St. Peter and Paul Catholic School." Sonny added, "Sit down, partner, this is good stuff."

Nick positioned a chair so he had a good view of the computer screen and sat. "I hope so."

"Okay, it seems they were a well-to-do family. Her husband was an oncologist. The boy went through the Catholic school and on to the seminary. Saint Mary's in Baltimore, to be exact. The doctor's name was Colin J. Masters. The boy's name is . . ." He turned the computer screen for his partner to get a good view. It read: Jason Brett Masters.

Nick couldn't believe what his ears had just heard and his eyes had just seen. He looked at Sonny, and then at the computer as he read the words again. He leaned back in his chair, took in a deep breath, exhaled, and said, "Holy fucking shit!"

"Yeah," Sonny said. "You got that right."

"We gotta talk with the parents," Nick said. "I'll tell the chief we gotta take another plane ride."

"Uhhh, not so fast. The parents took their own plane ride, and it didn't end up so well."

Nick looked at his partner. "What do you mean?"

"It seems the doc was a pilot," Sonny answered. "He had a twin-engine Piper. He and his wife were on their way to a convention in

Atlanta. It says he was supposed to be the keynote speaker, but he never made it. Their plane went down in the Smokey Mountains in North Carolina. They both were killed."

"When? How long ago?" Nick asked.

"Ten years ago. And everything went to the kid: lock, stock, and bank account. He's loaded. He's got more money than the man he works for. He paid for his own schooling and everything."

"Did I say holy shit?" Nick asked.

"Uhhh, sort of," Sonny answered.

"Anything on the sister?"

Sonny shook his head. "Nada. Now what?"

"Let's go talk with the chief."

The two detectives went to Chief Mannion's office. They were informed by Tricia that their boss was in a meeting in Scottsdale and would not be back until tomorrow.

CHAPTER 39

The Plan

Deputy Chief Bruce Mannion leaned forward and listened intently as his two detectives explained their findings from the day before. When they were finished, he leaned back in his chair, locked his fingers behind his head, and thought for a moment. Finally, he let out a deep breath. "Whew! That's a lot to swallow." He shook his head. "You're telling me a priest, a Catholic priest, a man of the cloth, is a serial killer?"

"We think so," Nick said. Sonny nodded.

"Wow," the chief exclaimed. "This is one for the books." He shook his head.

"Here's what we think," Nick said. "We think Father Brett Masters, or his twin sister, or perhaps both of them, witnessed their mother take out their father. Missy Webster said the perps would likely have been involved in or witnessed something traumatic. She even gave an example of a violent death of a sibling or a parent."

"If their mother whacked their father in front of either of them, that would fit the definition of traumatic," Sonny said. "We think it all has to do with unfaithfulness."

"We know the victim in Pennsylvania was a rover," said Nick. "The sheriff's investigation said he had an eye for the ladies, even though he was still technically a newlywed."

"Maybe she found out her husband was messing around. And she took him out, just like Mama," Sonny said. "We think the brother probably helped her dump the body in the lake."

Nick spoke, "The description we have of Catherine Ayers Widmann makes her pretty small. It's doubtful she could pull it off without help."

"What about Baltimore?" Mannion asked.

"We don't know for sure," Sonny answered. "Maybe she had a boyfriend who cheated. Maybe the brother had a boyfriend who cheated. We know he was in the area when the Baltimore victim was killed. We don't know where she was then. But it's only a few hours drive from Beaver County, Pennsylvania, to Baltimore, Maryland. And she does fit the description of the lady in the boat."

"Bruce, we know that Pete was having an affair," Nick said. "We think the Pennsylvania vic was doing the same."

"And the lady in the lake had a spotty past," added Sonny. "She was married when she started banging her boss, and ended up marrying him. He was out of town a lot, and she liked to party. We don't know about the rest, but I'll bet they all had one thing in common."

"So you think they were all screwing around," said the chief. "But what connects them to the priest? What would he have to do with any of it?"

The room was quiet until Nick said, "Madeline Meade went to St. John's in Scottsdale. Father Brett Masters was there around the time she was killed. He was transferred to St. Michael's after that, and two of our victims went to St. Michael's: Perrotta and Marquez."

"What about Pete?" asked Mannion.

"Uhh, we don't know," answered Sonny. "That's got us stumped."

"Well, Detectives, what's the next move? We can put a tail on the priest, I guess."

"I don't know, Bruce," Nick said. "If we do, we better be careful. If we spook him, it's all over. Right now all we can do is put him in the vicinity of each killing at the time. The DA won't be able to do much with that."

"What if we can get a DNA sample? We can see if there's a family tie to the blood we took from the Marquez place."

"We'd need a warrant. If we couldn't get one for the Meyers woman, I'm not even going to ask the judge for one for a priest," said Mannion. "I can hear the bishop now, and you know he's friends with the mayor." He looked at Nick. "You've been down that road."

"How well I know." Nick's mind wondered back to last year when he and Sonny worked the case of the murdered priest. Bishop O'Malley fought them all the way.

"I don't know what to do," Nick said to his boss. "We don't want any more killings and catching him in the act is wishful thinking."

"Wow, accusing a priest of being a serial killer is weird." Sonny grinned. "It gives me chills." He shrugged and shook his head. "It makes me feel like we should all go to confession. Even you, Chief, and you're not even Catholic."

Nick sat straight up in his chair. His mouth partly opened, and he barely moved except for his eyes slowly moving from one spot to another, up and down and from side to side. The room became eerily silent as both Mannion and Madison stared at the lieutenant, who finally broke the silence and looked directly at his partner. "You're right, Sonny." Nick nodded. "You do need to go to confession!"

Sonny pushed himself back in his seat, squinted, and looked at his friend like he was deranged. "Huh?" He looked at the chief and asked, "Has he taken a piss test lately?"

"I'm serious, Sonny," Nick said. "Does Father Brett Masters know you? Have you ever met him? Would he recognize you? Does he know you're a cop?" He fired all the questions all at once, like emptying a clip at the shooting range.

"Uh, no, no, I don't think so, and no." Sonny looked at Nick, then at their boss and back at Nick.

"When was the last time you went to confession?" Nick asked Sonny.

"Uhh, I don't know. Not for years. I don't do that anymore. Why?"

"Well, you're going to now." The lieutenant explained his plan to his boss and to his partner.

CHAPTER 40

They Meet

The mortuary was packed with friends and fellow police officers. The funeral was scheduled for tomorrow, but, as is customary in the Catholic church, there would be a rosary in about an hour. Nick Greer and Sonny Madison were standing at the rear of the room. April Madison and Sue Kim were sitting on a sofa talking with Elena Mendoza. The three Mendoza children were scattered throughout the room talking with friends and relatives.

The two detectives saw Spencer Lovett as he was signing the guest book. Sonny said to Nick, "Here comes Captain Hard-Ass."

As he entered the room, Nick greeted him, "Good evening, Captain."

Sonny followed with, "Good evening, Captain Lovett."

The captain ignored them and walked over to the deputy chief, who was talking with three other officers. "Look at him," Sonny remarked. "Instead of going to the family or the deceased, he's kissing up to the boss." Sonny grinned. "I think we should change his name to Captain Kiss-Ass."

Nick was about to comment on his partner's remark when he saw an unexpected, but familiar face walk past the guest book without signing it. Carmen Cruz greeted the two detectives as she came into the room. "I didn't know if I should sign the guest book. I wanted to, but I didn't know if I should, you know, the family and all."

"Do you think it's a good idea for you to even be here?" Nick asked.

"I had to see him. I tried to let it go, but I had to see him."

Nick responded, "That's your call, Carmen. I understand, I guess."

She looked across the room at Elena. "Is that her?"

"Yeah," Nick answered.

"Does she know?"

"She suspects, but doesn't know who."

Carmen looked at the two detectives, took a deep breath, and walked to the front of the room. She knelt, crossed herself, and prayed. After a few moments, she crossed herself again, rose, and stood in front of the coffin. A tear rolled down her cheek as she stared at her deceased lover lying in the copper coffin. She didn't hear or see the person come over and stand beside her as she looked at the large array of red roses covering his lower body. The gold ribbon across it read: Loving Husband and Father.

"Did you love him?"

Carmen was startled by the voice. She turned her head and saw Elena Mendoza looking at her. Many thoughts ran through her mind as she stood there. What's going to happen now? The widow meets the mistress. Is there going to be a scene? She should never have come here. But as she looked into the widow's eyes, she saw no anger, only gentleness and pain. Carmen was silent.

"Please, tell me, did you love him?" Elena asked again.

Carmen looked at the body in the coffin and nodded lightly.

"Did he love you?" Elena asked.

Carmen looked at the array of roses, then back to Elena, and said, "It was you whom he loved. No one could ever break that."

Elena's eyes began to well up with tears as she said, "Thank you for coming. I don't know if you were planning on going to the funeral tomorrow, but the kids don't know about you. I would rather they didn't. Please respect that. I think it would be best—"

"I understand," Carmen interjected. "Thank you." She turned and left the room.

Nick and Sonny had been watching from the back of the room. They both walked up to Elena. Sonny embraced her, then Nick embraced her and asked, "Are you okay?"

She lifted her glasses and wiped her eyes with the tissue in her hand and stated more than asked, "You knew it was her, didn't you?"

Both detectives nodded in unison. "We couldn't say anything, Elena. You know that," Nick said.

"I know. Thank you for handling it the way you did. You're good friends."

Later on that evening, Jordana came over to Nick, and said, "Mama is finally starting to show some emotion, other than anger. Who was that lady she was talking to?"

"Just a police officer paying her respects," Nick answered, as the announcement came that the rosary was about to begin.

* * *

The funeral Mass was the next morning. The procession to the grave site was long. Just about every cop not on duty was there. The news stations covered it; however, not so much as a fallen officer, but more as a victim of the serial killer. The flags at all city facilities were still at half-mast.

As the priest was sprinkling water over the casket, Sonny turned around. His eyes saw a car parked across the road, and someone sitting in the driver's seat. He nudged Nick, who turned and saw Carmen Cruz sitting behind the wheel. The car drove away.

CHAPTER 41

Sonny's Confession

The Saturday night Mass would begin in a little over thirty minutes, and there were still five people ahead of him in line for confession. Maybe this wasn't such a good idea, after all, he thought. He didn't want to be rushed. This had to go off without a hitch. Perhaps they should rethink their strategy.

Sonny Madison was a life-long Catholic. He was baptized, confirmed, and married in the Catholic church. Although he didn't go to Mass every Sunday, he was as faithful as he could be to the rules of the church, but confession was one of the things he had problems with. He felt his sinfulness was personal, and it should be between him and his creator, and no one else. He felt like a hypocrite because of what he was about to do. But he knew the importance of finding the killer, and taking him off the streets before he had a chance to strike again. He figured God would forgive him.

It was four-forty-seven when he stepped into the confessional. It had been a long time since he had gone to confession, but a cradle Catholic never forgets how. He tried to remember how long it had been, but he couldn't. He decided it wasn't important, because he knew this one wouldn't count, anyway.

Sonny knelt, crossed himself, and said, "Bless me, Father, for I have sinned. My last confession was a little over ten years ago."

"Go ahead," said the priest.

Sonny continued, "I missed Mass on Sunday a few times. I have lost my temper. I took the Lord's name in vain. I committed adultery."

There was a moment of silence between them. "Is there anything else?" the priest asked.

"No, Father, that's it."

Sonny thought this whole thing was a failure until the priest asked, "How long have you been married?"

"Twenty years," Sonny responded.

"Do you have any children?"

The detective knew his answer must be believable. "Just one, a son. He lives in California. We don't see him much."

"Is this the first time you've ever strayed?"

The priest's question caught Sonny by surprise. He hadn't expected the third degree from a priest. He thought for a moment. He knew his response had to be right, so he poured it on as thick as he thought would work. "Uhh . . . no, Father. It has happened before."

"Are you aware of the sanctity of marriage and the vows you took before God twenty years ago?" the priest questioned, gently but sternly.

Sonny thought for a moment. He hadn't been to confession in years, and he thought this approach was a little unusual. "Uhm, yes, Father, I am."

"How often do you do this?"

"Uhm, Not real often, I guess. Once a week, maybe?"

"Is it always with the same person?"

"This time. We have been seeing each other for the last few months."

"So this isn't your only time."

"Uh, no. There have been others."

"How many?"

"Uh, not that many. A few, I guess."

"Is she married?"

Sonny wondered why this priest was asking so many questions. "No, Father, she's not."

"Do you love her?" the priest asked.

"Uhhh, not really."

"So why do you do it?"

Again, Sonny was caught by surprise by the priest's question. "Uhh, I don't know. I just do, I guess."

"Are you truly sorry for your sins, and are you willing to accept your penance, repent, and sin no more?"

"Yes, Father. I'll give it a try."

"Give it a try? You must do more than try." His voice was raised a little. "I would like to help you. First, I want you to say five Our Father's and ten Hail Mary's and make a good act of contrition. Then, as part of your penance, I want you to call me tomorrow and make an appointment for us to talk."

"Talk? Talk about what?"

"You seem to have a problem and with a little help, I think you can overcome it. You will call me tomorrow?" He reached around the screen and handed him a note with a phone number on it.

"Uh, yes, Father, I will."

"My last Mass should be finished by one-thirty. Please call me then. The number is my personal cell phone."

"One-thirty," Sonny repeated.

The priest lifted his hand, made the sign of the cross over Sonny and said, "I absolve you of your sins in the name of the Father and of the Son and of the Holy Spirit. Go in peace."

"Thank you, Father," Sonny said as he got up and left the confessional. He got into his car, and as he drove away he pushed the call button on his steering wheel and said: Call Nick.

Nick Greer was waiting for his call. "How did it go?"

"I think he bought it," Sonny answered. "Now I kind of feel like I should go to confession for going to confession."

Nick laughed. "I'll bet a priest never heard that one before. Do you want to call Bruce, or should I?"

"I'll call him. You need to concentrate on tonight. By the way, good luck."

"Thanks," Nick said as he disconnected the call.

CHAPTER 42

The Question

After the funeral, Nick and Sue Kim went to lunch together. They talked about Pete, Elena, and the Mendoza family. "Who was the strange woman at the funeral home last night?" she asked.

Nick looked at her. "Pete's friend."

"I thought so, but I wasn't sure," Sue Kim answered. "Elena sure handled it well. I'd have ripped her face off." Nick was silent. "I saw her talking with you and Sonny. Did you know her?"

"She's on the force in Tempe," Nick said. "She was the investigator on the case of the lady pulled from Tempe Town Lake."

"I see. Do the kids know?"

"Elena says no. I'm not so sure about Jordana; she's pretty perceptive. Elena doesn't want them to know. The kids adored their father, and she doesn't want to tarnish their memories."

"I can respect that," Sue Kim responded.

Nick looked into her eyes and said, "There's something I want to talk to you about."

"Okay, go ahead."

"Not here. I have reservations for two at Rusty's tonight. Let's talk there."

"Okay, I guess. What time should I meet you?"

"Sue, I can't do that. I want to make this work, but I'm not going to meet you there. Either you meet me at my place, or I'll pick you up at seven-thirty, and I'll take you home afterwards. No obligations, but we go together and leave together."

She leaned back and looked like she was in deep thought. "Okay."

* * *

Nick had taken care to reserve the same table as the last time they were there. They sat down and were approached by Robert, who remembered them from their last visit. "Welcome back, sir. Would you like to see our wine list tonight?"

"Cabernet Sauvignon, please," Nick ordered.

"Yes, sir," the waiter responded as he left the table.

Sue Kim looked out the window at the city spanned out below. "I love it here."

"I know," he responded.

"What did you want to talk about?"

Before he had a chance to speak, the waiter returned with the wine. He opened it, picked up Nick's glass, and poured a small amount into it. Nick swirled it a little, sniffed it, lifted the glass to his lips, tasted it, and said, "Fine, thank you, Robert."

The waiter took Sue Kim's glass, filled it, and then filled Nick's. "Would you care to order, sir?" Nick ordered for them both and the waiter left.

"How is it going with the case?" Sue Kim asked.

"I guess it's going okay. I'm waiting on a call—" His words were interrupted by the ring of his cell phone. He pulled it from his belt and saw the text message. It was from Deputy Chief Mannion and read: *Let's do it. Tomorrow morning nine a.m. my office. BTW good luck tonight!*

"That Sonny! I'm gonna kill him!"

"Huh?" She looked at him puzzled.

"Nothing. We're meeting with the chief in the morning, that's all."

"Sunday?" she said. "Tomorrow is Sunday, you know."

"Yeah, I know."

"Are you making any headway in the case? At least anything you can talk about?" she asked.

"I should know more tomorrow," Nick answered.

They were both unusually silent as they ate dinner. The waiter came over and refilled their glasses.

Finally, Nick laid his fork on the table and broke the silence. He looked into her eyes and said, "Sue Kim, I messed up. I know that. I hurt you, and I hurt me. I promise, it will never happen again." He reached into his pocket and pulled out a small box. He got up from his seat, dropped to one knee, looked into her eyes and said, "Sue Kim Lee. You are the love of my life. I promise to spend the rest of my life making you happy, if you will be my wife." He opened the box, lifted it up for her to see the sparkling diamond ring it offered.

Suddenly, her eyes became as big as golf balls, and her mouth opened as she peered at the beautiful diamond as it reflected the lights from the room back into her eyes. Her hands began to shake, and she dropped her fork onto the table. Though she tried to speak, no sound came out. She looked into his eyes and nodded her head three times. He took the ring from the box and slipped it onto her finger. Standing, he bent down and gave her a long, lingering kiss. They heard the sound of applause as the whole room celebrated.

Robert came to the table, popped a bottle of champagne, and said, "Congratulations! This is compliments of a friend."

Nick asked, "A friend? Who?" He looked up and saw the back of a male figure leaving the restaurant. Even walking away, be recognized Sonny Madison!

A few minutes later, Robert came over to their table and asked, "Would you or your lady like some dessert?"

Nick looked at her. She shook her head. He looked at the waiter and said, "No, thank you, Robert."

As the waiter walked away, Sue Kim reached across the table and took Nick's hand. "You know, this time he's right."

Nick was puzzled at her comment. "What do you mean? Right about what?"

She held out her hand in front of her, looked at the sparkling diamond on her finger, and looked back to him. "I really am your lady."

CHAPTER 43

The Trap

Deputy Chief Bruce Mannion was waiting for them. "Sit down, Detectives. How did it go?"

"I'm supposed to call him after one-thirty this afternoon and make an appointment to see him," Sonny responded.

"Good," Mannion said. "I'll call for a van and have it put on standby. We can park it down the street from St. Michael's. We'll need to get you wired."

They discussed every scenario they could think of and how they would handle each one—all except the one that would unfold.

* * *

It was one-forty when Sonny phoned the priest. "This is Father Brett," came the answer.

"Uh, you asked me to call you," Sonny answered. He tried to sound as humble as possible.

"Yes, sir, I did. How is your schedule this evening?"

"Uh, okay, I guess."

"I have the teen Mass at five o'clock. Can you meet me after that?"

"I guess so. What time should I be at the church?" Sonny asked.

"Can you meet me at Cortez Park? You know where that is, don't you?" the priest asked.

"Uh." Sonny thought for a moment, then asked, "Yeah, I do, but why there? Why not at your office?"

"You know, sometimes even a priest needs to get away from the church. There's a little lake there. It's quiet and serene. Sometimes I like to go there to relax. I'll see you around seven o'clock by the lake." He disconnected the call.

Sonny texted Nick and Chief Mannion: *7 tonight Cortez Park by the lake.*

* * *

It was seven on the dot when Sonny pulled into the empty parking lot. He had driven April's car, just in case the priest would notice the chase lights in his. A plain police van was parked on the other side of Thirty-Fifth Avenue. They were a little farther away than they would have liked, but it was as close as they could get without being seen.

Lieutenant Nick Greer and Deputy Chief Bruce Mannion were in the van, along with two technicians. A pair of cruisers were positioned three blocks north, and two more were two blocks south. All had been briefed and were well out of sight, but in radio contact. They were ready to roll when called. An EMT crew was close by just in case things got out of control.

Sonny's eyes scanned the park as he sat in the car and waited. There wasn't a soul in sight. He periodically checked his wire. He knew if he got into any trouble, he was to speak a code word. If the cops in the van heard him say the word "bananas," they would respond immediately, and the place would be overrun with police in seconds.

It was almost seven-thirty. The chief told Sonny, "It looks like he isn't coming. Maybe he's on to us."

Sonny was about to answer when he heard a car pull up next to him. Father Brett got out and came over to Sonny. "I'm sorry I'm late," he said. "Sometimes the teen Mass goes longer than expected."

Sonny got out of his car and said, "I wondered what happened. I was just about to leave."

"Thank you for waiting. I picked up a couple of bottles of water. It's been a hot day."

He held out one of the bottles to Sonny, who said, "Thank you, Father, but I have my own." He lifted his can of Pepsi and took a sip.

The priest pointed to a picnic table a few yards away. "I'm tired. I've been on my feet all day. Let's have a seat."

They sat on the tabletop. The priest began, "Please know this is all still privileged communication. Let's call it an extension of your confession."

Sonny nodded. "That's good. That'll work."

They sat there in silence for a few minutes until the priest finally spoke, "Let's take a walk." He got up and began walking toward the small lake, and Sonny followed him. He didn't see the tiny body leave the car and covertly sneak over to the picnic table as he and the priest walked toward the water. The car's interior light had been disabled. The surveillance team, whose attention was directed on their detective, didn't see her as she crawled swiftly under the table. A few seconds later, she reached up and dropped something into Sonny's Pepsi can. As she saw them beginning to come back, she crawled back under the table and huddled there in the darkness.

The night was starless, and the only illumination came from a few wooden poles scattered sparsely throughout the park. A tree had grown in front of the closest pole, causing a shadow to be cast over the table.

The two men soon returned to the table and sat next to each other on the bench. The priest began, "What made you first stray from your wife?"

Sonny thought for a moment, reached for his Pepsi, and took a long drink. He needed to answer the priest's question correctly. "I really don't remember the first time. It was a long time ago. It just happened, I guess."

There was about a minute of silence before the priest said, "Why do you do it?"

"I don't know, Father. I know it's not right."

The shadow over the table made it difficult for the surveillance team to see what was happening, so they relied on the communication from the wire on their detective.

Only the sounds of passing cars could be heard as the priest sat there in silence. Finally he said, "You have to stop, you know."

Sonny began to answer, but all of a sudden he was unable to speak. He felt dizzy. He barely felt himself fall from the bench as the priest caught him and laid him on the ground. Sonny was trying to speak. He tried to say bananas, but all he got out was: "Ba—"

She crawled out from underneath the table with an ice pick in her hand. She looked at the priest and nodded. He nodded back and she took the ice pick and carefully placed it in the center of Sonny Madison's chest. She held the ice pick there, looked up at the priest, and said, "Do it! Do it!"

He reached down and was just about to thrust the ice pick into Sonny's chest when a shot rang out. Lieutenant Nick Greer's aim was perfect. The priest fell to the ground.

She froze as she saw him fall. She was stunned, but only for a brief moment, until she looked at the ice pick she still held against his chest. She straddled Sonny and sat on his stomach as she wrapped one hand around the ice pick and cupped it inside her other hand. She lifted her hands as high as she could above her head, looked up into the dark night sky, and let out a loud, piercing scream. Then, as her eyes targeted Sonny's chest, and she began to bring her arms down, a shot rang out. She fell backward to the ground.

In only a matter of seconds, all four police cruisers descended upon the park. The undercover van was followed by the EMT vehicle, all with their lights flashing red and blue.

Father Brett Masters was lying on the ground, writhing in pain. Deputy Chief Mannion was running toward them, pointing his gun at the woman who was lying motionless on the ground. Nick was holding his gun on the priest.

Nick Greer's aim was deadly. The bullet had hit her directly in the chest. Her lifeless body now lay facedown on the ground. One of the uniformed policemen shined his flashlight onto her. Nick reached down and turned the body over, wondering if he would recognize the face. He froze for a moment as the light illuminated a face he had only seen once before.

He looked up at Bruce Mannion, who asked, "Do you know who she is? Have you ever seen her before?"

"Yeah," the detective answered. "She works at the Phoenix diocese. Her name is Diane Harding."

All of a sudden the priest sat up and lunged at Sonny. None of the police officers had seen the ice pick fall from Diane Harding's hand and land on the ground next to the priest, who had quickly grabbed it and hid it under his leg. He yelled, "Adulterer," as he plunged the ice pick deep into Sonny's chest. Several shots rang out, and the priest fell backward to the ground.

CHAPTER 44

The Hospital

The paramedics ran to Sonny as fast as they could. They packed the wound, lifted him onto a gurney, loaded him into their van, and rushed him straight to Phoenix Thunderbird Hospital. The Rohypnol dose had been a strong one. Sonny had never felt the ice pick as it invaded his chest.

The emergency room doctors worked hard. By the time Nick arrived, April Madison was already there. She saw Nick coming and ran into his arms. He held her for a moment, and then she pulled away. Tears streamed down her face as she looked at Nick with angry eyes and began beating her fists against his chest. She yelled, "You're supposed to protect each other. You were supposed to have his back! How could you let this happen? It's all your fault!" Nick just stood there and took it until she finally ran out of energy and stopped. He held her again as she lay her head against his chest and sobbed.

Sue Kim had just walked in, but she saw it all. She came over to Nick and April and hugged them both. "How is he?"

April answered, "They said he coded in the ambulance on the way here, but they brought him back. He's in surgery now, but it doesn't look good."

Sue Kim, Nick Greer, and a sobbing April Madison stood in the middle of the emergency waiting room, hugging each other. After a few minutes they sat down and were soon joined by the deputy chief.

It was ten minutes past eleven when a doctor finally came through the door. April immediately jumped up and ran to her. Nick, Sue Kim, and Bruce Mannion followed.

"Mrs. Madison?" she began.

"Yes," April answered as her eyes welled up with tears.

"Your husband had a bad chest wound. There was a lot of bleeding. It was touch and go for a while. Fortunately we were able to stop the bleeding and repair the damage. He'll need some rest, but he should make a complete recovery."

April's legs became wobbly. Both Nick and Bruce caught her before she fell, and they held her up as the doctor continued, "Your husband was lucky, Mrs. Madison. It's a good thing it was an ice pick. If it had been anything thicker, like a knife, we might be having a different conversation. It missed the heart by less than a centimeter."

"When can I see him?" April asked.

"He's in post-op now. Then we'll move him to intensive care. You can see him then."

The doctor turned and walked away. April called out to her, "Thank you, Doctor. Thank you very, very much." They didn't see the smile on the doctor's face as she raised her hand and stuck her thumb into the air.

CHAPTER 45

April's Rules

It was Monday, mid-morning, when Nick Greer took the elevator up to the third floor of Phoenix Thunderbird Hospital. The doors opened and he turned left. The room he was looking for was the second one on the right. Sonny was sitting up in bed with an IV in his left arm. His chest was bandaged, and an oxygen tube was running around his ears and into his nose. April was sitting in a green vinyl chair next to him. She had a newspaper in her lap.

"Well, look who's here, the great Gumby," Sonny said as Nick walked in through the open door. Sonny's voice was noticeably weak.

"How are you doing, my friend?" Nick asked.

"I'm great! I want to go home. I want to find the bus that ran me over."

Nick looked at April. "How is he, really?"

She smiled. "The doctor says he can go home in a couple of days, but he can't go back to work for at least six weeks."

"I ain't taking no six weeks off!" Sonny stated.

April leaned forward, looked straight into her husband's eyes, and stated, "Oh, yes, you are, Jasper James Madison. As soon as the doctor signs your release, we're leaving this hospital. You're going to park your ass in the car and I'm driving you home. You are going to stay there until the doctor says you can go back. You will put your gun in the safe. You will not call the station, and you will give me your cell phone." She looked at the lieutenant. "Nick, if you want to talk with him, either come over or call the landline, which I will answer."

Sonny grinned as he looked at his partner and said, "Hmm, it looks like I'm grounded!"

Nick nodded. April put her hands on her hips and said, "Yeah, that's right. Detective Sonny Madison is grounded!"

"Uh, Jasper James Madison?" Nick asked. "How come you never told me?"

Sonny looked at his friend. "My name is Sonny. That's all anyone needs to know." He changed the subject and looked at his wife. "I'm keeping my cell phone. And maybe we'll go to Florida."

"What are you talking about," April questioned. "What's in Florida?"

"Fish. I wanna go fishing!" April shook her head. Sonny continued, "And maybe while I'm recuperating at home, I'll do some studying."

"Studying?" April looked at her husband. "What do you want to study?"

"Oh, maybe I'll look at taking the lieutenant's exam. That reminds me. Would you drop by Walmart and pick up something for me?"

April looked at her husband. "Sure. What do you want?"

"A bolo tie. I need a bolo tie."

"What the heck do you want with a bolo tie? You don't wear ties," she responded.

He grinned. "I want to send it to a cop I know in Baltimore."

Sonny looked at Nick. "You wanna tell me what's happening? I heard the priest didn't make it. April was just going to read the newspaper article to me."

She held up the paper, revealing the headlines: Serial Killer Priest Killed—City Relieved.

"Yeah, Jack has him, and the sister, too. He's going to try to have the autopsies finished by this afternoon. Sue Kim is assisting him."

"By the way," April interjected, "congratulations on your engagement!"

"Thank you," Nick responded.

"Does she know what she's getting into? Marrying a cop, I mean?"

"I think so. Did you?"

"I learned to cope." April looked at Nick. "Nick, I'm sorry I lost it last night. I know it wasn't your fault."

"Don't worry about it," Nick answered. "Just take him home and take care of him."

He left the room and went back to the station. He knew the drill. He would have to go through an internal affairs interview, and then a psych evaluation with Missy Webster. He would be on paid leave until everything was cleared. This was not his first shooting. But it was the first time he had actually killed someone.

CHAPTER 46

The Right Cross

Sonny had gone home and was recovering well. Sue Kim told Nick she had spoken with April, who had said Sonny was becoming a pain in the ass. Nick just laughed.

They spent the next weekend in Prescott with Nick's girls. Cassie made it a point to avoid Sue Kim the whole time.

It was Sunday afternoon, and the girls wanted to go to a festival at their church. Nick and Sue Kim said good-bye to them, and they left with their grandparents. Nick went out to the front yard and waved as the Lexus drove away. Just as he walked back into the house, he heard a crash. It came from the backyard patio. He ran out to see what had happened.

He couldn't believe what he saw. He thought for a brief moment his eyes were playing tricks on him. Cassie was sprawled out on the floor and looking up at Sue Kim, who was standing over her with clenched fists. A slightly bent lawn chair was overturned next to her, and Cassie's mouth was bleeding.

"If you ever even think about it again, remember this day!" warned Sue Kim. She turned to walked away, but stopped when she saw Nick standing there with a "what the hell?" look on his face.

Cassie looked up through angry eyes and said to her ex-husband, "Arrest her! The bitch assaulted me. You're a cop! You have to arrest her!"

Nick looked at Sue Kim who was just barely over five feet tall and might weigh one hundred ten pounds soaking wet, and then down at his ex-wife who was five feet eight and weighed about one hundred fifty pounds. Though he tried, he couldn't hold back the amusement he felt. He smiled as he looked at his fiancée and asked, "What happened here?"

She shrugged and said, "Uhh, she tripped?"

He looked at Cassie, then at the lawn chair, then back at Cassie. "You know, Cassandra, you should really try to be more careful." He pointed to the bent lawn chair next to her. "You're supposed to sit in those things, not sleep in them."

Cassie glared at her ex-husband. If looks could kill, the Prescott police would have had a double homicide on their hands.

Sue Kim looked at Cassie lying on the floor, walked over to her, and extended her hand to help her up. "Get away from me, bitch!" Cassie yelled.

Sue Kim shrugged, turned, and headed toward the door with Nick beside her. Then came the cry from the patio floor: "Nick, aren't you going to help me?" She held out her hand to him.

He looked at Sue Kim, then at his ex-wife. He stroked his chin as if in thought and said, "You had your chance. I hope you have a better day, or"—he shrugged—"maybe not."

Neither of them spoke a word as they got into the car and drove away. Sue Kim was holding her swollen hand up to her lips when he finally broke the silence: "There's a Circle K a couple of blocks down the road. We'll stop and get some ice on that hand."

She nodded. "Good idea."

"Do you want to tell me exactly what happened back there?"

Sue Kim answered, "You know I love the kids. I thought I could try to make things a little smoother for all of us if Cassie and I could agree to at least try to be civil around them. But she got defensive."

"That doesn't surprise me. Exactly what did she say that caused you to go off on her?"

"She said I was just a fling and that she could have you any time she wanted."

"So you decked her," Nick said.

"No. Then she said there was nothing I could ever do about it, because I was just a gook bitch that you would throw away when you were done with me."

"Ahh, I see. So that's when you went Muhammad Ali on her."

"No, silly." She looked at him. "Sticks and stones, you know." She paused. "Then I told her she better stay away from you."

"Okay. I give up. So why the hell did you punch her?"

"She laughed at me!"

"Uh oh," he commented. "That wasn't very smart of her."

AFTERWORD

The Beginning As the End

Monica Spivey reached up to the kitchen wall and hung up the telephone. The news she had just received made her legs feel wobbly so she sat on one of the wooden bar stools lined up against the kitchen island. Soon, angry tears filled her eyes and spilled down her face as her mind and heart processed the news her ears had heard moments before. Her husband was having an affair. How could he?

She was still sitting there when the front door opened, and he came in, laid down his briefcase, and dropped his keys into a bowl sitting on the small buffet table that sat against the wall of the row house. "Hey, babe, I'm home. I'm starved! What's for dinner?"

He walked into the kitchen and saw his wife sitting there crying. He hurried to her and said, "What's wrong, babe? Why are you crying? What happened?"

She stood and screamed, "Don't you touch me, you son of a bitch!"

He reached out to hug her, but she stepped back and almost fell over one of the bar stools. "Stay away from me, you lying, cheating bastard!" she screamed.

"What are you talking about, Monica?"

"Don't act so innocent! I know what you've been doing with Carol Ferguson. I just talked with Janie Caruso. She told me all about your afternoon flings. How could you do it?"

He walked toward her again. She reached into the sink, grabbed a plate, and threw it at her husband. He quickly ducked. The plate crashed against the kitchen wall behind him.

He laughed as he moved toward his wife. As he did, she opened a kitchen drawer and grabbed the first thing she could find, an ice pick, and plunged it into his chest. He gasped and tried to hang on to the kitchen counter, but he fell to the tiled floor with blood oozing out around the weapon that was still buried deep in his chest.

Anger was building inside her. She was a bomb about to explode as she stood over him. She took hold of her husband's feet and dragged him out of the kitchen, down the hall, and into the bathroom.

Emotion can often provide unexplainable strength. And it came through in spades for Monica Spivey as she lifted her husband's limp and lifeless body up over the side of the bathtub, shoved him into it head first, and turned on the water. That's when she saw it. His left hand was dangling over the side of the tub, and his gold wedding band caught her attention.

She dropped to her knees, grabbed his left hand, and tried to pull the ring off, but it wouldn't pass over the knuckle. She tugged and pulled with all her might, but to no avail. Then, she remembered the kitchen drawer and the meat cleaver stored in it. She ran to the kitchen, reached into the drawer, ran back into the bathroom, and again knelt by the body. She grabbed his left hand. She bent his fingers into his palm, except for the ring finger, which she held on the edge of the bathtub. She raised the meat cleaver and brought it down with all the force her anger could produce. The cleaver did its job and sliced through the skin and bone. The finger slid across the floor. As she reached for the wedding ring, she looked up. That was when she saw them.

Her seven-year-old twins were standing there. The boy had tears rolling down his cheeks. "Mommy! Mommy! Why did you hurt Daddy?" His twin sister just looked. Her face was expressionless.

Their mother didn't know it, but they had seen and heard it all.

Monica Spivey was arrested, tried, and convicted of second-degree murder and aggravated assault. She was sentenced to twenty years to life and was incarcerated in the Maryland State Penitentiary. Four months after her incarceration, Monica Spivey was found hanging in her prison cell.

Both children were admitted into foster care. The boy was eventually adopted by his father's sister and her husband. The girl remained with the foster family.

Lisa and Colin Masters were devout Catholics and raised their son in the same manner. It was this attachment to the church that spawned his interest in the priesthood.

Catherine Spivey was eventually adopted by her foster family. They had her name legally changed to Ayers. She didn't care to be called Cathy, so she went by her middle name, Diane. She was a brilliant student. The state had her tested once, and her IQ was in the genius category. She graduated at the top of her high school class and decided to enroll in college. Her superior grades would provide her scholarships in just about any school she wanted. She had chosen Vassar College, just north of New York City.

Growing up, she often thought of her twin brother and wanted to contact him. But no one was able to help her with any pertinent information. Someone had once told her that he had heard her twin brother had been adopted by a doctor in Pennsylvania, somewhere near Philadelphia.

One day, she saw an article on the evening news about the crash of a small airplane in the Smokey Mountains near Asheville, North Carolina. There were two people on board, the pilot and his wife; neither survived. The reporter said the plane was registered to a doctor in Huntington Valley, Pennsylvania, and that they had one surviving son, age eighteen. The doctor's name was Masters.

Curious, she did more research on the family and finally contacted the young man. After several emails and phone conversations, they decided to meet. He sent her a plane ticket to Philadelphia. They meshed immediately. They knew they were twin siblings. The bond grew exponentially, especially as they shared their experience and feelings about their mother and about their father's death.

Though he was an intelligent young man, she was the one who was in control of their relationship. She cared for her brother, but he adored his sister. The two siblings, as Missy Webster had stated, completed each other.

Diane liked the area and decided to stay. She applied for a scholarship at Penn State University, where she graduated in three years, during which time her brother had entered the seminary. Though her schooling was paid for by the scholarships, her brother saw to it that she had a nice place to live, a nice car, and plenty of money.

While in college, she met James Widmann, who was a star running back for the Penn State Nittany Lions. James was considered by many sportswriters to be a Heisman trophy candidate until, in the beginning of his senior year, he was carried off the field due to a serious back injury. He recovered from the surgery, but the doctors said he would never play football again. They said another injury, and he could spend the rest of his life in a wheelchair.

Shortly after she graduated Magna Cum Laude, Diane married James. They moved to Beaver County, Pennsylvania, where James had grown up.

Brett Masters liked his brother-in-law and loaned him twenty thousand dollars to start his own construction company. It wasn't long before Diane started to wonder where the money was going, and why her husband was spending so much time away, but he wasn't showing much for it in the way of income. Diane didn't want to take any more money from her brother, so she took a job at a local bank in order to make ends meet.

One night the truth came out by way of a friend. James Widmann was playing around and not only with one woman. Childhood memories that had remained dormant inside her suddenly surfaced when she heard the news. That was when she concocted her sinister plan.

The argument between them was intense. She bought a plane ticket to Philadelphia and stayed with one of her foster sisters. From there, she called her brother, and put her evil plan into action.

Brett Masters, who was temporarily working at St. Luke's Church in Philadelphia, picked up his sister, and drove to Beaver County. While the three of them were having dinner, she put a large dose of Rohypnol into her husband's iced tea. Soon he fell out of the chair and onto the floor. That was when she took an ice pick from the kitchen drawer, and remembering where her mother stabbed her father, she took care to place the ice pick in the exact spot and tried to push it in. The cartilage was hard, and she looked up at her brother.

He understood the look in her commanding eyes. He bent down and pushed on the weapon until it was sunk all the way into his brother-in-law's chest.

They wrapped the body in a blanket, put it in the trunk of Brett's car, and drove to the closest large body of water: Brady's Run Park.

As they pulled the body from the trunk, she saw something sticking out of a plastic bag and asked her brother what it was. He explained it was a Japanese tanto, and he told her what it was used for.

Diane pulled the instrument out of the bag, and handed it to her brother. Then she grabbed her dead husband's left hand, held up the ring finger and said, "Take it! Cut it off!" Her brother followed her order. They dumped the body into the lake and drove back to Philadelphia. She waited until the body had been found, then flew back to Beaver County. Diane phoned her brother who was still at St. Luke's. Brett Masters practically camped out in a back office of the church and watched the phone lines. When it finally lit up, he provided her alibi.

Two years later, she had moved to Baltimore. Her brother's substantial inheritance took care of her financial needs. She was dating a man by the name of James Pennington. Upon finding out he was married, she called her brother and they took him for a boat ride. They had just dumped the body into the harbor when they saw the two bicycle cops. She decided if they were thought to have found the body, they wouldn't be suspects. She was correct. Fortunately for them, the cops never looked inside the boat. They would've found a bloody Japanese tanto under one of the seats, along with a severed finger.

Catherine Diane Ayers Widmann decided to continue her studies and obtained a master's degree in education at the University of Arizona in Tucson. When her brother finished the seminary, he moved to Phoenix and was ordained by Bishop O'Malley. Diane subsequently took a job with the diocese in order to be near her brother. It was there she met and married J. Michael Harding, a hedge fund manager.

Diane Harding had become friends with Morgan Montgomery. One day while they were having lunch, Diane found out that Morgan had been having an affair while her husband was out of town. Diane talked with her brother, and Montgomery became victim number three.

The others were confessions heard by Father Brett Masters. Pete Mendoza was feeling guilty about his affair with Carmen Cruz, but he did not want to confess to his own priest, so he went to St. Michael's.

The police searched the trunk of Father Brett Master's car and found several bloodstains and a double-edged Japanese tanto. The lab matched the blood to Pete Mendoza and Richard Perrotta. The DNA, from the bloodstain taken from the Marquez patio, was a perfect match to Diane Harding.

The subsequent search of the Harding residence revealed four men's wedding bands and one woman's wedding set. They were hidden in Diane Harding's jewelry box.

* * *

What goes around, comes around, is a saying we often hear, and it is certainly appropriate in this case.

When the autopsy was finished, Nick read it over. His aim was not just deadly; it was perfect. The bullet hit her dead center in the upper aortic arch.

Quick read ✱
FUN TO READ ABOUT LOCAL PLACES.

quick, easy to read
nice to read about
Beaver County.

CPSIA information can be obtained at www.ICGtesting.com
Printed in the USA
LVOW08s1659060214

372652LV00002B/386/P